TUCKER'S
MONSTER

S.S. WILSON

Published by
Real Deal Productions, Inc.
P.O. Box 142
Wadsworth, IL. 60083

Library of Congress Control Number: 2010905101

ISBN 978-0-9827222-0-6

INTRODUCTION

By Seth Whitney

My grandfather, Gerard Whitney, was a zoologist. While he was respected by his peers for his field notes, he was renowned among his grandchildren for his wonderful Tucker Stories, as we called them. They were culled from the time he spent as "Chief Zoologist" for the eccentric Oklahoma rancher and adventurer, Harold B. Tucker in the early twentieth century. Grandpop happily told and re-told the tales verbally but, despite repeated requests from family and friends, he wouldn't commit them to paper, grumbling, "That's too much bother for a bunch of fluff." He was first and foremost a scientist, satisfied to publish his zoological papers (see Whitney, G. "Venezuelan Tree Frogs: Four Species' Tadpoles Identified," et. al.)

So it was with considerable surprise that, more than a half century after hearing the stories as children, my siblings and I found the manuscript which follows. Grandpop's old house, then owned by our aunt, was being sold, as she could no longer afford the upkeep. As some families do, we all showed up to help sort through decades of accumulated junk. Prosaically enough, this small stack of paper was discovered in the attic. Bound with string, it was in the bottom of a large cardboard box, buried under reams of his technical writing.

We believe it was written sometime in the 1950s, because it was typed on a manual machine pre-dating the IBM Selectric typewriters he loved in later years. If we are correct, it's frustrating to realize that it probably sat untouched in his desk for at least twenty-five years until his death in 1981 at age 93 (we know the attic box was packed after that); and remained "lost" for three decades more in our aunt's attic.

So much else we don't know. We don't know who the child is to whom he refers in his prologue. When we were older, any kid who crossed Grandpop's path was fair game for a Tucker Story. This boy he must have met prior to 1956 (before we were born). That's when, sadly, the photo to which he also refers (reproduced on the cover of this book) was damaged in a fire. The surviving portion shows only the smiling Tucker himself with his wife beside him, her back to the camera, and a painfully tantalizing glimpse of the monster's tail behind them.

We don't know why Grandpop never mentioned that he had written this, or if he ever approached publishers with it (though the first sentence of his prologue hints that he did not). We like to think it was his plan that the manuscript would be discovered by accident, just as it was. But it is also possible that his scientist side won out and he chose not to publish it for fear of embarrassment in the halls of learning. If that was his decision, we have overruled it with apology, for the benefit of kids and dreamers everywhere.

Here are Grandpop's Tucker Stories. As written by him, they contain a wealth of detail which was not in the simplified tales he told his grandkids. That has caused us to wonder if in fact there was more truth to the sagas than he claimed. But as you will see, some patron saint of all things mysterious and wonderful seems determined to eliminate all tangible evidence of Tucker's discovery. So we leave it to the reader to decide how much of what follows is "fluff."

TUCKER'S

MONSTER

Events Leading to the Discovery of
TUCKER'S MONSTER

by Gerard Whitney

PROLOGUE

Should this writing come to light, no doubt many of my dear friends and family will congratulate themselves in having persuaded me at last to expound on my experiences with Harry Tucker. Honesty decrees, however, that I note the real force which impels me to set down these events so late in my life. I had occasion to meet a young boy, ten or twelve I suppose, who engaged me in a discussion of paleontology, a subject in which clearly he was better versed than I. Inevitably, we touched on Tucker's Monster, and of course I produced my print of the old photograph of same. The lad then astonished me by explaining, in detail, how the photograph could have been faked! Indeed, it was this young's man's opinion that it *had* been faked. He referred me to certain artists of the motion picture industry (notable among them a Mr. Harry Hausen) who have been accomplishing feats of much greater complexity and imagination for years.

Alas, there is nothing to substantiate the existence of Tucker's Monster except the photograph and the testimony of a few eyewitnesses, most long dead. These do not constitute proof. The skepticism of the scientific community is unfortunate, but inevitable. The rules must be followed. Even though I know the truth, I must accept this.

But this child's skepticism somehow cut deeper than any I might have endured from my peers. For it was, all those years ago, a young boy's fantastic, illogical dream that led us on our long and ultimately successful search. So, not for science, but for the dreams which drive us beyond its rigid boundaries, I here document, or perhaps I should say "tell the tale of," the search for Tucker's Monster.

CHAPTER ONE

I Arrive

The sign on the door said, in small neat letters, "Beware of Snake." I looked round myself. I was standing on a shaded veranda stretching fifty feet along the front of the substantial main house of the DH Ranch in north central Oklahoma. Seeing no serpents, but only moderately reassured, I prepared to knock.

I had come to this door just as hundreds of others had, in answer to one of Harold B. Tucker's advertisements. He had placed thousands of ads in hundreds of languages in dozens of countries throughout the world, though the one to which I had responded was unusual, in that it was for employment.

So, at the age of 21, on this warm early August day in 1903, I knocked. The door opened quite suddenly and I was faced with the largest snake I had ever seen, a green anaconda (*Eunectes murinus*) more than twenty-five feet long, coiled menacingly at the entrance. I leapt back, jerking my satchel up in front of me.

The snake made no move. I realized, much to my embarrassment, that it was stuffed.

A man stepped from behind the door. "Well, at least you didn't keep running," he said in a gruff baritone voice softened somewhat by the Oklahoma drawl. "You my new zo-ologist?" (He pronounced it as though it were two words.)

He was stocky, even burly, about five foot ten, wearing a rather long frock coat, tailored to fit him closely, and a broad-rimmed "cowboy" hat. He also sported an enormous black handlebar mustache, but his black bushy eyebrows competed with it in size. Decades of prairie sun had set them in a permanent scowl above vivid gray-blue eyes that regarded me intently, unnervingly, unblinking.

While I was a bit taller, he was looking down at me, and I

2

realized that I was still crouched, ready to spring away from the snake. Straightening awkwardly, I said, "I did come to discuss my taking up a position. You are Mr. Harold Tucker?"

"I am. Can you shoot?" The advertisement I was answering had in fact required, in addition to a knowledge of zoology, proficiency with firearms. "You'd best tell the truth. The only other fellow who's come out here couldn't. Said he didn't think it was really necessary. It is. And I'm going to make you prove you can do it, so let's have it straight right now."

"Well, I wouldn't claim to be an excellent shot, but I'm reasonably familiar with fi —"

"All right, come on. He turned walked away down the hall, boot heels clicking authoritatively on the solid oak flooring, the sound echoing off the dark mahogany walls. I followed, eyes fixed on the great snake. Mounted in a marvelously natural setting that stretched many feet down the entrance hall, it was magnificent, perhaps a foot in diameter at its widest.

"Plenty of time to gawk at that later," Tucker said impatiently. I looked up and saw him framed in an open door at the opposite end of the hall, which ran straight through to the rear of the house. I walked down to join him, passing a mounted grizzly bear (*ursus arctos horibilis*) I had failed to notice before.

He was now holding what I took to be a large double-barreled shotgun. "You can set your bag by the door there for now. You can't shoot, you'll be leaving." He disappeared out the door. Flustered, I set down my bag as instructed and followed him out into the Oklahoma sun, wondering why shooting ability had such a significant bearing on employment as a zoologist. I had ridden on horseback for several hours since entering Tucker's property, a cattle ranch for which a term like "vast" was an understatement; and I had rather expected the offer of a chair and perhaps some lemonade on my arrival, not a test.

We walked a considerable distance from the house, collecting on the way, four cowboys who had been working with some corralled horses. Following at a discreet distance, they chuckled among themselves and appeared to think that great sport was at hand.

We came eventually to the foot of a typically Oklahoman hillside of vivid red clay. There Tucker had a makeshift shooting range which consisted of two saw horses with a board laying across them. Set on the board was a large adobe brick.

Tucker stopped some fifty yards from that target and held up the gun he was carrying. "Know what this is?"

"A shotgun?" I ventured. The cowboys behind us snickered.

Tucker gave me a squinty look, "When did you last see a shotgun with rifle sights?" He indicated the gun's sights, which in fact I had not noticed. I felt my job interview was not going well.

But then he added, "Never mind. Not many people have seen one of these." He snapped open the action and held the gun out to me with satisfaction: "600 Nitro Express. Custom built by John Rigby and Company of England." I must have looked as though I needed more explanation, as he added, "An elephant gun."

I took it gingerly. Thinking of it as a rifle instead of a shotgun made it seem absurdly large and heavy. Tucker produced two enormous brass cartridges from his pocket and handed them to me. At this point, I was becoming somewhat annoyed with his brusque manner and the requirement that I show off like some Bill Cody trick shooter.

"Is this really necessary?" I asked.

"Yes. I must know that you are a decent shot. Plenty of time for explanations *if* you prove competent. I don't expect you to shoot flies off a buffalo. I just want to know you can handle yourself in a worrisome spot. If you can hit that brick from here, you'll do — that is, at least as far as shooting goes. Now, please —" He gestured toward the target. Besides his obvious impatience, there was a curious urgency in his voice that commanded action. It was a tone I would come to know well.

So I fumbled the over-large cartridges into the gun's cavernous chambers and raised the ponderous thing indecisively to my shoulder.

"Shoot either barrel. They're regulated to fifty yards. And hold it tight into your shoulder. Weighs sixteen pounds, but that don't shave much off the kick."

His last remark was unsettling, for it was just what my father had said to me when I was taken out for my first trial with the family 10 gauge shotgun — its recoil had knocked me down. And this rifle was twice the weight of any "normal" game gun. I resolved to concentrate and get the silly affair over with.

I set the sights on the adobe block and squeezed the rearmost trigger. The gun slammed me back and wrenched itself from my left hand, tilting up until it was nearly perpendicular.

I managed to hang on with my right hand, but was dismayed to find that I was falling over backwards, just as I had as a child. Tucker caught the rifle with one hand, caught me under the arm with the other and eased me down into a sort of chair-less sitting position. Through the ringing in my ears I became aware of a gurgling noise. I glanced behind me to see the four cowboys trying to control uncontrollable laughter.

Still with one hand, Tucker then effortlessly lifted me so my feet slid back under me. He was startlingly strong, I thought, parenthetically.

And he was obviously surprised, "Well, looks like you're a man of your word. Blessed good shot. Made you some talcum powder there." I had forgotten about the target. I looked, and sure enough, in place of the brick was a large cloud of red dust drifting slowly away in tandem with an equally large cloud of blue-white powder smoke.

I loosed myself from his grasp and straightened my clothes, determined not to evidence the throbbing ache in my shoulder. "I'm not in the habit of misrepresenting my capabilities, Mr. Tucker."

"And I apologize sincerely for my mistrust," said Tucker, bowing with a smile that gleamed startlingly under the black mustache. "You'll find that I'm a man who has learned to believe little that people say. Working for me, you'll see why in due time. Right now let's get out of the sun and down to business. Can offer you a drink?"

But a thought had occurred to me, prompted by the mounted anaconda and bear. "Mr. Tucker, perhaps I should make it known now that I do not engage in, nor do I approve of, trophy hunting. If that is to be our purpose —"

"I'll state my purpose in full, and it is not that." He held up the rifle. "And I'll assure you that if you ever have to use this thing, it will be in defense of your life or someone else's." He took my arm, steering me toward the house. "It's my turn to prove my mettle. Now you've come all this way, least you can do is hear me out."

Indeed, I had traveled some thirteen hundred miles for this interview. "I suppose so," I said doubtfully.

"Good man!" He snapped open the elephant gun, ejecting the spent case, pocketing the unfired one, and laid the rifle casually over one shoulder as he strode briskly for the house. Tucker's every movement in life was brisk.

As I started unsteadily after him, one of the cowboys came alongside me. He was a very tall gangly man with a long gait and a wiry gray-shot mustache that seemed somehow uneven.

And there was a smile in his eyes as he said, "No hard feelin's, mister, 'bout our laughin' I mean. Me and the boys, it just starts our ribs seeing anybody shoot that thing. And you done all right; better'n most dudes we get out this way. Hit what you was shootin' at."

He held out his hand, "Name's Luddy Sedlak."

Thankful for this unexpected apology, and flattered that my embarrassing display had earned any respect at all, I took the proffered hand. "Why, thank you. Certainly no hard feelings. If I looked at all as ridiculous as I felt, I'm sure it was quite the sideshow." This started a new round of laughter and brought resounding clap on the back from the group spokesman.

"You're all right, Mr. Whitney. Ol' Harold, he's gonna take a shine to you. I'm predicting it."

The cowboys did not accompany me into the house, but veered away and let me follow "Ol' Harold" inside alone.

The home was large, but not ostentatious, at least not in frivolous ways. It had the rooms that any wealthy person's abode was expected to have in that time. More than style or fittings, it was the *manner* of construction that stood out. The place was built, or rather overbuilt, on a monumental scale. This was far more apparent indoors than out.

Tucker led me again down the dark, museum-like hall past the record-breaking grizzly and the world-class anaconda. This time I noted that the hall's cross beams were not mere lumber, but whole trees, rough-hewn and somehow man-handled into place above us. Doors were at least four inches thick. The wood-paneled walls proudly wore the marks of great mill saws.

We entered Tucker's library. It was as rough and cavernous as the hallway. Here were huge leather chairs which could barely be moved by one person; hulking book cases of solid teak; a towering stone fireplace that would have been the envy of an English king. Even the reading lanterns were of the strongly built wind-proof type seen on seagoing vessels, with iron fittings and thick glass.

While it all made me feel small, as though I had wandered into the domain of some brooding giant, none of it was done out of a need to intimidate or impress. It was simply, I would find, the way Tucker did everything — thoroughly and to excess. "Wouldn't want the place to blow away in a good wind," he would later say.

As daunting as the library was, even here were sights that trumped the room itself; I was dismayed to see more examples of the taxidermist's trade. The head of an enormous elk (*Cervus Canadensis*) thrust out above the fireplace. A massive cougar (*Felis concolor*) was mounted in a low crouch, teeth bared, on a great boulder that dominated the center of the room (and was itself so large it made me wonder, *Was the house built round this thing?*). These trophies rekindled my doubts about Tucker's hunting habits, but I resolved to keep an open mind.

He pointed me at one of the elephantine chairs. As I sat, I saw a long row of finely made wooden filing cabinets lining one wall. More what one would expect to find in an expensive lawyer's office, they were certainly incongruous in this otherwise rustic setting.

But outshining all else, *everywhere* were fossils — bones, skulls, plants, trilobites, dinosaur tracks — and one very beautiful and nearly complete fossil ichthyosaur (an aquatic dinosaur), about four feet long, framed in oak on the wall adjacent to the fire place.

Without asking my preference, Tucker handed me a drink which proved to be straight bourbon.

"Here's the deal. I'm looking for a dinosaur, been looking

for one coming up on twenty-five years. That snake out there is the closest I've come."

"Beg pardon? A *dinosaur?*"

"Don't interrupt. I have to tell this story a lot, and it bores the warts off me."

"Sorry."

"I'm forty-three years old, young fella. My mam passed at forty-seven. My pap left us at fifty-three. *Fifty-three!* And I'm forty-three! Don't have time to waste."

"I shall not interrupt," I said quickly, afraid that any shine Tucker had taken to me was tarnishing.

He grunted his acceptance. Clasping his hands behind him, he stood stiffly in front of the distracting cougar and began again.

"Caught up with the snake down along the Orinoco in South America after two and a half months of getting eaten alive by bugs. People claim all kinda critters are in the jungles down that way. But that's the best I did. And it ain't a dinosaur is it? It's just a big snake. You know that better'n me. Anyway, I still don't have a dinosaur, but I've sure got a reputation. And that's of a man who's looking for any monster, never mind dinosaurs. A man with *money* who's looking.

"People send me stories about sea monsters, mermaids, ogres, trolls, yetis, hide-behinds, leprechauns, ghosts, vampires and what not. Can't understand why they go so far off the track. My advertisements say 'dinosaur' as plain as you can in any known language. Problem is, as my fame has spread, folks have started showing up with all sorts of blessed things — two headed chickens, three tailed pigs. They'll say that these are just the babies and the *real* monster, the mama monster, well it lives just out back of their place somewheres and wouldn't I give that the thousand now on their say so."

"The thousand — *dollars?*"

He nodded, "I've got a standing reward posted in every civilized country of the world; for any information that leads me to a real dinosaur."

He stepped to a writing desk (made of walnut thick enough to serve as a butcher's block) and snatched up a hand-bill to show me. This particular one in French, it announced the reward of which he spoke.

"That's how serious I am about this. Now, here's how I've come to advertise for someone of your calling. Eight months ago September, I paid a man a hundred-seventy-five bucks for the thing in that case over there."

I followed the brisk jerk of his head to a glass case, unnoticed up to now due to the other more imposing features of the room. The case was about three feet long, and inside was mounted a preposterous creature with the head of a crocodile, the body of a dog or other canine, and four stork-like legs.

"I keep it to remind me how stupid a man can be," he growled. I looked back at him. He was regarding the cased creature with a dark expression, lips pressed in a frown.

"Fella sold me a real bill of goods. Said he found a herd of these, much bigger of course, 'way up in northern Washington. This was the littlest one he saw, but it was the biggest he was willing to chase after on his own. They can run like the wind on them skinny legs, don't you know," he rasped, apparently imitating the sharper.

Tucker went on, "Well, next he says he'd be glad to lead me back up there but he had a debt he had to cover in Seattle first and wouldn't I just advance him the stake to cover it and he'd be right back. Hold on, I says, I want to take a closer look at his monster, and that's where he hooked me. Told me this here was an airtight case to keep the thing perfect. These animals spoil in only one day and he hadn't wanted to pickle it, of course. That'd dissolve all the fur and — aw, bless it, I don't know why I'm going through all this. I paid him the one-seventy-five in silver and off he went.

A few weeks later, I've got some friends over here looking the new beastie over, and one of 'em spilled his drink on top of the case. And we seen it runnin' down the *inside*, right through the "airtight" seal. Opened up the case, and the thing's held together with balin' wire. Bless it! I still don't know why I fell for it. I'm not an educated man, Whitney, but I used to know enough not to get flat-out hoodwinked. People brought me plenty other phony critters and I spotted 'em. But I'm gettin' old. Gettin' more desperate. Thought I could *make* the thing be real if I paid him. Word must've got around, too, 'cause they show up in droves now."

I had gotten up and was looking at the "beastie" more closely. "Well, in all fairness to you, it *is* a remarkable piece of handiwork. Have you noticed how carefully the hair is placed on the legs and head. It looks exactly as if it's growing there."

"I said I was uneducated, not blind. But never mind that thing. What do you say?"

"Say? About what?" I had completely forgotten what we were supposed to be talking about.

"About workin' for me. Don't you understand my situation?"

I wasn't sure I did, so I returned to the most alarming part of what I'd heard so far, "You're looking for — dinosaurs?"

He nodded vigorously, "I want to see one for real, up close, alive."

"But you realize, of course, that dinosaurs are —"

"Extinct, I know. I know the word. But the world's big. Huge. A thousand and one places civilized folk have never been. I'm looking under every rock, like they say, till I find one."

"Yes. But I'm afraid I still don't see how I can help."

He testily rapped the glass case. "You know about animals. You can spot things like this before I pay for 'em. You can tell what can't be true from what *might* be true. You can keep me from wastin' my time. I'm forty-three years old, man! Four years till I'm as old as my mam when she died!" He raised his arms in a gesture of desperate helplessness. It was moving, but even so, I really couldn't imagine myself becoming involved with this outlandish, if not unbalanced man, and his search for creatures that had not existed for millions of years. It might reflect badly on my hoped-for reputation in the scientific community.

"Mr. Tucker, I think that it was a mistake for me to come here. For many reasons I don't feel I'm suited to — "

"Why *did* you come?"

"Well, actually, to be quite frank, it was more that I was dissatisfied with what I was doing rather than actually expecting to find — "

"What were you doing?"

"As my references state, I was serving as assistant to Professor Collins at the University of Delaware, and I didn't feel that —"

"And what do you *want* to do? Really."

I noted that to converse with Tucker was to start many more sentences than you would finish, but I muddled on, "Well, I suppose one would call me idealistic, but I feel that teaching does not directly contribute to increasing our body of knowledge and, since I enjoy working in the field, I felt that I could perhaps find a position which allows —"

"'In the field'" he interrupted yet again. "Does that mean 'in zo-ology' or 'out of doors?'"

"Oh, 'out of doors.' That is, actually engaged in finding, studying and classifying animals of a given region, perhaps discovering more about how they —"

"Well fine! You can do that here, can't you?"

12

"Well I don't see how, I mean, not if my time is to be taken up exposing the work of charlatans and," I gestured at the stuffed cougar, "trophy hunting."

"Bless it, man, I told you we'll not be hunting. If I find what I'm lookin' for, I'll try to take it alive, I promise you. As for that cat, he's only here 'cause he killed my father-in-law." He paused, apparently expecting an outburst, which he got.

"And you had it *mounted!*"

"That was her daddy's dying wish. He wanted everybody to see how big a cat it took to break his hold on life. The elk's just up there 'cause it's the biggest I ever saw, but I was after food when I come up on it, not trophies."

Then he suddenly bellowed, "And what difference does it make, anyways?! If you're gonna throw a fit every time you see some dead animal, you sure as rain don't want to hang around *me!* I don't go out of my way to kill 'em, but I've got a short temper, I like fresh meat — and stop changing the subject!"

I closed my mouth, which did not seem to be serving me very well anyway. Tucker inhaled deeply and re-clasped his hands behind him in a seeming attempt to calm himself, then spoke more quietly.

"What I'm tryin' to say is, we don't get tricksters in here every day. Most of 'em *I* can see through on my own. What I need you for is the ones I'm not sure about. The rest of the time, which is *most* of the time, you can do whatever you want. If you can find enough on these plains to classify, then classify 'til you're sick of it. My only conditions are that you be available, say within two days, whenever I need you. Oh, and you'll have to be ready to go on trips."

"Trips?"

He nodded, but a sadness flashed across his face for an instant. "I don't go on 'em much any more. Not much use. But we might be off to anywhere, anytime, depending on what news we get, and we could be gone as long as a year if we go."

He glanced at me with a trace of nervousness, as though this news might put me off, and added hurriedly, "But you ought to have a yen for that. I mean, you'd spring at a chance to study and classify in some other country, wouldn't you? You ever spend six months in India on your teacher pay?"

"Hardly."

"Well there you are. Now what do you say? I'll pay you whatever you were makin' as a teacher, minus your room and board, of course. You'll live here on the ranch, and do mostly nothin' but classify, probably eighty percent of the time."

I had been mentally preparing another firm refusal, but was suddenly jolted by the possibilities. Court magician to an eccentric but benevolent king? Free to explore the vast ranch but for an occasional consultation? All my needs provided for? *Heavens, man, this situation isn't ridiculous, it's more than you could ever have hoped for!*

"You're thinkin', aren't you?" Tucker was watching me intently.

"Well — what you have outlined is certainly attractive. Let me be sure I understand you. I will have most of my time to myself?"

"Right," he held up a finger, "except for trips now."

"Of course, but as you guessed, I would welcome the opportunity to travel. How about facilities — an appropriate space in which to catalogue, preserve and store specimens?"

"I got spare rooms in the house. I got barns, sheds, and root cellars. Pick any one you want. He grinned, apparently sure of me, and turned to pour himself another bourbon.

"Marvelous!" I said, "But, one more thing?"

"Yeah?" He swiveled his head toward me with a wary expression, as though expecting me to try to take advantage of him now. I considered dropping this last point, but then decided that I should try to protect myself. I had surmised that this man could easily decide he did not need my services and dismiss me as suddenly as he had hired me.

"Do you think you could give me some assurance of time to find another position, in the event that you should, for whatever reason — "

"Drop you like a hot rock?" He let out a single, distinctive snort, something like, "Pfhuh!" I would come to know the sound as the closest he usually came to actual laughter. His eyes smiled slightly, and I sensed I'd come up a small notch in his estimation.

"Pretty shrewd, Whitney. I guess I do move kind of fast. But I try to be fair, too. Would say, five months severance cushion your fall enough?"

"Dear me. More than adequate."

"It's a deal then?"

I drew a slow breath, held it for a moment, and then nodded, "Yes."

"Fine!" He held his glass toward me. "Why don't you have a little of that drink you've been avoidin' all this time." I complied, raising my glass to him, and taking a small sip. I tried to look composed, but I have never cared for the bar liquors and apparently this was quite evident to my keen-eyed employer. He smiled and adopted a fatherly tone, "Teetotaler? Or do you fancy a different spirit?"

"I am more partial to port," I admitted.

"We'll lay some on quick as she'll come by rail. Would that suit, Mr. Whitney?"

"Very much, Mr. Tucker."

CHAPTER TWO

Life on the DH

I was an official staff member of the DH (the letters, I now realized, standing for "Dinosaur Hunter"). Tucker provided me a room in the servants' end of main house, simple and comfortable, not far from the kitchen. I sent for the rest of my meager belongings (since he would not hear of my taking the time to return east for them) and we then set about choosing my work place.

It was just a former tack room, one of the ranch's many outbuildings. But it was fifteen by seventeen feet, with a sturdy plank floor and three north-facing windows that provided a nice even light all day long. Upon the addition of a small desk (purchased second-hand from the Post Office in Ponca City), ample shelving, a potbellied stove, and a work bench, I had a delightful little domain in which to write notes and prepare specimens. It even came with a well established family of mice which I did not have the heart (or tenacity) to displace. Tucker christened my new office "the Science Building," and so it would be known for the next seven years.

Toward the end of my first week, as I was organizing traps and preparing new books for field notes, Tucker strode in to ask how things were proceeding. I'd just begun an answer when Luddy rode past us, calling to Tucker, "Jenny's back, Harold. Up in the front barn."

Tucker nodded, and it seemed to me that he tensed ever so slightly as he said, "You should meet Jenny, of course. She's been off on a visit to her mam. Come on." He set off immediately, for he always acted on decisions immediately. I hurried after him toward the indicated barn.

It was the primary horse barn. Inside, as the warm yeasty smell of hay engulfed us, Tucker squinted around.

"Jenny?" he called.

A woman stepped out of one of the stalls, carrying a bridle she'd just removed from a beautiful and feisty chestnut mustang. She wore a no-nonsense leather riding skirt; leather vest; boots, well broken in; and a broad-rimmed leather hat. All this brown was offset by a vivid maroon shirt and a downright garish multicolored bead necklace which culminated in a sunburst round amulet of reds, blues and blacks, with dangling tassels which rustled softly when she moved.

She was slender, barely over five feet; yet her bearing was strong and confident. To my eye, she was most exotically beautiful, or perhaps handsome is more correct. Her hair, straight and hanging well past her shoulders, was gleaming black, as were her eyes. Clashing with this otherwise arresting vision were two scars, one running down the right side of her forehead and bisecting an obsidian eyebrow; and another, on the same side of her face, starting at her cheekbone and running jaggedly back toward her ear.

The pale scars contrasted with her very dark skin. At first I thought she was deeply tanned, but then realized she was an Indian — the first I had ever seen (except in photographs, and once at a distance in a Wild West show).

Tucker stepped over and put his arm round the woman. "Jenny, this is Mr. Gerard Whitney. He's our new zo-ologist. Whitney, I'd like you to meet Mrs. Tucker." He fixed me with a stare, clearly watching for some negative reaction. In truth, while I was quite surprised to learn she was his wife, I was too naïve to realize the extent to which an interracial marriage was looked down upon in that country at that time. Thus, luckily for me, I simply reacted as my social training dictated.

"I'm delighted. How do you do, ma'm?" She nodded very slightly, her expression quite unreadable.

"Are you now?" Tucker pressed, still staring at me.

"Well, of course!" I insisted. Jenny's eyes flicked to Tucker for an instant in what might have been reproach. Then she stepped forward, and with the hint of a smile, extended her hand.

"I am happy to know you, Mr. Whitney." The English was curiously accented, slow and precise. Her voice was startlingly soft and musical coming from this imposing, stern-looking little figure.

As I took her hand and bowed, I was surprised to note that her slim fingers were calloused and marred with more tiny scars. So different from the pampered ladies of the eastern city in which I had been raised. But I maintained formalities, "The pleasure, and honor, are mine, I assure you ma'm."

I straightened and looked squarely at Tucker, "And I assure *you*, Mr. Tucker." His mustache tilted with a slight smile.

In the months, even years, to come I would gather more snippets of information about Jenny, as I came to know Mrs. Tucker. She was a fascinating opposite to Tucker's bombast. She spoke English quite well, but she seldom spoke. I judged her to be considerably younger than he, who constantly announced his current age to anyone within earshot. Once, I asked him privately how old she really was. He raised his eyebrows and pretended to peer about furtively.

"Well now, you know, Whitney, I'll tell you this: I was twenty five when we met, and she swore she had seen eighteen summers. But seemed like she grew about two inches *after* we were married. So I've always preferred not to press the point."

She was, as Tucker often said, a "cipher." Born on the Cherokee (she would say *Tsalagi*) reservation in the Eastern Oklahoma territory she grew into, by her own telling of it, a rebellious youth, caught not only between two civilizations but between two eras. Her path crossed Tucker's during the time he was building the ranch. She saw in him a kindred free-thinking spirit. He saw in her a strong-willed independent mate, and their course was set.

He called her Jenny because he had always liked the name, and could not pronounce her Cherokee name. She christened him *"Kiyuga."* (Technically, it was pronounced something like "kee-you-u-gah," but that does not convey the swift guttural way she said it.) Tucker later told me she gave him a Cherokee name because his nickname, Harry, made her hysterical with laughter when she learned the English word "hairy." As I tried to imagine this sober woman laughing at all, Tucker went on, "I know, I know, you'll be lucky to see her laugh once in a year, and then it'll be at something you won't understand. But that was one of the times."

↔↔↔↔↔↔↔↔↔↔

Having unknowingly passed the test of meeting Mrs. Tucker (and not reacting inappropriately), I was fully welcomed into the ranch routine, and I enjoyed it thoroughly. I rode with the men (real cowboys!), and often lunched with them in the cook house or out on the range. I also became friendly with Eugenia, the main house cook (who indulged me in making soft-boiled eggs to perfection). I met "Jurgen the German," a wild-haired, taciturn blacksmith who kept the horses shod, wagons tired, and all the ranch's metal work in good repair. It was he who had crafted the elaborate branding irons which marked every cow on the sprawling domain. It was in the shape of a trilobite.

But it was Luddy Sedlak who became a close "compadre," as he liked to say, taking it upon himself to improve my horsemanship, introduce me to proper knot tying, and teach me ribald songs (he seemed to know at least one from every state of the union, and not a few from other countries). As Tucker's oldest friend and most trusted hand, he had traveled widely with "Harold" in the tireless search for a dinosaur.

Day to day, of course, most of Tucker's time was spent tending to the ranch. Highly respected by his employees (many of whom, like Luddy, had been with him since the founding of the DH in 1881), he was known to pitch in even with the menial task of fence mending.

And, true to his word, my time was entirely my own except when some report or "beastie" required my services. In my first months, I acquired many books and treatises on the fauna of the region. Determined to verify or enlarge upon the information I found therein, I tramped fully to the four borders of the empire. Among my finds was an enormous "town" of black-tailed prairie dogs (*cynomys ludovicianus*). I constructed a blind close to it in which I spent many absorbing hours observing the frenetic creatures. I also began collecting and mounting insects. Tucker found this amusing, one day proclaiming, "You talk down from your high horse about trophy hunting, and here you've killed and mounted more critters than I could in four lifetimes!"

I learned more about Tucker's network of dinosaur seekers. In addition to the rewards posted for information leading to the capture of exotic beasts, (dinosaurs preferred, lesser critters considered), ship captains of every nationality on every ocean were on notice to report sea monster sightings. He kept in touch with expedition outfitters and hunting guides, and had write-ups sent to him of their forays into unexplored regions. Most importantly, he employed what he called his posse, seven men who, like Luddy, ranged across the globe running down rumors of particular interest; "To date, all wild goose chases," he ruefully commented.

While nothing of significance transpired for many weeks,

there were frequent responses to the advertisements Tucker continually placed round the world. Mostly these were letters. Almost every evening, he would sit in the library in the shadow of the perpetually snarling cougar, his glass of ferocious bourbon on his side table, and patiently read each one. In various forms, but with remarkable similarity, they described some fantastical creature which had recently been sighted in the writer's area and exhorted Tucker to come see it for himself. When he had finished, he would rise and slip them one by one into his voluminous file cabinets, filed first by country, then by creature type.

To me, in these early days, each tale sounded exciting and worth investigation. But Tucker invariably dismissed them cynically, "All hearsay. Been to a hundred of these places. Nothing ever there. Trolled up and down Lake Champlain two seasons. Nothing there. Cold, rainy, and the fishing wasn't worth a hoot. These days, I'm getting older. If something sounds like there might be a shred of truth, I'll send one of the posse to check it out. See if it's worth going myself. Luddy goes a lot of the time. He's a good fella and he likes to travel to godforsaken places. Turns up somethin' unusual now and then. But never a dinosaur."

With somewhat less frequency, packages arrived with curious artifacts — a claw, a large tooth, a mummified piece of skin, a mat of coarse moldy hair. Always these were claimed to be from some great beast the likes of which the world had never seen. While I could not consistently identify the specific animal from with the pathetic samples had been taken, I was able to certify that they were not from unknown monsters, certainly not from dinosaurs.

In the meantime, my shed (the Science Building), with its ever-growing collection of local fauna, became a showplace for visitors to the ranch. Having a college-trained "zo-ologist" on staff was a point of pride for Tucker. Always quick to point out how little formal schooling he'd had, he now felt he was making a contribution to science and learning. Like so many self-taught men, he seemed unable to appreciate what he had learned on his own. His enormous, and enormously successful ranch was little compensation. Ironically, I learned much more from Tucker about cattle, horses, their diseases and habits; and about the ebb and flow of life on the rangelands than I could have discovered in many years of "book learning." But he could not be persuaded that this teaching was of any value. "That stuff — that's just life," he would say.

On most days, after dinner and mail reading, Tucker and Jenny settled in the library to read books. On many evenings it was my pleasure to join them, he with his bourbon, I with a glass of the outstanding port he had shipped in for me, Jenny with water (all she ever drank).

Much time was passed in quiet contemplation of our respective tomes. Though Jenny had attended an Indian school as a youngster, Tucker hired a tutor after they were married so that she might improve her reading skills. Thus they now both read extensively. Between their chairs, on its own pedestal, sat Webster's International Dictionary (with supplement), and it was well used. Jenny and Tucker meticulously looked up every new word they encountered and tried to commit its meaning to memory.

Of course there was occasional conversation, too. One night, I was quite surprised to learn the meaning of the nickname Jenny had given to Tucker. *Kiyuga* is Cherokee for "chipmunk." This was baffling to me at first, for if anyone was ever more bear than chipmunk, it was Tucker. Jenny only smiled, and let Tucker explain, "It's 'cause I'm restless. Always searching. Can't never set still."

The most memorable evenings were those when Tucker could be induced to speak at length. I had become accustomed to his abrupt manner and short temper, and had quickly learned that it was folly to press him on a subject which did not interest him. Nevertheless, when the mood seemed right, I attempted to draw him out. A well-aimed question, especially on his favorite subject, could elicit a variety of rambling and utterly fascinating replies. I dearly loved his tales. They could be about anything — the cattle drives, drilling a water well, building the ranch, petitioning of the Cherokee elders for permission to marry Jenny.

For example, one night I heard the shocking conclusion to the tale of the mounted cougar on the rock. Jenny had been *with* her father when the cat attacked! The scars on her face were the result of her own counter-assault on the animal! Tucker delighted in dragging me over to it and pulling back the hair behind its left ear to reveal a jagged scar. "From Jenny's knife," he said. "Gave as good as she got, eh?" He raised his glass to her. "She run that cat off all right. He didn't get no meal." He rubbed the scar, "This is how we knew we had the right one when we tracked him down." Such was the matter-of-fact way Tucker described life-threatening situations.

Too, there were tales of Tucker's travels; to Russia, Egypt, Europe, Africa. These tended to be brief and negative, as they all ended in not finding a dinosaur. But on one grand evening, I at last drew out of him the genesis of the passion which drove his life. I began with a carefully worded question.

"Given the energies and devotion required to build the DH, how did you ever develop such a fascination with dinosaurs?"

Tucker glanced up at me from his copy of Jules Verne's *The Steam House*. "Oh, that fascination happened long before I ever dreamed of being a rancher. You can blame that on my Pap. Now, he had no schooling at all, and it bothered him plenty. Worked the big cattle drives that used to go through this country. To him, schoolin' meant learnin' to read, and that's what he set out to make me do." He smiled, gazing into the ship's lantern on his side table, flame glinting in his eyes, obviously seeing a vivid image of his father.

Jenny put down her own book and watched him intently. I got the impression this was a story of which she never tired.

"I fought against just about every word," Tucker went on. "He sent me to a school, but after I run away from there three times, he took me — I'm ten, eleven years old, mind you — on a drive with him! Texas to Kansas on the Chisolm. My Mam, now she's fit to be tied, you know? But he was trail boss by then, and if he said something was gonna transpire, well, it transpired.

"So he hires him a cowhand who could read, and makes him my teacher. Every night, going and coming, he makes us sit by the fire, you see? Stands there looming over the two of us while that poor fella tries to teach me what he could barely do himself. But son-of-gun, it finally started to take. And I kept at it — partly just to keep Pap off my back, but partly 'cause I was gettin' proud that I could make sense out of books. First time he seen me pick one up, I mean, one I ain't ever seen before, and just start reading it — well, I guess it was the proudest day of his life.

"Biggest day of *my* young life was a year or so later. He took me to a real library in Kansas City. A great old lady there, Mrs. Carlton Weathers, taught me how to use a *dictionary*. Up to then I thought the only way to learn new words was to find a cowhand who knew more than the first fella. So then I wanted a dictionary more than anything. Closest I ever seen Pap ever come to hittin' a woman was when the old lady wouldn't sell us her big library dictionary."

Tucker laughed at this and shifted his gaze to the floor. He glanced at me and added, "But she gave us an old one she had, little kinda pocket book, and for free."

He opened a drawer in his side table and took out a small book — the very dictionary of which he was speaking. He flipped through it. It was wonderfully tattered, edges frayed and rounded from years spent in saddle bags, nearly every page smudged by a boy's hard-worked, dirty fingers.

"Well, that gift calmed Daddy some. And she told us how we could mail-order us a big one like hers. 'Course it was a few years before we had *that* kinda money." He smiled at Jenny and patted the Webster's on its stand.

Then he looked back at the floor. When it was apparent that he wasn't going to continue, I risked prodding him to return to the original question.

"So then, when exactly did your interest turn from reading to dinosaurs?"

"What? Oh, well I didn't turn to it; that's how I got it."

"I'm afraid I don't quite —"

"I got that interest from readin'. See, every time we'd go to Kansas, I'd ask old lady Weathers for interestin' books. First she tried to get me to read stuff about history, or George Washington, or English high society." He turned to Jenny, "What's that lady's name, Dickens?" (Tucker sometimes called Jenny "Dickens." This was both because she was small and headstrong, as in "you little Dickens," and because she was an avid reader of Charles Dickens' work.)

"Jane Austen," she replied, in answer to his question.

"Yeah. Well, I tried some of that but it didn't make much sense to me. Bored me to death is what. I told her I didn't like it, and she says well, that's great literature, son. Everybody should read it. And I says, well in that case, ma'm, I think I might as well give up readin'.

He laughed (in his way), "Pfhuh! Well, that prodded her, you know? She started offerin' up real good books, then. She got darn on target at guessin' what I'd like." He suddenly looked at me defensively, trying to decide how I would react to something. At last he asked:

"You ever heard of *Moby Dick*?"

"Oh, indeed I have," I replied.

"Yeah? I thought you college men read high society stuff. That Jane Austen, and Charles Dickens."

"It bored some of us to death."

"Pfhuh! How about Jules Verne?"

"I've read everything he has written to date."

At this, Tucker was positively glowing, "Well, there you are!" He pointed a triumphant finger at Jenny, "Jules Verne!"

She shook her head with disdain, "The boat *cannot* go under the water."

Meanwhile, I played a hunch. "Are you familiar with the work of H. G. Wells, Mr. Tucker?"

Tucker's head tilted back slightly and his chin jutted out, lips pursed under his mustache. This, I would find, was a rare and coveted reaction. It meant that he had encountered something he found impressive, something he considered worthy of note. In this case it meant he was pleased that I was aware of Wells.

"Monsters from Mars!" he exulted, pointing his finger at me.

I nodded.

"I'll be jiggered, Whitney. You know a lot more than I thought."

"Thank you. But, if we might return to dinosaurs, you are not looking for monsters from Mars, correct?"

"No, no, of course not. That's just nonsense. But it's the kind of thing that got me started. See, old lady Weathers always tryin' to get me to read history, and I wouldn't do it. So she started mixing it with something that I *would* read. By then I was thirteen or fourteen. She knew I liked readin' about whales and elephants — stuff I'd never seen — so one day she gets out this big leather-bound book just chock full of pictures. *Johnson's Natural History.* And I'm balkin' and buckin' — 'History?' I says. But she flips it open to these woodcuts of the dinosaur sculptures over in Syndenham, you know, England. Anyways, there they was, Megalosaurus, Iguanadon, Hyleosaurus and the rest!"

He jumped up, hurried to a bookcase and lovingly withdrew a copy of the book of which he was speaking.

"This the very book!" he beamed. "Years later I went back and bought it from that same Kansas library. 'Course Mrs. Weathers had left us by then. But it was still there, and the fella in charge, well he let it go for a proper donation."

The book fell open, well trained, to illustrations of the Benjamin Waterhouse Hawkins' sculptures on display in Syndenham. As did Tucker's first dictionary, the pages of this book bore multiple smudges from his younger hands. Each page had clearly been studied innumerable times before.

He went on, "Jenny and me, once we was set better, went on over to England and seen'em in person." He jumped up again and from one of the file cabinets produced a photograph of himself and Jenny in front of the Syndenham Megalosaurus.

Suddenly he was as a child, eagerly showing off a prized collection of tin soldiers. He rushed about the library. More documents, publications and photos flowed out.

First came issue upon issue of the *American Journal of Science.* "Luddy found out about this magazine on one of the posse trips. They've printed up a bunch of science articles, just like what you do, by Othniel Charles Marsh. You know him?"

Certainly I knew of the famed fossil hunter, and I quickly asserted, "I know *of* him, and a bit of his contentions with Edward Cope."

"Them two didn't get along and that's a fact. I had'em

both out to the ranch. Different times, of course! Pfhuh!" he laughed as he handed me a photo of Marsh and his 1870s fossil-hunting party, amusingly (though I suppose necessarily) armed with rifles.

Tucker pawed through the journals and flipped open an 1884 edition to a page showing the fearsome skull of the carnivore Ceratosaurus.

"Look at that there!" Tucker enthused. "Ceratosaurus! You'd want to be carrying my Rigby if you met up with that son of a gun, eh?"

"I might, indeed," I smiled. And, behind Tucker, I thought I glimpsed Jenny's dark eyes smile, too.

He flopped back into his oversized chair, gesturing again to *Johnson's Natural History*.

"Well, anyways, when I seen them things, after that I couldn't think of nothin' else. Up to then I'd been interested in anything sort of, what, you know — fantastical. Griffins, dragons — Martians later on. But when I found out about dinosaurs, they seemed far and away the best bet."

"The best bet for — ?" I began.

But of course Tucker interrupted: "Why, for catchin'. For bein' *real*."

↔↔↔↔↔↔↔↔↔↔

While privately I lamented that Tucker would never find his dinosaur, I almost daily thanked the Powers for my good fortune, and was happily lost in my research and the comfortable atmosphere of the ranch. So used was I to my pleasant routine, I was quite unsettled to awake one day to find it all changed. It was a blustery December 2, 1903. As I strode merrily from my quarters, I noticed that I did not smell the usual coffee and bacon, but thought nothing of it until I reached the kitchen and found it deserted. Eugenia and other cooks were not there. The stoves were stone cold.

I turned about and went down the great entrance hall. There was no one in the library. A bit more hurried now, I rushed back to my room, grabbed my jacket, and walked out the rear of the main house. Once outside I was somewhat reassured to see at least some movement; a ranch hand was leading two horses toward one of the barns. But I quickly noticed that he did so with an uncharacteristic trepidation, whispering to the animals as he urged them on. It seemed he very much wanted to keep them quiet.

I walked on to the bunkhouse where, by this time of morning, the cowboys should be saddling up for the day's chores. There was no one there.

In the milk shed, a few hands were tending to the cows, which was a daily necessity of course, but these men, too, carried out their task with a quiet, intense nervousness wholly antithetical to the normal jovial tenor of Tucker's well-paid workers.

I passed the blacksmith shop, where on any day but Sunday, Jurgen should be firing his forge. He was not there.

Wild thoughts ran through my mind: *A hand's been struck down by the smallpox or some such, and the staff have all fled!*" But I knew full well the staff would not desert Tucker if Satan himself were battering at the doors, so I really had no idea what to make of all of it.

At last I saw Jenny. She was riding out of the main barn on Hadrosaur (by then I knew her mustang's name). When she spotted me, she wheeled him in my direction.

"Jenny!" I blurted, "There's no one — not in the kitchen, not at the blacksmith's —" She held up a dainty gloved hand to stop me.

"If you see *Kiyuga*, don't speak to him."

"But why? What on earth has happened?"

"Only time has happened. It is his birthday."

Thus I learned that, one day each year, the Tucker empire was plunged into deep mourning. Another 365 days had passed without the master achieving his life-long goal. He did not want to be seen, celebrated, congratulated, toasted or even spoken to. For him, a birthday was simply a milepost on a bleak road to an inevitable early grave and ultimate failure. On this particular December 2, Harold Tucker had turned forty-four.

The next day, normalcy resumed with a swiftness that was eerie in itself. The cooks cooked. The hands rode out. Jurgen's anvil rang. Tucker arrived at breakfast, cheery as ever (or what passed for cheery with him), as though nothing had happened. Indeed, it was his way of denying that anything had in fact happened.

↔↔↔↔↔↔↔↔↔↔

1904 arrived, and spring came with no creatures of any interest being reported. In midsummer, Luddy was dis-patched on a "posse trip," this one to Louisiana to look into claims of a mysterious beast that had reportedly been sighted in that region. While a dour Tucker gave slight odds for his success, Luddy left in high spirits, for he truly loved these ventures, fruitless or not.

Dinosaurs remained elusive, but the time was hardly wasted as far as I was concerned. I published a paper on my prairie dog town, and though it hardly shook the foundations of zoology, it was an enormous delight to Tucker, who sent copies of it to all of his neighbors.

In support of that patronage, I arranged a meeting between Tucker and some paleontologist friends of mine, with the ulterior motive of perhaps channeling some of his wealth into their work. This was ill-fated. While he did pay well for up-to-date reports of new fossil findings, and especially for detailed drawings of what living dinosaurs were assumed to look like, he was not about to finance any "bone digging parties."

"I ain't interested in dead ones," he said, "and it's strictly cash-on-delivery for live ones."

In spite of this strict policy, a seemingly endless line of would-be hoaxers found their way to Tucker's door. Most brought only tales of far-off lands populated with horrendous creatures. Some brought elaborate constructions like the one which had resulted in my being hired. One of these latter raised Tucker's hopes quite cruelly.

A Norwegian circus owner arrived unannounced one day, accompanied by an interpreter and a large cage. In the cage was a stuffed Allosaurus standing easily twelve feet tall. Tucker identified it immediately, familiar as he was with every dinosaur then known.

On close examination, I exposed the Allosaurus as yet another fake, made of caribou bones, lynx teeth, and cleverly assembled reindeer hides. Tucker took the news well outwardly, but I could see that he was very disappointed. Almost as upset as he, however, was the owner of the sham dinosaur, who was himself apparently convinced it was genuine. He had acquired it from Siberian nomads who claimed it had been found frozen in the tundra. Via his circus, the creature was now quite famous in northern Europe. He left very dejected.

↔↔↔↔↔↔↔↔↔↔

I had now been in Tucker's employ almost exactly one year. It was one of those muggy Oklahoma August evenings where any breeze seems only to add to the discomfort — like a big dog breathing hot damp air in your face. I was returning from an afternoon of prairie dog observation. My usual route to the barns took me past the main house. There I saw Tucker standing on the front porch, avidly reading the mail. This was unremarkable since, if the letters were few, he often read them the moment they arrived. But as I rode past, he suddenly growled, "What?" and tromped inside shouting "Jenny! Jenny!" I quickly tied up my horse and hurried after him.

I caught up with Tucker in the great hall by the python as Jenny was rushing from the kitchen to meet him, drying her hands on a dish towel, unspoken concern on her face.

Tucker waved the letter, which was several pages long, "Luddy's got himself hurt down in Louisiana."

She took the sheets of paper and started reading as she asked, "Is it bad?"

"*He* don't think so, but you know Luddy — looks on the bright side like a moth. Hurt his ankle is what. Didn't know sprained or broke when he wrote. But the smart Alec says he's gonna wait there for me to come down! Ain't even seen a doctor! And this letter's already —" he looked at the postmark "— a week old!" He threw off his overcoat and marched angrily into the library. Jenny and I followed.

Tucker paced fruitlessly in front of the cougar. "Blessed fool. Could end up lame, or lose his leg, or die with the gangrene. I'll send him a telegram in the morning. That's what. Tell him get back to New Orleans and —"

Jenny interrupted, asking quietly, "Did you read all of his letter?"

"Not past the blessed fool part!" Tucker never used blasphemy, no matter how angry he got.

Jenny maintained her low, steady tone, "You will want to go."

"What?"

"Luddy knows you will want to go. He is right." She proffered the letter. He snatched it back and continued

32

pacing as he read, occasionally emitting his guttural "Pfhuh." Gradually he slowed down until at last he stopped, head tilting back, chin jutting out, lips pursed.

He seemed to notice me for the first time. "Whitney, good man. How long you been here?"

"Actually, I came in with you."

"No, no, no, how long you been here on the ranch?"

I had to think, then said, "About thirteen months."

"And we ain't once gone on one of them trips I promised."

"Well that's no matter," I offered, "I've had more than enough to occupy my —"

But he had turned away and was re-reading the letter. "Yeah, this one sounds better'n usual. You ever hunt werewolf, Whitney?"

↔↔↔↔↔↔↔↔↔↔↔↔

The three of us sat close round a lantern on one of the library tables. An appropriately eerie wind had come up. It whistled, raked branches on the walls outside, and even inside coaxed a ghostly flickering from the lantern's flame. Tucker, his face lit orange, mustache casting theatrical shadows up his cheeks, was giving us the details of Luddy's current adventure.

"I will say, reading a letter from Luddy is as good as standing there asking him questions and having him answer'em, if you know what I mean."

"He writes a thorough report?" I asked.

"He does that. So, seems this little town down there, place called Sombre Foret, has had a werewolf worrying them for almost two years. First victim was killed that long ago. Two more have been killed since then.

"Some wolf or bear turned man-eater, of course."

"You don't have to tell *me*. But nobody can track it down. And it ain't like they haven't tried. Here's the part I like." He began to quote from the letter, "'They tried many times after both the first and second killings to track the critter down. Every time, the trail led to the same big oak tree and was lost there. The finest hounds, brought in for the purpose, were unable to pick up the scent beyond the tree. The townspeople are certain it's because that is where the wolf changes into a man.

The last man killed was a volunteer, an expert 'coon hunter in his own right, who staked out the tree not too long before my arrival. On the third morning of his vigil, he was found killed on the spot, terribly mutilated, his gun drained dry.'"

Tucker sat back and snapped the letter with one finger. "Now that's pretty good, I'll admit."

"Good?" I asked, not bothering to hide my disapproval of his lighthearted tone. "What's good about a man being killed, if I may ask?"

"Oh, don't get all prissy. I read and hear about this kinda stuff all the time. I just mean that this situation is a lot different from most. Usually there ain't a shred of proof of anything. Anyway, Luddy goes on to say that he hired some dogs and tried to track the thing himself. Had to go it alone. Townspeople are a hundred percent cowed after that last killin' and won't even go out nights. Darn Luddy's gonna get killed himself huntin' alone like that, even if it's just a mangy lame bear."

"Well, he was not killed this time. What did happen?"

"Well, the dogs led him to the same big oak tree." Tucker again read from the letter: "'They was running pretty far ahead of me and I heard them fighting before I caught up. And, Harold, blamed if they wasn't all three dead when I got there! Strong, seasoned dogs every one. Someone or some — " here Tucker hurriedly turned to the next page, " — thing had tore them up real bad.'"

34

We silently contemplated the admittedly spooky tale. Then I asked, "Was that how Luddy injured himself? Chasing the dogs?"

"Naw, tripped on the hotel stairs when he got back. Says a local Gypsy woman must've cursed him. Pfhuh!"

Tucker stared into the lantern flame. There was energy in his eyes, an alertness to his rigid body. For the first time since I had known him, he was genuinely interested. He shook his head, trying to resist, "Doggone Luddy. I said I'd never waste time on supernatural nonsense again."

Jenny had remained silent until now, "But we are going to Louisiana."

"That we are," Tucker nodded.

CHAPTER THREE

My First "Trip"

Preparation for the expedition was swift, Tucker's employees executing a well-rehearsed program. By noon of the next day I was introduced to Triumph, his massive expeditionary freight wagon. With the name emblazoned in bold gold-and-black on either side, she was reserved exclusively for his dinosaur hunting journeys and, like so many of Tucker's belongings, was custom made, in this case by the Studebakers. With steel wheels six feet tall, oversized frame, iron strapping throughout, she was pulled by a duo of stupendous Belgian (Brabnet) horses named Taft and Bronto. Tucker had taken team and wagon quite literally round the world, transported by rail and water when necessary. Where others made do with prairie schooners, Tucker set forth in a juggernaut.

By the time I saw her on that day she was already loaded with what I took to be an inordinate amount of gear. As Tucker strode out of the house, carrying even more paraphernalia, I simply had to ask, "What is all this for? Surely you're better equipped than Magellan."

"And I pride myself on it. Just odds and ends I've learned to have handy." In his travels seeking the unusual, Tucker had encountered many unique and often dangerous situations. As a result, he had built up an daunting list of items he deemed it necessary to have with him at all times.

Over time I would learn that "odds and ends" included, in addition to the normal camping and food supplies, medicine, fuel oil, trading goods, plaster of Paris (for casting footprints), whole cloth, sewing equipment, a portable desk for letter writing, and seemingly enough raw materials to build a modest-sized town. I also noted a black metal keg stored right under the wagon's seat. It bore a starkly disconcerting white stenciled label.

"Blasting powder?" I asked, in a quavering tone far less cavalier than I'd planned.

Tucker nodded casually, "Used to carry dynamite, but, like I say, I don't go on these treks much any more, and dynamite don't age well. Gets touchy. Powder stays reliable."

Finally, of course, there were weapons. I immediately identified the sturdy, brass-bound case I knew to contain Tucker's double-barreled express rifle. Beside it was an identical case, which I assumed contained artillery meant for me.

"You always take those?" I asked. "Even in America? I can assure you no game on this continent is worthy of them."

"Well now, you never know, you never know." He leaned toward me, opening his eyes wide. "What if them folks just *think* it's a werewolf? What if it's really an Allosaurus?"

"Even so, if you insist I go armed, might we not select something less punishing?"

Now he caught my drift. "Pfhuh!" he snorted. "That second double's not for you. It's Jenny's. Had the Rigby fellas custom fit it to her. 'Course it's not a 600 like mine. She don't care for the recoil. It's only chambered for the 450 NE, but it'll still send any elephant to his maker."

"One should accept nothing less."

"Exactly," he said, missing my sarcasm. "Anyways, I *do* insist you go heeled, so come on in and take your choice from my humble stock."

I followed him into the house mumbling, "You make me feel like I'm going into battle."

He shook his head, "Bless it, Whitney, *I* don't believe it's a werewolf, *you* don't believe it's a werewolf, but whatever it is, it tears people and dogs to pieces. Now, if we are lucky enough to find it, *I* might do somethin' stupid and uneducated like shoot it. *You* —" and here he turned on me so abruptly that I nearly ran into him, "are welcome to try to classify it to death." He laughed abruptly, as though taken by surprise by his own joke, then strode briskly off again.

We went down a corridor past his and Jenny's bedroom. I'd not been in this section of the house before. Just beyond the bedroom we entered a dimly lit study. It had only one window, and that was covered by a red curtain through which the sun gamely forced a faint firelight-like glow.

I say "study" because the room contained a desk, reading lamp, and arm chair. But "armory" would be more appropriate, for here was where Tucker kept his cache of personal firearms. Elegant glass-fronted gun cabinets lined two walls. The other two were fairly festooned with guns on hooks. While it was evident that considerable thought had been given to the room's original design, it was also evident that the weapons had long ago overwhelmed and conquered the original space. They overflowed the cabinets and exceeded the wall hooks. Several cluttered the desk top. Not a few simply stood stacked in bivouac-style pyramids, making navigation in the room a dicey proposition.

Tucker gestured broadly to the room and stood back, leaning against the door jamb, arms folded, watching me like a skeptical parent. I didn't even recognize most of the guns; so after a moment I reached tentatively for a Henry repeater which was similar to my father's.

Tucker immediately grunted displeasure, "Pfhuh. Forty-four rimfire? Why not just choose a handgun and be done with it?"

I withdrew my hand. "Perhaps you'd care to make a suggestion," I said, daring more unheeded sarcasm.

"I would!" He eagerly stepped forward and hefted a bulky rifle from its wall hooks. "Since you appear to favor the lever action, would you cotton to the President's gun —

Winchester 1876 in 45-75? It's got a bark with the bite to back it up." He reached into a drawer and withdrew one of the fat cartridges for the rifle — not the cannon-like rounds for his express rifles, but still worthy of the term "overkill."

He worked the gun's lever and aimed out the window. "I met T.R. once in the Dakota Territory. A man I much admire, by the way." This was not surprising. Roosevelt and Tucker were certainly of similar drive, physicality and philosophy. "He spoke so highly of his big bore Winchester, I right away ordered one for myself. Took that elk in the library with it, in fact."

I felt it was wise to concede quickly, "Well then, I could hardly do better than to carry such a highly recommended weapon."

"Well, so you know, Winchester makes a bigger one. Express model they call it, done up in 50-95. T.R. said he had a couple of them, too. Beats the 45-75 all hollow, when it comes to knock-down power. I could order up one for you." He seemed genuinely concerned that I might feel slighted not to have the largest lever action gun available. I shook my head.

"This will do fine." Thus, the Winchester 1876 in 45-75 became my expeditionary rifle.

↔↔↔↔↔↔↔↔↔

We set out at dawn the next day, making one stop at a distant neighbor's place to borrow a coon dog. This was Luddy's suggestion. He'd paid $150.00 for the slaughtered dogs he had borrowed, and doubted that we could convince anyone else in the area to provide more. Our dog was named Joker (he'd been won in a card game as a pup, the owner claimed), and was a sturdy, rather serious, black-and-tan hound.

It being the twentieth century, we thankfully did not have to jounce in stiff-sprung Triumph clear to Louisiana. Tucker, impatient with all aspects of life, would have chafed at the wagon's leisurely pace over so great a distance. Also he was not averse to traveling in style and comfort when those were to be had. Thus, he, Jenny and I went by rail in the finest Pullmans, while Triumph, her steeds, and Joker trailed behind us in freight. We were soon in St. Louis, and as quickly on to Lake Charles, where Tucker had arranged rooms in a hotel of the best class.

To his surprise, Luddy had heeded his telegrammed advice about seeking medical attention. Upon our arrival at the hotel, there he was waiting for us on crutches. When Tucker spied his old friend, the deep bond between the two men was instantly apparent in the relief on his face.

Luddy's mere presence was reason enough for Tucker to modify his otherwise relentless travel schedule. He announced that we would repair to the hotel's lounge and drinks would be ordered. I felt privileged to be invited. Jenny, on the other hand, predicted an evening of boisterous talk ahead and excused herself.

In his stoic way, Tucker showed more affection for Luddy than for anyone else in his circle, save Jenny. This affection was, of course, expressed in an odd, rough-and-tumble fashion. One conversation of that long and late evening in Lake Charles will hopefully serve as an example.

"Breakin' an ankle is a sorry way to get out of working," began Tucker as he poured tumblers of bourbon (I declined, having commandeered a glass of port before joining them.)

"Ain't broke. Doctor says sprained," Luddy shot back, raising his glass.

"Oh, so you're a lollygagger?"

"My job invites it."

"How so?"

"Well, you see, Harold," (Luddy was the only one who called Tucker by his proper first name), "there's this crazy man in Oklahoma and, you won't believe this, he *pays* me to look for monsters. He don't seem to know there's nothin' to it!"

They laughed uproariously over this and tipped their glasses.

Tucker rejoined, "No foolin'? Well if the work's that easy, what'd you need to sprain your ankle for?"

"I figured I might as well. He pays for that, too!" They laughed some more.

I was able to coax them into telling me a little more about the early days of building the ranch, but soon it was clear that, like Jenny, I should excuse myself and let the old friends share time as only old friends can. But just as I was about to do so, Luddy turned serious on the matter of the werewolf.

"You know, Harold, I'd feel better if you'd wait till I can go back down there with you."

"Lord's not granting me what little time I have left to set around waitin' for you to mend."

"Well know this, you'll get no help from the townsfolk."

"They like usual?"

"Worse. But you can't blame'em. It ain't like most places, where it's all rumor and hearsay. There's something in them woods, and it's a pretty damn mean something."

"We leave at sunup, Luddy, without lollygaggers pretending to have come up lame."

Luddy nodded, obviously knowing that would be Tucker's response. He glanced at me.

"Falls to you then, Gerard. You keep him out of trouble, you hear?"

"I'll do my best," I said, and bid them goodnight.

The following morning, I found myself, for once, ready ahead of Tucker and Jenny. The hotel staff had hitched up Triumph and she was ready and waiting in front of the hotel. Stoic Joker, the hound, was perched somewhat unsteadily on top of our mound of gear.

Soon Tucker came down from their room with two of his cases, Luddy hobbling gamely along behind with a third case slung over his shoulder. Seeing me, Tucker seemed to feel the need to explain, "Jenny'll be a minute. It's usually best if she changes before we reach these small towns."

"Changes?" I asked?

"Um hm." He volunteered nothing else. I caught a faint smirk from Luddy, and surmised that Tucker was setting me up for some surprise. This proved to be true, but that did not lessen the shock.

A moment later, Jenny strode swiftly out onto the hotel porch. She was wearing a broad Stetson like Tucker's, a finely fitted fringed deerskin jacket, one of her colorful maroon riding shirts, her dazzling Cherokee necklace, glossy riding boots — and *trousers*. She paused on the steps, tucking the hat between her knees and readjusting her hair under a bright red headband. Completing the startling transformation, a Colt Army revolver hung in a black military flap holster belted round her slim waist.

I must have looked astounded indeed, for Jenny actually smiled as she walked to where we stood on the boardwalk. "You are embarrassed," she said.

I was more than embarrassed, but that was accurate enough. My reaction no doubt seems quaint to the reader of today, but proper ladies didn't wear pants in that time. It felt almost indecent to see her in such, well, detail. In my defense, I might add that the hotel liverymen were gawking more blatantly than I.

"I am sorry," she said, and glanced reprovingly at Tucker, "Kiyuga, you are cruel."

Tucker was suddenly all wide-eyed innocence, "Me? I never said a thing." And, turning to me, "I guess she means I should've warned you about her work clothes."

Jenny shook her head with mild annoyance and explained to me, "He has been waiting to see this look on your face since we left Oklahoma."

That I could well imagine, and I thought quickly in an attempt to minimize the success of his game. "Mrs. Tucker, I'm only surprised — surprised because my limited, or rather one-sided, social upbringing compels me to be so. Certainly I have nothing but respect for your choice to wear the dress of your people."

To my dismay, Tucker and Luddy exploded with laughter. I think Jenny almost laughed herself, for I'd made still more the fool of myself. As Tucker thudded into the wagon seat he said, "You'll never see a Cherokee, or any Indian woman dress like *this*."

Luddy added, "That there's Jenny's own concoction. Hers alone. She takes what she wants from her people and ours, and the hell what any man, woman or dog thinks of it!"

Tucker held his hand down to Jenny. She ignored it and swung herself effortlessly into the high wagon seat. Blushing, and altogether less graceful, I clambered up into the seat on the other side of Tucker.

We waved goodbye to Luddy, and as Tucker started the horses, he leaned close to me, "Tell you the truth, Whitney, used to make me jealous as all get-out to see her in that outfit among town folk, but she laid down the law. If I wanted her come along on these shindigs, she was gonna dress sensibly or just not come. She hates dresses and all that. I had no choice but to get used to it, so I swung the other way. Now it starts my ribs seeing folks go goggle-eyed. You watch their jaws swing when we hit this one-horse swamp town we're headed to."

In truth, there was no need to wait for that. All along our route through the refined neighborhood of the hotel, heads turned and wide-eyed whispers were spoken behind white-gloved hands. True to his word, Tucker enjoyed this immensely. Every few minutes he jabbed me to point out yet another shocked couple. "Looky there. Look at'em," he chuckled.

Jenny endured with her usual stoicism, except to say, "You are a child."

"Don't I wish that were true," he retorted. "I'm nothing but a frustrated old man. Mam gone at forty-seven. Pap at fifty-three. My time's running out. And I'm gonna die without ever seein' a werewolf or a sea monster or any other blessed thing of fantastical stature — much less a dinosaur. Gotta get *some* fun out of life."

By now, I was well used to Tucker's frequent laments about his age. Also, Jenny had earlier confided to me that his obsession with early death was baseless, at least where his parents were concerned. He was not from "weak stock." His mother had been struck down by smallpox, as might happen to the strongest of us. His father, a tough, hardworking man to the end, was killed in a horse fall. Even his grandparents were long-lived on both sides. In telling me this, she had sighed, "Yet still he thinks death comes early for him."

CHAPTER FOUR

Obtaining Lodging

We left Lake Charles heading south. Never having been in this country, I was fascinated by the dark, dramatic, dreamlike forest through which we passed. Spanish moss was draped everywhere, like macabre Christmas tinsel. The trees were alive with myriad birds of which I could catch only fleet, frustrating glimpses.

But for Tucker travel was measured only by pace, and ours was slow. The road was muddy and Triumph was a challenge to move over even the best road. After several punishing hours on the seat, Jenny made a more comfortable half-bed half-chair from our array of gear in the bed, covered it with blankets, and lay in it with her hat over her face. Joker seemed happy for the company and quickly nestled beside her.

Tucker grew increasingly agitated as it became clear we would not reach the village before sundown. After many annoyed glances at the sun, barely visible through the dense forest, he muttered, "Bless it! This is gonna be a tussle."

I thought him rather petulant and dared to comment, "Surely you've been on a many a trek more difficult than this."

"It's not the trek, it's the need to bust into the rooming house at the end of it. I hate to cause trouble right at the start."

"Bust in? I — don't understand."

He seemed not to hear me for a moment as he scowled at the darkening road ahead. Then he said, "What? Oh, well, places like this, where they think they've got a werewolf, or vampire, or witch — take your pick — the people just start acting like blessed fools. Won't talk to you. Won't help you. Tell you to go away. Keep sayin' you don't understand."

"But, I should think that they would appreciate an offer to hunt the creature down for them."

"Pfhuh! You would think so, yes. I used to think so, too. But ain't ever like that. I told you, I've looked for these things in maybe a dozen different places, back before I lost interest in the supernatural. And Luddy and the other posse boys have hunted'em in dozens more, all over the world. The people are always the same, tight-lipped, unfriendly, and dumb enough to make you wanna to shoot them instead of any werewolf. I don't know, maybe it comes from being scared all the time, and these people *will* be scared, I promise you."

At that moment, Triumph took a bad bump. Jenny, who had been asleep, sat up instantly.

"It is dark." She said it flatly, but was clearly unnerved. Seeing the implacable Jenny unnerved, I was unnerved all the more.

Tucker growled his reply to her, "I know, I know. We're late. Just have to make the best of it."

We paused to light the wagon's carbide lanterns. Softly hissing, they thrust their beams into the inkiness ahead, rimming our horses in otherworldly yellow light.

Though a bright full moon struggled upward, it was unable to pierce the forest, and now a dense ground-fog rolled heavy across the road. It gave the impression that the wagon was afloat on ghostly waters.

We suffered with the eternity that is travel in darkness, eyes straining ahead, aching to see something in the blackness beyond our lumbering horses.

What came first was not sight, but sound. A ghastly, moaning howl suddenly wafted out of the woods, seemingly from all directions. The up-to-now implacable Joker leapt up and snarled savagely.

Taft and Bronto started. As Tucker fought to rein them back, he said, "Glory be! A wolf it is! This far south!" For indeed, to anyone who has ever heard it, there was no mistaking a wolf's howl. Jenny drew her revolver and patted Joker comfortingly on the head.

A mere moment later, to my great relief, we saw the pale glow of a lantern in the distance. Luddy had told us that one was kept burning in front of the small rooming house on the main street of our destination. The light seemed to float unsupported in the path ahead until we finally drew near enough to make out the shadowy shapes of low buildings, rising out of the mist like islands.

The village of Sombre Foret hovered in the marshy nether world between the open waters of the Gulf and the solid ground of Louisiana. At first, I thought I saw more dim lights in the windows of some houses, but as we drew nearer, I heard the dull thump of shutters closing — and no light shown as we passed them. The moon had finally topped the trees, adding a sepulchral gray luminescence to the scene. By that minimal light I could see that every door and window was hung round with ragged wreaths of some plant. Why, I could not imagine.

The town was absolutely silent. We approached the rooming house. It was two stories, a relic of more prosperous times, when sulphur mining was thought to be the town's future and fortune.

A fresh, chilling howl of the wolf slithered down the deserted street. Tucker shook his head, annoyed. "Bless it! As if these folks weren't on edge enough. You'd think somebody hired the critter to sing on cue."

He halted the horses well back from the lantern and held out his hand to Jenny, "Let's have the Le Mat." Then he changed his mind. "Naw, no need to show off yet. Just gimme one of the Smiths."

Jenny swiftly opened a case and handed Tucker one of several holstered Smith and Wesson handguns inside (it seemed that all major gun manufacturers were represented in their arsenal). Her own pistol was still drawn. She opened the loading gate and spun the cylinder, checking that it was full.

I was appalled at this show of arms, and whispered urgently to Tucker, "*Guns!?* What on earth is your intention?"

He climbed down from the wagon. "My intention is to knock on the door. After that, it's up to them. And I'd prefer you hold a weapon yourself."

Jenny proffered me another of the handguns. I recoiled as if it were a snake.

"I will not!"

"Suit yourself," shrugged Tucker.

I was becoming downright panicky. "Mr. Tucker, this is *insane!* We're seeking rooms, not laying siege to Troy!"

Tucker unexpectedly whirled and glared at me, eyes glowing yellow-orange in the carbide light, "Look, we've done this before and you haven't. Now shut up."

He turned toward the rooming house, then turned back, his manner faintly apologetic, "I told you, these people are scared. They're scared every day and night of their lives, and they're gonna be extra scared of a bunch of strangers ridin' in *after* dark under a full moon! Now I don't really expect them to start shooting, but you never know."

I must have looked as pale as I felt, even in the darkness. He shook his head with what I took to be disappointment, "Good night, the way you look now, I wouldn't trust you with a gun anyway. Can you do this much? Just hang onto the reins. *If* there's any shooting, start the horses, I'll hop on and we'll high-tail it. Do you think you can handle that?"

"Yes. Yes, of course," I stammered.

"All right, then." He glanced at Jenny, "Dickens, you set?"

48

I turned to look at Jenny who was crouched behind one of the large trunks, pistol ready. She nodded at Tucker and then looked at me. I could not read her expression, but I felt ashamed because I suspected she thought me cowardly, and angry because I didn't think I should feel ashamed. After all, who in his right mind expects violence when knocking on a rooming house door? Thoroughly flustered, I simply faced front and took a tight grip on the reins.

Tucker strapped on his side arm and stepped to the door. With one more glance back and Jenny, who nodded, he knocked firmly, then stepped quickly to one side.

"Hello the rooming house!" he yelled, his voice seeming terribly loud in the fog-muted silence. "We're looking for Morgan Tumley, proprietor! This here's Harold Tucker, his wife, and college-trained zo-ologist Gerard Whitney!"

Only the oppressive silence answered him.

"Come on. We know you're in there. And you know you're expecting us. Mr. Luddy Sedlak made all the proper arrangements. Now, I'm sorry we're late, but it couldn't be helped. So how about you just open the door?"

There was still no response.

I couldn't see Tucker's features in the flickering lantern light, but I saw his body straighten, a movement I already knew to indicate growing impatience. Indeed, now he stepped to the door and delivered several fierce blows with closed fist.

I'm, gettin' tired of standin' out here!" he bellowed. "Now it's worth good money to you to open this door, 'cause in about a minute I'm gonna break it down!"

I felt Tucker was being quite unreasonable and I spoke up in a loud whisper, "At least give them a moment! Perhaps they were asleep." But instantly I felt the gentle pressure of a hand on my arm, and looked round at Jenny. She fixed me with an insistent stare and gave one quick shake of her head.

49

Just then a pitiful, low voice came from inside the rooming house. At first it sounded like a woman, but then I realized it must be an old man.

"Please, please, go away!"

Tucker turned to look at me, raising his hands in a gesture that said, *What did I tell you?* Then he turned back and spoke sternly to the door.

"You Tumley? Open up!"

"You must go. It is not safe," came the tremulous reply.

"Nope. Ain't goin' away. Now look, I'll give you ten dollars, that's on top of our room rate, if you open this door right now." Tucker patted his money belt, which was always stocked with ample currency for the given locale.

"You don't understand. I cannot."

"I do *too* understand!" roared Tucker. "I know more about what's botherin' you than you do. You got a werewolf in your town. Well, I'm gonna kill it for you. That's my business, killin' werewolves. I'm an expert. Got silver bullets and everything. But I never kill one without I get a good night's sleep first. Now open the blessed door!"

We heard shuffling of feet inside and then another voice. This time it was in fact an old woman, "No! It's a trick, Morgan!"

Tucker turned toward me and again raised his hands helplessly. In his mind he was being given no choice.

Now he squared off with the door, stepped back three paces, and threw himself against it with such force that the walls trembled and the window shutters rattled. There was a cry from within, but the door held absolutely firm. Tucker staggered back, rubbing his pained shoulder. "Bless it! That's sturdy built, that is."

Then he shouted, "All right, all right, that's it! You open that place up or I'm gonna burn it to the ground!" There was more silence. "You hear me?"

50

The old woman spoke again, "Please, please — we must not! Come back tomorrow, in the daylight!"

A cloud passed over the moon at just that point, and blackness rushed in round our little pool of lamplight. It could not have more vividly underlined Tucker's darkening mood.

"Aw, curse you people!" he snarled. He stalked to the wagon and grabbed out an old woolen blanket and one of the five-gallon tins we carried. The blanket he soaked with water from the tin, then draped it over the wagon wheel. Next he yanked out a second tin, twisted off its cap, marched onto the boardwalk, and sloshed liquid from the tin on the nearest window shutter. I was horrified as I smelled the thick odor of kerosene!

"Good Lord, Tucker you can't —!" But my frantic yelping was again cut off by Jenny, this time with her hand clamped roughly across my mouth.

She whispered, "He will not let it burn." But even as she said it, Tucker struck a match and lit a corner of the window shutter. Slowly, then more rapidly, the deep orange, oily flame climbed and spread. Jenny kept her hand tightly over my mouth.

Meanwhile, Tucker shouted, banging his fist on the rooming house wall, "Better take a look out this window! "Your place is burnin' right now, and you know none of your Christian neighbors gonna lift a finger to help you!" I squirmed. Jenny's other hand slammed down on my shoulder with surprising force.

"Quiet!" she hissed. I kept still, but was as fully shocked as if my traveling companions had suddenly announced they were bank robbers.

Tucker snatched up the water-soaked blanket and stood ready. Meanwhile, a terrified moan rose from the unseen woman inside the house, climbing in pitch to a wail.

The man's voice came again, "Dear Lord, protect us!" We heard a heavy bolt shot back, a wooden bar thud to the floor, then still another bolt slide; and at last the door swung inward to reveal an old man in a nightshirt backing fearfully away, and a woman, on her knees behind him, eyes tightly closed, hands clasped in prayer, rocking and moaning.

"About time," was all Tucker said as he swung the blanket in a wide arc and slapped out the flame on the shutter with a single blow. Then he dropped the blanket and strode swiftly through the open door.

Jenny released her alarmingly powerful grip on me and, as though it were a perfectly normal evening, gathered her things to carry in. Thus I learned a Tucker maxim: propriety, subtlety and caution were unacceptable where rudeness, brute force, or rashness would save time.

Through the door I could see the old man had backed all the way to the far wall and was literally trembling with fear. Tucker shook his head with disgust but spoke in a kinder, softer tone, "Now do I look like a werewolf? Besides, don't you know werewolves can't talk?" The woman opened her eyes and gazed dazedly at him. Tucker walked past her to the old man, who shrank back even harder against the wall.

"Take it easy, take it easy," said Tucker. "Now here's the ten dollars." He held it out, but the old man hesitated. "Go on, it's good American money. It'll pay for any damage I've done and maybe put back some of the years I took off your life. When did a werewolf ever offer you money?" The old man timidly took the coins.

At that point the woman suddenly rose and ran to the door, which she started to close. However, she jerked back as though it were electrified, for she had come face to face with Jenny who was just stepping inside. The woman recoiled, making an incoherent yapping noise.

Tucker sighed, "Calm yourself, ma'am. She ain't a

werewolf. Just an Indian. Now we've got things to bring in. I know you don't like leaving the door open, but we won't be long. We'll sling oat bags on the horses and leave them and the dog till mornin'. I don't want to have to burn down the town's stable, too."

↔↔↔↔↔↔↔↔↔↔

Once we were moved in, and the door downstairs was again bolted, barred, and bolted, I went purposefully to Tucker's room and knocked on the door. For this was the closest I ever came to resigning Tucker's employ. He called to me to enter.

Jenny was hanging clothes. Tucker was sitting on the bed with one boot off, looking at me with an anticipatory expression which said he already knew why I was there. "Okay, Whitney, what is it?" I closed the door and faced them, planting my feet and clasping my hands behind me. I looked at Jenny and was somewhat encouraged when she avoided my eyes and sat down lightly on the bed, watching Tucker. I thought smugly, *Clearly she knows I have a case.*

"Mr. Tucker," I began, being careful to keep my voice low enough that we would not be heard, "I must tell you that I am outraged by your display of — of bad manners. I'm afraid that if this is what I must expect of you every time we travel, then our association should perhaps —"

"Now, now, Whitney, now just hold it," said Tucker, raising his hand. He drew a breath, frowned at the wall, seemed to decide upon an approach, and looked back at me.

"I told you I was hard to get along with sometimes. And those times are usually when I meet up with fools like those two."

"I had no idea you meant that you become completely unreasonable."

"Unreasonable? I swear, with all your education, I think I know more about people, these kind of people anyway, than you do. That old man and woman wouldn't have opened that door if we'd been dying out there. Jenny could 've been having a baby on their front steps and I tell you they'd have left her lay."

This last image was unfairly dramatic, and it distracted me for an instant, but I was able to regain logical footing.

"Even so, was it so important that they let us in? We could have simply set up camp, or slept in the wagon."

"I slept under the stars, boy," he waved his hand in a graceful upward arc while his lips twisted into a sneer, "for most of the first fifteen years of my life. Never did care for it that much. Still don't. Bless it if I'm gonna sleep in the street just because some old geezer's scared of the moon!"

"And that's reason enough to frighten them nearly to death? I'm sure the situation could have been handled in a more civilized —"

"Forty-four years old, Whitney. Got no time to coddle cowards. And these people are *already* scared to death. They've got their whole world built around it. I swear, sometimes I think folks like these, they *like* believing in nonsense. Makes their lives more interesting. I tell you, the only way to get'em to do anything is to scare'em worse than what they're scared of."

"I refuse to believe that is the *only* way!" I fired back with all the haughtiness I could muster.

"Well, it's *my* way!" Tucker roared in counter-attack. "You go chase after a dozen werewolfs and see how far you get being friendly!" Now he was standing. Jenny put a restraining hand on his arm.

We were silent for a moment. I glanced at Jenny and found her watching me with her deep, black eyes. I looked away. My initial anger was spent. Some of what Tucker said made sense. Certainly the people had acted just as he had predicted they would.

Finally I queried, "I don't suppose it would be profitable to try to elicit a promise that you won't go to these extremes again."

Tucker shook his head slowly and defiantly, "Oh no." I looked at Jenny. She was almost smiling, no doubt at the absurdity of my suggestion. I tried to think clearly. Could I really afford to be associated with a madman, who not only was looking for dinosaurs but set fire to people's homes when they didn't do as he asked?

After another awkward moment, Tucker said, "Whitney, I'm not a bully by nature. I promise I'll do only what is really necessary. But I *will* do that." I didn't answer, but was listening.

"Why don't you think on it. You might as well stick with us until we get back. We won't be here more than a week or two. And this is almost sure to be the worst trouble we'll see." He paused, started to speak, stopped, then shifted his gaze back to the wall and said in a quieter voice, "You know I like having you around. Jenny does, too."

In spite of my outrage at his methods, I admit I was flattered that he seemed upset at the prospect of my quitting. I reminded myself of the work I was able to do at the ranch, and of the fact that Tucker had said these trips would be relatively rare in any case. I sighed and conceded.

"I suppose there is no harm in continuing as we have, for now."

"All right, then."

As I turned to the door, Tucker added, "Oh say, Whitney, I heard you start to speak up when I was setting my little fire. Glad you had to good sense to keep quiet and let me play my bluff."

I kept my nod nonchalant, but made the mistake of

looking back at Jenny, who winked at me. Such an overt facial comment had double the impact coming from her, and I retreated quickly, blushing, to my room.

The following day was bright, clear and warm, but it brought little change in the morale of our landlords, who served breakfast in sullen silence, avoiding us as much as possible. As the woman, Cordelia (who was in fact Tumley's younger sister), scuttled away from us after serving our breakfast coffee, Tucker nodded after her.

"See? Now didn't I tell 'em I was going to kill their werewolf? Don't they look tickled?"

"Well, if they really believe in the creature, and I must admit they certainly seem to, perhaps they feel that you can't do it."

"Oh come on; the rule is all you gotta do is plug'em with a silver bullet. Some say it's gotta be melted down out of a cross, but I'm not goin' that far — be sacrilegious."

"You mean, you really have silver bullets?"

"I've got two. Used to have ten. Made'em up years ago before I understood what a lot of hooey it all is. Just keep the two over fresh powder, now." Then he shrugged, clearly a tad embarrassed at the revelation.

I smiled, "So even cynicism so well entrenched as yours has its limits."

"Well, I told you. Pride myself on being ready for anything. I'd look pretty silly if I did run up against a real werewolf and — aw, stop lookin' at me like that."

But I continued staring, and smiling, "As though you'd ever meet anything you couldn't utterly annihilate with one of your elephant guns."

"Pfhuh" he grunted. Then stretched expansively. "I guess it's about time we got to work."

Work, it turned out, meant walking out to the desk in the hotel lobby and getting the attention of old Tumley, who obviously hoped we'd leave without noticing him.

"Listen, mister," said Tucker, "sure do want to apologize for bustin' in like I did. But you couldn't expect me just to stay out there, I mean with the werewolf and the full moon and all. Anyway, like I said before, I aim to kill off this werewolf. Now, I wonder if you could tell me where I can find the old Gypsy woman, Mordia, that Luddy, that's Mr. Sedlak, told us about?"

The old man busied himself with a dust cloth, going over the same area on his desk again and again. "I — I know of no Gypsy woman around here."

Tucker reared back and seemed to expand with anger. Then he glanced at me, let his breath out slowly, and spoke evenly. "Mr. Sedlak already told me you know her, and that she knows something about where to hunt for the werewolf. Mr. Sedlak is not in the habit of lying." At this point, Jenny, who was of course in her "work" clothes, paced over to the desk with what could only be described as a swagger, pushed her hat far back and leaned on the desk top with one elbow, dropping her chin into her hand and gazing coldly at the old man with her impenetrable expression. He drew back, a pathetic picture of nervousness, folding his hands round the dust cloth. She followed him with her eyes only. He looked pityingly at Tucker.

"Why do you ask these things? Why don't you just leave this place?"

Tucker shot another look at me to be sure I was noting the trials he endured. I granted him a helpless shrug. He looked back at the old man, placing both hands on the desk top and leaning slowly toward him, spoke in a low, menacing tone.

"Now look. You ain't gettin' rid of us til you tell us how to get to Mordia's place."

Terribly afraid, poor Tumley clutched his dust rag as

57

though it were some sort of life vest, hung his head, and spoke quickly and softly.

"It is about a half mile south. The road forks once; take the right fork. Her place is the first you'll see."

Tucker leaned back and shot me another look, "Like pullin' teeth. Every time."

Outside in the street, there was actually life in the little town. People set about daily chores and errands, yet their very movement was pervaded with a sense of unease. Nor was it the comical alertness of a small mammal on the watch for predators. Rather it was a somberness borne of having lived with fear so long that it had been reduced to a dull ache of acceptance. There were no smiles. No "good mornings." Everywhere we were met with sullen scowls, as though to intrude on their misery was an affront. It was quite unsettling.

Also, I could now identify the plant of which the ragged wreaths were made. It was wolfsbane (*Aconitum cammarum*). Jenny explained that it was thought to ward off the werewolf.

As we prepared to set out I was in for still another surprise from Tucker. Before he climbed up onto the wagon, he withdrew from one of his trunks a custom holster which he strapped on. What made it surprising was the size. Where Triumph had a certain elegance, like a dreadnought, this enormous, misshapen holster seemed like something a circus clown would wear.

"Good Lord," I blurted, "is there only one gun in that thing?"

So used was Tucker to this accoutrement, it took him a moment to understand the question. Then he brightened, that child with tin soldiers re-surfacing, "Oh, you ain't seen the Le Mat have you?"

He opened the holster and brought forth a handgun which indeed fully filled it. It was a very large revolver, but it had two barrels, one above the other, the lower one being at

58

least twice the size of the upper.

"See, it's kind of like a howdah pistol."

"Howdah?" I asked.

"Yeah, you know, that little chair you sit in when you're riding elephants."

"I've never had the pleasure."

"Hm, well anyways, them Limey hunters going after tiger and whatnot in India, they thought up the idea. You keep a hefty handgun handy in case you make a bad shot with your rifle and that riled-up tiger goes to climb into your howdah with you."

"Clearly an essential accessory."

You know it. Trouble is, the Brits' howdah guns are big old double-barrel jobs — only two shots. So I done 'em one better. Got the idea from a gun Pap saw during the Civil War. They called it a grape-shot revolver. Built by a fellow name of Le Mat. 'Course those were cap and ball, and only forty-one caliber. So I had this made special for me, on his patent, oh, quite a few years ago now." He spun the big cylinder. "Nine rounds, 45 Long Colt." Then he swung aside the cavernous lower barrel, "One round, 10 gauge shotgun."

I had to laugh, "Hunt buck and bird with the same gun."

Tucker's head tipped back and his chin jutted out. The concept pleased him. "Something like that," he smiled.

"From you, not so surprising."

"You're getting to know me. See, I got to thinkin' what if sometime I was in a fix like got Jenny's Pap killed — some good-sized critter catch me without a rifle, and maybe isn't gonna be impressed with any pint-sized wheel gun. Well, I just set the ten bore under his chin and let fly. I load it with number two buck."

"And have you ever had occasion to use it?"

Here he winced ever so slightly, "I'll tell you the truth. Never shot a blessed thing with it but snakes. Took it bird huntin' just for the smile a few times. But it ain't exactly comfortable to handle or shoot." Then he was defensive, "'Course, it's not meant for comfort." He returned the pistol to its holster. "Could have one made up for you if you like."

"I'll stick with Mr. Roosevelt's preferences."

↔↔↔↔↔↔↔↔↔↔

The Gypsy woman's home, really a one room hut, almost seemed to be part of the thick vegetation of the area. Moss and multicolored fungi splotchily covered the gray wood plank walls. Vines were doing their best to swallow the little building. A tree had grown leaning against one side so long that its branches had lifted the roof several inches.

We walked a narrow path to the door, barely discernible through high weeds. The hut's single window was shuttered and, like the doors and windows of the village, hung round with wolf's bane.

Tucker knocked lightly on the sagging, low door and, as was his habit, stepped to one side (lest someone shoot through it on provocation of the knock alone). After a pause, from inside we heard a woman's voice utter the single word, "Enter." Jenny took a position where she would be out of sight when the door opened, unsnapping her holster as she went. For myself, I simply prayed that the door would be unlocked.

Tucker pushed on it. It grated inward on the dirt floor. A single candle could be seen inside, but that was all. Tucker stepped in and Jenny nodded to me to follow.

The air inside was thick, reeking of mildew, mold, vermin and a pungent incense, perhaps used to mask the first three. I noted the stick, burning on a small pressed-tin stand in a corner.

The Gypsy, Mordia, a short, heavy, olive-skinned, thick-lipped, middle-aged woman, sat facing us across a tiny slanted table. She was wearing a tumultuous gaudy array of beaded necklaces that made Jenny's seem positively understated. These were draped over an equally gaudy print dress. Her long graying hair was pulled back and tied severely behind her head. Her eyes were small, and black, and scowling from a deeply-lined face.

Tucker surveyed the barely visible interior of the small cabin and, satisfied no immediate threat was apparent, called to Jenny, who slipped noiselessly in behind us.

Tucker turned to Mordia. "How do, Ma'm," he said, in an uncharacteristic jovial manner. "My name is Tucker, this is my wife —"

"I know who you are," she snapped. "And I knew you were coming." Her voice was husky with an accent my untrained ear could only catalogue as vaguely European.

Tucker theatrically placed a hand to his chest in apparent astonishment and exclaimed, "Why, how did you know that?"

"I know many things," said the Gypsy.

"Well, you must be just the woman I want to talk to. Where can I find that there werewolf tonight?"

The woman's eyes narrowed in a deeper scowl. "You must leave this place. This place is evil." And I confess I was by now astonished at how predictably the locals played upon this common theme.

"Well, if it's so ee-villl" said Tucker, mocking her drawn-out pronunciation of the word, "how come you don't leave?"

She did not answer. Tucker proceeded in his usual clipped way, "Well, never mind. Point is, I came here to kill your werewolf for you. Got silver bullets, the whole shebang. I've killed werewolfs all over the world, and I'd be glad to kill yours if you'll just tell me what you know. Might be a little money in it for you, too."

"You make jokes," hissed Mordia. "Foolish unbeliever!"

61

She glanced down and suddenly her eyes went wide with terror.

But Tucker only rolled his eyes wearily skyward. Then he sighed and held out his hands to her.

"Why, what ever is wrong?" he asked.

Mordia shuddered, barely breathing, "The *mark!*"

Tucker nodded. "Yes, Ma'm. Sign of the pentagram, is it? Uh, which hand?" He turned his hands palm up for her to inspect.

She trembled as she gestured stiffly toward his right. "The mark — of the Beast!" she hissed.

Tucker glanced at me, "Pentagram, beast — same thing, more or less. Funny, it was my left hand last time." The woman struck her table with a closed fist, startling only me. Then she rose slowly out of her chair, glaring at Tucker, pointing a stubby accusing finger at his face. Her mouth contorted grotesquely with each word. "You are a great fool! If you stay in this evil place, you — will — *die!*"

I could see Tucker was fighting to control his temper. But he maintained an even tone.

"Not if I can help it, Ma'm. Now if you could just give us a general idea where to start looking —"

"Unbeliever! You do not know!" Mordia gripped the edge of the table and leaned forward as though her next words were to be nothing short of transcendental, "Even a man who is pure at heart, and says his prayers at night —!"

That did it. Tucker exploded. He lunged forward and bellowed in her face, "may become a *WEREWOLF!*"

Mordia was so startled she recoiled backward, tripped over her chair and crashing heavily to the floor. Tucker grabbed the small table and threw it out of his path. As it shattered against the wall, he leaned over the dazed woman, concluding with quiet menace, "when the wolf's bane blooms, and the full moon shines bright."

Now he took her under the arms and lifted her to her feet. She jerked away and fixed him with a withering stare, either too stunned or too outraged to speak.

Tucker touched the brim of his hat. "Sorry, Ma'm. Sometimes I get so scared I can't hardly stand it." Then he turned and walked out, followed by Jenny. I remained for a moment, thinking I should say something apologetic. But I could think of no simple statement which would explain Tucker to anyone, so I settled for looking apologetic and leaving quickly, or would have if I'd been able to drag the awkward door closed more gracefully.

When I caught up with Tucker and Jenny I said to him, "You knew the rest of her odd poem."

"I keep tellin' you I know what I'm doin'. This visit was more for your benefit than mine. There's always somebody like her around. I've come to believe that a lot of times it's folks like her gets these stories going in the first place."

↔↔↔↔↔↔↔↔↔

We returned to town. Tucker set about trying to find someone to guide us to the large tree which Luddy had described, the tree where the trail of the "werewolf" was inevitably and mysteriously lost. Tucker wanted to scout the area in daylight before we returned there in darkness.

And so he strode purposefully to a low log structure at the far end of the little town. Though no sign proclaimed it, the building was the local saloon.

Without slowing, Tucker marched in. Jenny hurried after him, and I after her; but once we were inside, she took a subtle side-step and stopped, indicating to me that we should remain near the door.

It was quite gloomy and oppressively hot inside, the air choked with tobacco smoke overlaid with a musky sweetness arising from decades of spilled beer. The floor sloped noticeably; and while the curiously trapezoidal room was large, its low-beamed ceiling, at barely six feet, made it very claustrophobic. As my eyes adapted to the darkness, the figures of drably dressed local men emerged, hunched at rude tables, hovering over greasy beer mugs — and all bearing scowls.

Tucker stepped unhesitating to the center of the room and faced the scowlers squarely, "Now let's not be pretending you don't know we're the new folks in town. And that you don't know our purpose here. I'm offering ten dollars, gold, to the man who'll take us to the tree. And let's not be pretending you don't know which tree."

Silence as oppressive as the air was the only reply. But eventually one man spoke up. He was a clean-shaven young fellow with unruly blond hair and bright blue eyes (currently a bit brighter due, no doubt, to an abundance of alcohol in his system). He was quite burly, and seemed to be in the process of outgrowing his overalls.

"You had no call to treat Tumley like you done."

"A misunderstanding, sir. I had gained the impression he was seeking to deny me lodging duly contracted for. By way of reparation I have paid him well in excess of his rate."

Another man spoke from a dark corner, "Get on out of here. You're gonna make trouble for us."

"I intend to cause no trouble. Come now, ten dollars for a walk in the woods."

The burly young man abruptly slid forward off his stool, snatching a beer bottle from the bar and holding it by the neck.

"We done told you to move on!"

While I expected a certain negativity toward us for the nature of our arrival, I was appalled at the anger and violence implied as the young man now stepped menacingly toward Tucker.

But a crisp metallic click halted him. Jenny had produced

her Colt from under her jacket and held it leveled steady at the young man's head. To my utter astonishment, she abruptly grinned, curtsied, and then instantly resumed her usual unreadable expression. She moved sideways a few steps so that she could see behind the bar, and shook her head at the bartender. Naïve as I was at the time, I did not know that it was common in those days for them to keep weapons handy.

But if this bartender had been planning some counter-attack, he swiftly abandoned the campaign, backing away from his bar and tightly folding his arms lest they get any ideas of their own.

The young blond man was clearly cowed as well, but tried to maintain his bravado. "Oh, you don't mean trouble, but you's carrying guns in here?"

Tucker nodded his head at the beer bottle, "And in your hand, son, that a libation, or a weapon?"

"Fine talk," rumbled the young man. "Hiding behind a *woman*."

Tucker, granted him a condescending smile, "That particular woman could take any so-called man in this place. Saves me time and bother."

The insult hung in the air like blasphemy in church. My heart pounded as I tensed for a stampede from the seething men. But none moved. Tucker knew his foes well.

He went on, "Now, what in my sorry fate is the matter with you men? Sulphur mining so good none of you has need of some extra spending money? Twenty I'll say now! Double eagle! Twenty days pay for an afternoon's work showing a man one blessed tree!"

Indeed, in that time, this was an extravagantly rich offer. Yet still the man in the corner growled, "Ya ain't listening. Nobody gonna help ya!"

But in contradiction, a voice blurted from another corner,

"I'll take you." Everyone turned to stare at a man seated near a narrow window. Amid unanimous grunts of disapproval, he rose shakily. He was perhaps forty, plump, with thin graying hair and drooping, life-weary eyes.

The man in the corner snarled, "Ed, it'll do for you like it done for Jacob."

The man we now knew as Ed stared at the floor. His reply was mumbled, but quick and somehow defiant, "Do Tumley first, for puttin'em up. And anyways, what do you care?"

Tucker hurried over to Ed and led him toward the door, "Well, at least one among you has the entrepreneurial spirit. Glad to see it. Come along, Ed."

Outside, we walked quickly away from the saloon, Tucker urging Ed along lest the man lose courage. Ed studiously avoided one's eyes, looking always at the ground when he spoke, as though, if he raised his gaze, he might see something he'd rather not.

He declared there was no road to the fabled tree and the only way would be on foot. This meant we must abandon Triumph and board our horses. That done, we returned to the boarding house to gather our gear, including the new Repalfly insect repellant Tucker had obtained from Canada.

As we came out of the hotel, Ed's eyes flicked high enough to appraise our weapons (he wore none himself), but even in that fleeting glance I clearly saw his disdain. To me this was astonishing for, in addition to Tucker's Le Mat, he and Jenny carried their ponderous double rifles and I had my big-bore Winchester 1876. I felt we would be intimidating to an army, never mind a lowly werewolf.

Tucker untied Joker from the porch post and we set off down the street with jittery Ed. Tucker was either in, or affecting, a jovial mood, perhaps at least partly as a result of my recent complaint. He attempted time-passing conversation with our monosyllabic guide.

"Ed, I want to thank you for helpin' us out. People around here don't seem too friendly on the whole."

"Need the money is all," Ed mumbled.

"Well, you'll sure get it. I'd say you are a little smarter than your neighbors. I can be downright generous if people'll just cooperate with me."

Ed did not respond. We walked a bit in silence. Then Tucker began again.

"You don't think much of our firearms, do you, Ed?"

Ed stared even more resolutely at the ground, apparently debating whether or not to voice a negative opinion and possibly place his potential earnings in jeopardy. Finally he said, "Won't do you no good."

"So I've heard, so I've heard. I heard a man emptied his gun at this critter and it still got 'im."

Ed visibly tensed, but continued to walk as he said quietly, "Yeah. I was there."

Tucker's eyebrows went up. "Were you now? Well, there's a story I'd like to hear."

It was many more shuffling steps before Ed spoke again. "We were fools. We didn't listen."

"Didn't listen — to that crazy old Gypsy, you mean?"

Ed suddenly looked at Tucker with an expression of equal parts anger and fear. Then he quickly turned his eyes back to the ground. "She knows. She *knows*."

"Oh she knows, all right." Tucker's voice was fast losing its friendly tone. "She knows enough manure to keep you people scared. And I bet she don't ask nothin' for her wise words and sage advice — except that she don't have to work a day in her life for anything. Am I right?"

"You oughtn't make fun. It don't like folks makin' fun. It'll come after you sure. And Tumley. And maybe — prob'ly me too for helpin'."

67

"I wouldn't worry about it. If it gives either me or Jenny a clear shot it won't be comin' after you."

Ed suddenly stopped, and looked at Tucker for the second time. "My brother was a good shot. A damn good shot!"

He seemed to have startled himself as much as us. His eyes shot back to the ground and be began his shuffling walk again. At first it seemed he wasn't going to say anything else, but suddenly it poured from him.

"My brother, Jacob. He was the last one killed. I used to live with him, but my sister-in-law, his wife — widow — she done threw me out now. Don't want me around. Anyways, there was a bunch of us out after it. Thought we could kill it. Each had silver bullets, too. Melted down from the cross in the church."

Ed's eyes rose, but now they were fixed on inner visions. "He'd been out three nights with his dogs. Before daybreak that morning, I was bringing him some food. But before I got there I hear him go to shootin' and shootin'. He had a Winchester 73." He nodded at me. "Not big as yours, but a fifteen shooter. Then I hears him yellin', but I couldn't find him right off. Too dark in amongst the trees. And I could hear the — the thing just growlin' and growlin'. Such a sound you never heard." Ed stopped speaking, shook his head slowly. Eventually he added, "All tore up."

Tucker whistled. "Silver bullets an' all, huh?"

This seemed to make Ed even more nervous. He nodded hesitantly and said, "That's right," in a low voice.

Tucker's brow furrowed and he looked closely at the man. Then his head went back, his chin jutted, and a knowing look spread across his face.

"He didn't use his silver bullets, did he, Ed?"

Ed started to protest, but Tucker's ever-certain attitude overpowered him and his expression became one of pleading.

"Don't tell no one! I found'em in his pocket afterwards. Guess he was gonna keep'em. Sell the silver, you know. Good money in these parts."

"Hah!" Tucker slapped his holster, "sounds like a man after my own heart! No offense meant there. God rest his soul."

Ed was not thrilled with the compliment. He went on, "Anyways, I wanted no part. Jus' chucked them bullets in the crick."

Ed's sad solemnity seemed to put Tucker off from asking further questions. We trudged on in silence.

Unfortunately, our trek took us down the trail past Mordia's cabin. As it came into view, much to Ed's consternation, she appeared in her doorway and glared at us, hands clenching a shawl pulled tight round her face. Poor Ed stared even harder at the ground, I suppose trying to be invisible. It was socially awkward, to say the least, except for Tucker, who chuckled softly to himself as we trudged along.

Just before we were out of sight, Ed unexpectedly whirled and called to Mordia in a trembling voice.

"Don't you be puttin' no hex on me! Don't you do it. My family's in a bad way with Jacob gone. We need money."

Mordia slowly shook her head, and pointed at Tucker with a bony finger, calling back, "It is not me who wakes the evil. It is him."

With another chuckle from Tucker, we pressed on. I found myself feeling sorry for Mordia and Ed, living in their narrow worlds, plagued by fears of unnamed demonic forces which could strike at any moment. While I have, and had then, a healthy respect for the way in which chance can impact one's life, I did not ascribe to it a malevolent intelligence, nor spend my energies on charms and spells to dissuade bad luck from my path.

A mile or more past Mordia's, at last our guide turned off

the road and led us into the dense, dripping forest. His hang-dog manner changed. He began to look around constantly and even walked in an unconscious half-crouch, as though ready to spring at any moment.

It was quite miserable trekking. Our boots caught on every root and vine. The perpetually damp forest reeked of mold, fungus, and rotting vegetation. I hadn't gone a mile before I regretted choosing my heavy 45-75. Carried at port it strained the wrists. Slung over either shoulder it bruised the shoulder blades. But of course I couldn't complain, given that Jenny was carrying an even heavier gun with no apparent strain.

Onward we pushed, until Ed suddenly stopped and faced Tucker nervously, "Look, I cain't go no further. Just head east from here. You'll find it all right. It's a great big tree. Cain't miss it."

I was at least as surprised as Ed when Tucker's twin-muzzled pistol materialized in front of his face. Tucker's voice was grating and absolutely fiendish.

"No, *you* look. I didn't hire you for good cash money so's I could come out here to waste time wandering around on my own."

Ed seemed unable to speak. He drew a constricted breath and then faltered, "P-please, Mr. Tucker. I told you — shouldn't even be helpin'."

Tucker jerked the Le Mat's hammer back! I flinched on Ed's behalf, thinking, *Tucker's gone mad again!* Tucker's face was as frightening as his gun; his left eye had gone wide open, while the right was squinting. He had started to speak out of the right side of his mouth, so that his mustache was tilted crazily. His voice shook.

"Ed, the sun is shinin'. There ain't no moon. And right now the most dangerous thing in these woods is *me!* Now, let's all find the big tree — together."

Ed was ashen. His hands opened and closed uncontrollably. He managed a spasmodic nod.

Keeping his gun aimed right at Ed's face, Tucker let the big hammer down with unbearable slowness. Then he bowed slightly, swinging the pistol down and away in an "after you" arc. Ed moved quickly ahead of us.

I was furious and felt the fool for it. Only hours earlier Tucker had promised to curtail his violent ways and now he was threatening murder! Even so, I chose not to raise the matter in Ed's presence and trudged onward in ill-tempered silence.

We went at least another grueling mile and, given the faintness of the "trail" Ed followed, I had to admit we'd likely not have reached our goal without him as guide. But at last we arrived at an enormous oak tree. It was so huge its vast umbrella of foliage commanded a clearing in which lesser vegetation struggled for light. Its thick branches extended far out in all directions and made me think of an octopus, for many were exotically twisted and curled, almost knotted, perhaps from the old monarch having survived a century or more of hurricanes.

"All right, that's it," Ed quavered.

Jenny began to circle the tree, leading Joker by his leash, studying the ground.

Tucker turned to Ed, "So, trail goes cold here, every time?"

"Yes, sir."

"And people were smart enough to range around a bit. Try to pick it up?"

"Sure. We gone in ever direction trying to pick it up. Crossed the stream, too." Ed nodded toward a syrupy stream meandering sluggishly past perhaps thirty yards south of the tree. "Dogs never found nothin'."

"Any chance the critter backtracked on you?" asked Tucker?

Ed shook his head, "Folks followed the trail clean back to the road. Never found a cut right or left."

Tucker pondered for a moment, then said, "So, seems like that thing just disappears right here on this spot. I just don't see how that can be."

Ed lowered his always-low voice to a near whisper, "Well, you know — this is where he *changes*."

"From wolf to man?"

"Yes, sir. That's why the dogs lose him. Then he circles around, changes back, and makes his move on ya."

Tucker nodded. He was clearly dismissive of the superstition, but had no ready explanation to counter it.

"Please, can I go now?" asked Ed, glancing at the surroundings he feared so much.

"You can go," Tucker grunted.

Ed gratefully began to back away from the tree. When he was perhaps ten paces away, Tucker produced a twenty dollar gold piece and held it lazily out, "Don't forget your money."

Ed stopped, fought a mental battle, walked stiffly back, snatched the coin — and then ran into the forest. When his crashing steps had subsided, I gathered my faculties for yet another confrontation with Tucker.

"You must have a lot of enemies!" I announced huffily.

Tucker was looking up at the tree. He rolled his head round and gave me a weary look. "None that I have any respect for."

"Well you said you'd only do what was necessary. Was it necessary to pull a gun on the man?"

"I can almost guarantee it."

"Well — well, you didn't have to *cock* it. You might have shot him accidentally. Or, what if he had made a run for it? It would be pretty hard to explain wouldn't it? We shot a man because he wouldn't show us the location of a tree?"

Tucker now turned and looked at me directly, suddenly

incredulous. "You really think I'm crazy don't you?"

"I'm a scientist. I have to judge by the evidence." I raised my head triumphantly.

"Well here's some more evidence for you. First of all, I wouldn't have shot ol' Ed. Just gets things done quicker if people think you're willing. Can't you tell when I'm kiddin'?"

"Cocking a loaded pistol in a man's face is *kidding*?" I railed.

"Which brings me to evidence number two." Tucker drew the Le Mat. He opened the loading port and turned so that I could look into it. He cocked the pistol, and an empty chamber came into view. Then, looking at me with an all-wise expression, he lowered the hammer and cocked again. A second empty chamber appeared.

I was confused, "You keep *two* chambers empty?"

"That's right." He adopted the attitude of someone speaking to a very small child as he clicked the cylinder round and demonstrated again. "I keep the hammer on an empty chamber like most people with any sense. But I also keep the *next* chamber empty. So when I cock the thing, the hammer's still on an empty chamber. Now isn't that wonderful?"

I ignored his patronizing. "I must admit, I'm relieved." Tucker spun the cylinder to its ready position and holstered the gun.

"Good night, Whitney, I never shot anybody in my whole life. I shot *at* a man once, but *he* was stealin' my horse." He stared into the past for a moment, glowering, then added, "Missed him. Did a lot more shooting practice after that."

His eyes came back to me, and he almost smiled, "Pfhuh! You're quite a case, man. Never figured myself for much of an actor, 'cept for people who're already scared to death. You want to know if I'm kiddin' or not, just keep your eye on Jenny. Can't fool her."

I looked round and saw Jenny still methodically circling

the tree with Joker, apparently uninterested in this latest confrontation.

"What do you think, Dickens?" called Tucker.

Jenny shrugged, "The ground is no good."

"Yeah, I know."

"No good?" I asked.

"For tracks." He stalked over and yanked Joker's leash. "And if this mangy critter gets any more excited, he'll fall asleep. But let's look around a bit. The thing's led people here more than once, so it must hang around here a lot. Maybe we can turn up something."

We walked in ever widening circles round the great tree. We clambered along the banks of the stream. But we turned up nothing.

We returned to the base of tree and broke out some biscuits we'd brought for lunch. Jenny and I sat on a log. Tucker chewed and paced round and round the tree. Abruptly, he stopped.

"Looky here."

We joined him. The tree's bark was vertically scratched with what looked like claw marks, as though some animal regularly pawed at it for some reason. Joker gave the scratches a sniff and growled softly, the first sign he'd shown of interest in anything.

Tucker gazed up into the tree, then held his rifle out to Jenny. She took it, and he scrambled up into the tree with remarkable agility. He straddled a massive branch and looked down at us.

"Now if I was trying to get away from dogs, I'd head into that stream and go up or down a ways. But the trail never leads to the stream. Just the tree."

"So they say," Jenny commented.

Tucker began to work his way along the branch toward the stream. Somewhat mystified, we followed along on the ground. Soon he was out over the middle of the stream.

"Now, if I wanted to increase my odds, maybe I'd do like this and drop myself out in the middle of the stream, so the trail don't lead to the bank. What do you think?"

Jenny folded her arms with a dubious look, "I think you are a very smart wolf."

Tucker had to agree, "That I would be." He leaned forward and grasped the branch to let himself down. But just as he dropped into a hanging position, something caught his eye.

"Hello," he said, and reached up with one hand to snatch at something in the leaves. That caused him lose his grip and he dropped in a heap.

Jenny leapt forward, "Kiyuga!"

"I'm all right, I'm all right," he gruffed. "Looky here."

He held out what he had snatched from the tree as he fell, a small tuft of course gray hair. "Caught on a twig up there." He and Jenny studied it closely.

"Not raccoon," she pronounced.

"Not possum," he added. Then, to me, "Is it wolf?"

"It's from a good-sized mammal," I said. "That's the most I can venture."

"A wolf that climbs trees?" Tucker mused. He was as animated as I'd ever seen him.

A painstaking search of the area revealed nothing else. Tucker decided that if we got clear weather, we would cover the same ground that night as we had in daylight. He hoped that the creature might prove nocturnal, and that our dog would pick up a fresh trail. If we found nothing in the area of the tree, we would explore the east bank of the stream, playing Tucker's far-fetched hunch, to see if any trail exited from the water on that side.

There was little conversation on the long trudge back to the boarding house. But as we stepped out of the dreary forest on the relatively more open road, Tucker suddenly spoke, "Uh, Whitney, knowin' how you feel about huntin' and all — well, you don't really have to come back tonight." I started to speak but he stopped me with a raised hand, "And it isn't just that. Like Luddy told us, could be dangerous if we run into the thing, no matter what it really is."

"Please, I wouldn't miss it," I smiled. "I feel utterly safe in the capable hands of you and Jenny. Besides, thanks to you I have my own Naval cannon to wield should we get into a tight spot." I lifted my Winchester.

Tucker nodded, apparently glad to get an unpleasant task over with. "Okay, then."

It was true that I felt in no particular danger, but I was to learn that this was primarily because I did not really expect to find anything dangerous in the woods. I was in error.

CHAPTER FIVE

The Beast

Tucker delayed us briefly before we set out again from the boarding house. He could not find a favored pair of gloves — custom-made thick and strong, of course. He finally became convinced he had failed to pack them and bleakly chalked that up to the failing memory of an old man.

On the positive side of things, the moon had risen exceptionally bright. The road fairly glowed ghostly blue-gray and our walk was nearly as carefree as in daylight.

We again had to pass Mordia's abode. Dim lantern light shown through her sagging shutters. I was glad that she seemed unaware of our passing and was unavailable to cast her baleful gaze on us.

With Tucker setting a smart pace, we strode to the spot where Ed had entered the woods. While the moon lit the road we were on like a good gas street lamp, it barely penetrated the tangled forest, which looked considerably more forbidding than it had in daylight. And, adding to a growing sense of menace, the woods droned with the curious hollow "gonging" of tree frogs (mostly *Hyla cinerea*). Heaping on more unpleasantness, the night air was fairly choked with flying insects, buzzing in our ears and buffeting our faces despite our liberally applied Repalfly.

We had pushed not thirty yards into the forest when Joker startled us by baying excitedly, straining at the leash Tucker held. He had picked up a fresh scent exactly where others had before us. Jenny and Tucker shared one of their information-laden glances.

"Well, that's obliging. Wasn't there earlier," he said. "Whitney, you best go between me and Jenny. If the thing turns out to be behind us, she'll hear it comin' before you

77

will. You watch the sides, but don't let me get out of sight ahead of you. Oh, and I guess you know enough to keep quiet." I nodded.

Tucker walked into the shadows behind the eager dog, which he was keeping leashed in order to prevent a reoccurrence of the mysterious ambush that had claimed Luddy's dogs.

Jenny and I followed. The interwoven branches of the moss-draped trees reduced the moonlight to pale gray splotches in a world of impenetrable blackness. I could see Tucker only as fragmented silhouettes in the splashes of light. Occasionally his broad hat glowed as he passed through a moon beam.

There was no wind, but I wondered how Jenny could expect to hear anything coming from behind us over the din of forest creatures. Surely an elephant could sneak up on us in all that noise. Much less confident than I had been in the hotel, I chambered a cartridge and walked with my thumb poised over my rifle's hammer; and repeatedly shirked my duty to watch our flanks in glancing back to see that Jenny was still close behind me.

Pushing through the dense, damp growth was every bit as unpleasant as it had been during the day, and seemed to take twice as long. But, following the scent, Joker indeed led us to the big oak tree. Before we moved beneath its sprawling branches, Tucker stopped and spent a long moment carefully surveying them.

When he was satisfied that we were not to be attacked from above, he moved to the base of the tree where the dog's purposeful pulling suddenly became erratic and confused as he sniffed first one way then another. Tucker led him round the tree, but the trail was cold.

Jenny and I stood with our backs to the tree. I silently wished we had a campfire or lanterns to drive back the darkness. It was increasingly alarming to imagine some beast flying at us from out of the shadows, even if it were only a wild boar or rabid skunk.

Tucker dragged the straining dog over to us. "Let's cross the crick. I'm dead certain if we go far enough on the other bank, we'll pick up a trail." He hauled the dog in that direction, with Jenny and me close behind.

We pushed through the thick vegetation overhanging the stream and waded slowly in. Thick scum on the surface glinted the moonlight. The water flowed into my boots. It was surprisingly, and queasily tepid. I was thankful it was little more than knee deep. I imagined hoards of irritated water moccasins, invisible in the blackness, moving out of our path as we forded. Each step had to be very deliberate, for the bottom was a soft mud which permitted our boots to sink easily and then clung hungrily as we tried to pull them out. Sunken branches and roots abounded, making every step a stumble. I resolved myself that there would be leeches to contend with when I later removed my boots. (There were, but given the rest of the night's adventures, I was happy to be alive to see them.)

Tucker elected to try downstream first. We worked our way along the bank, all of us watching the dog for some sign that he had regained the scent. Our water-filled boots added their irksome squishing to the other noises of the forest.

But suddenly we heard a loud splash behind us. Certainly something very large had fallen or leapt into the water. We all spun about to look in the direction of the big oak.

"Heck of a catfish, wasn't it?" said Tucker. He unconsciously opened his Rigby 600 to run a reassuring thumb over the two fresh cartridges in the breech, a habit he'd acquired in hunting dangerous game. He snapped the rifle shut and then slipped two additional cartridges from his belt, holding them between the fingers of his left hand, ready for a fast reload if needed.

At the same time, Joker, facing in the direction of the sound, got wind of something. He stiffened. Even in the dark I could sense the poor animal trembling. His exuberance for the chase had evaporated in an instant.

Tucker tied the dog off to a bush near me as he whispered, "Spread out some."

Jenny quickly stepped several paces away and took cover behind a tree, snapping off the safety of her Rigby. There was no large tree near me and I was afraid I would make excessive noise if I tried to move too far, so I stepped behind an inadequate sapling and turned sideways, easing my Winchester's hammer back.

I tried to peer ahead of Tucker into the patchwork world of gray and black, but could see no movement. I tried to listen carefully, but succeeded only in becoming aware of blood rushing in my ears. My heart thudded erratically.

It was terribly disturbing that Joker had gone silent and trembling. It would have been reassuring if he had strained at his leash in a mad effort to confront whatever had crossed the stream. I had read of hunting dogs who fearlessly attacked grizzly bears. But this one cowered behind me, pressing his shaking body against my calf. What on earth was approaching us?

I strained to hear any sound of footsteps or movement. Tucker and Jenny were doing the same. "Bless these blessed birds!" Tucker hissed. "Can't hardly hear a thing."

"They're tree frogs," I corrected.

Tucker's silhouetted hat swiveled toward me, tilting with a sarcastic, "Thank you."

Then, cutting through the frogs' shrill chorus, we heard an unearthly growl. Low and ominous and ugly, it seemed to go on forever, as though the thing emitting it had no need to breathe. Joker whined pathetically, pressing himself harder against my leg and trembling all the more.

Eventually, the growl stopped. Tucker leaned toward me, speaking so softly I could barely hear him. "I'm stepping into the open. If it comes, let it come for me. Be ready. But if you decide to shoot, for my sake make sure you know what the blazes you're shooting at."

I nodded, but wondered how I could see to shoot at all. My eyes bulged, trying to force the black shadows before me to yield any image, however faint. Had it been this dark all along? I glanced in Jenny's direction, but could see only the faint glint of her rifle barrels amid dew-glistened leaves.

Tucker moved slowly, quietly forward into a small moon-lit clearing a few yards upstream. The growl returned, horrid, throaty, louder, more threatening, floating through the air, seeming to come from everywhere. Tucker stopped, poised in a half crouch, rifle held tensely at his hip.

The sound subsided again. How long did we all stand motionless? Surely it was many seconds. Perhaps a minute. Long enough that my mind actually began to wander. Why do the frogs keep singing? Are they not as unnerved as I at that dreadful growling? Why does Jenny come on these bizarre adventures? Luddy, the fool, had he not injured himself I would not now be standing —

Suddenly there was movement. A black shape streaked through patches of moonlight straight toward Tucker. I could ascertain only that it ran on all fours — and that it was big. The growl escalated into a ghastly snarling screech. A dog? A wolf? Something worse?

Tucker jerked his rifle up and fired. At night, the deafening roar of his 600 Nitro Express was eclipsed by the flame from the muzzle. It lit the woods like a photographer's flash pan. And frozen in that harsh instantaneous glare I saw the thing which charged headlong at him.

It was wolf indeed (*Canis lupus*), but such a wolf. It seemed big as a lion. Its hair was course and wildly flying. Its legs were long and skeletal. And its eyes, dear Lord, its eyes — they glowed hellish and pupil-less in the orange gunpowder glare.

All this my mind captured in the time it took for Tucker to move his finger from the front to the rear trigger of his Rigby. He fired his second shot, lighting up the forest in another Halloween tableau. This time the image was of the beast now flying toward him in mid air, jaws wide, teeth gleaming, blood-red tongue lolling to one side.

The night slammed back down as after a lightning stroke. Blinded by Tucker's muzzle flashes, I could only hear his breathy grunt as the monster collided with him. A heavy thud and the flutter of wet leaves told me that Tucker had been borne to the ground. At my feet, our hound split the air with a terrified howl and dashed madly against his leash, not toward the wolf, but frantically away.

To my right I heard Jenny barely breathe, "Kiyuga!" Neither of us dared fire our weapons into the darkness, so we sprang forward as one.

Ahead, we heard Tucker shouting and the thing snarling and growling with demonic ferocity. Worse, to my horror, I could tell that the creature's mouth was full.

Plunging ahead blindly, I had the thought that when I felt the thing with my legs I would club it relentlessly with my rifle butt. But I had taken only a few steps when the beast was yet again brilliantly outlined in an orange flash which was accompanied by a muffled whump. Even as the flash faded, I saw the animal's hindquarters jerk violently upward. The growling changed to a guttural moaning interrupted by hissing intakes of breath.

Then came jumbled, disorganized scuffling sounds. My eyes readjusted and at last I could see the creature as it crawled into a patch of moonlight, dragging itself painfully with its forelegs. Its back was broken. Intestines trailed under its useless hind legs.

That it was wounded was apparent, but this gave me no comfort. I yanked up my rifle and began firing. Jenny's elephant gun thundered simultaneously. We fired relentlessly as though facing the Spanish at San Juan, though the beast was surely killed with the first shots. Gun smoke billowed into the patch of moonlight, slowed, stopped, and hung like fog in the utterly windless air.

Shockingly, there were now no forest sounds at all. The gunfire had silenced the tree frogs and every other living thing in the vicinity. Our breathing and Joker's labored panting seemed loud as a steam engine.

I turned toward Tucker. With great relief, I saw him sit up shakily. Jenny was already on her knees at his side.

"I'm okay, Dickens. Okay. Just my arm — don't know how bad."

"Whitney! A match!" Jenny whispered.

I fumbled a strike-anywhere from my pocket and raked it across my rifle's butt plate. Though it created a pitifully small oval of light, the flame was oh-so-welcome in the crushing blackness. Cupping it in my hand, I knelt beside them.

Tucker's left jacket sleeve was shredded from wrist to elbow. The tattered white lining began to darken with blood.

"Take off your jacket," Jenny ordered, swiftly unbuttoning it.

As Tucker eased the jacket off his shoulder, he drew a pained breath, "Whew, wish your daddy could have seen that." With his good arm, he held up the twin-barreled Le Mat, broad smile glinting in the flickering light of my match.

"First time ever fired in need! And served me well, wouldn't you say, Whitney?"

I now realized that the shot which had so swiftly done in the wolf was in fact from the 10 gauge shotgun barrel of the Le Mat, fired point blank into the wolf's belly as the animal had pinned Tucker to the ground.

Then he added sheepishly, "'Course, I wouldn't have needed it if I'd shot straight with my blessed rifle."

"No one could have aimed squarely in the time you had, and in this darkness," I offered.

Tucker shook his head slowly. "Gettin' slow. Gettin' old. Ow!" Jenny was pulling his torn sleeve over his wounded arm.

"Well, help me, stupid!" she snapped. "Talk when your bleeding has stopped."

I struck another match as the sleeve came off, and was instantly dismayed; blood covered Tucker's entire forearm and ran in rivulets down his wrist, dripping from his finger tips.

Even unflappable Tucker was taken aback at the sight, "No wonder it hurts." Jenny did not pass judgment, but went to work, washing his arm with water from her canteen. At last it became clear that what looked like hopelessly mangled flesh was in reality a series of lacerations. Jenny pointed to several deep ones on top of his arm, then turned it gently and pointed to three more. "These are the worst. Here." She handed him a bandage which she produced from a small pouch on her belt. "Press hard on this one," she indicated one of the deepest gashes in which blood kept welling rapidly. Tucker obeyed and she began to wrap his other wounds.

Tucker glanced up at me, "Jenny knows a lot about stuff like this."

"I would know less if you would stay out of trouble," she grumbled.

I was feeling ill. Surely, I thought, the sight of Tucker's cuts could not alone so affect me. I became aware of an appalling odor. To the already acrid smell of the wolf's water-soaked fur, wet from its stream crossing, had been added the overpowering stench of its rent intestines.

Jenny leaned back from her work and sighed. "The blood comes more slow. But we should go back. Your arm should be cleaned more, with alcohol, or whiskey."

Tucker nodded, but looked off wistfully at the fallen wolf. "'Course, I sure hate to leave this big fella, though. Maybe we could at least dress him out and hang him up in a tree. Would you mind, Whitney?"

"Is that really necessary," I asked impatiently. "The smell may kill me at close range."

"It is sweet, at that," Tucker said, nose wrinkling. Then he nodded, "You're right, we'll forgo dressin' him out. Just throw a rope over a high branch, haul him up and leave him. We'll come back for him if we feel up to it."

So, I held my breath while I tied a rope round the wolf's neck. Death had left its great teeth bared in a snarl and a staring eye glinting from blood-matted fur. We later estimated it weighed one-hundred-sixty pounds. Supernatural or not, it had been a formidable animal.

Since we knew the stream flowed toward the road, Tucker insisted we follow it rather than return the way we'd come. This way he could search for the wolf's trail a little further. Surprisingly, Joker seemed in support of this plan, since, with the beast dead, he had fully regained his willingness to hunt. Jenny took over his leash to spare Tucker his incessant yanking. I trudged behind them, carrying Tucker's sixteen pound Rigby in addition to my own rifle. They hung limply at my sides. My wrists ached. I was in a misery of nervous exhaustion and whirling insects. Even so, a question still suddenly came to me.

"That wasn't silver buckshot in your Le Mat, by any chance?"

"Pfhuh! Two ounces of pure lead. The silver slugs was in the Rigby and I missed with both barrels! Besides, if he was the real article, he was supposed to change back to human when he died."

"Oh. You're disappointed then."

"I'm used to it."

"It doesn't make any difference that this must be one of the largest wolves ever recorded?"

"Well, that's ok, if that's what you're after."

"But it's not a dinosaur."

"Exactly."

At that moment, our newly intrepid dog picked up the trail of the wolf again. It appeared, as Tucker had suspected, that the crafty animal leapt into the stream from the big oak, and swam a considerable distance downstream before going ashore. This was why no one had been able to pick up its trail beyond the tree.

Soon we came to the road, not very far from where we'd originally left it. The dog led us straight across and wanted to enter the woods on the other side. Jenny began to drag him determinedly in the direction of town.

But Tucker paused, staring in the direction the dog wanted to go. "Hey, uh, Jenny — hold up just a second."

She stopped, turned half way round, dropped a hand on her hip, and tilted her head to one side. Even by moonlight the remonstration was palpable.

"Aw come on, Dickens. Nobody else has ever managed to backtrack it this far. Say we go just a mile in. I'm not gonna bleed to death goin' an extra couple of miles. Tricky wolf like that one must have a great hideout. Or maybe there's even pups. I'd hate to miss out just 'cause I didn't feel like goin' a little out of my way."

I thought she might challenge him, but instead, without speaking, Jenny wheeled the dog round and followed his lead into the woods. I then suspected that she had anticipated Tucker's curiosity and was unwilling to try to argue him out of continuing.

As he plunged into the woods after her, I hurried after him, asking, "Who wins the right to estimate when we've gone a mile?"

"Oh, no estimatin' to it. When she turns in her tracks and walks over top of you goin' the other way, that's a mile. She surveyed the whole upper west section of our ranch, after she got the hang of it from a professional surveyor workin' the neighbor fella's land. Surveyor thought it was cute, you know, the little Indian woman watchin' him every day. But she's got a mind like a sponge. He never suspected he was cheatin' himself out of getting to do *our* land. I ever tell you that story?"

"No, but I'm getting used to such surprises."

"Yeah, well she's full of'em all right. She's both wife and partner. A man couldn't do no better." Tucker spoke a trifle overloud, evidently aiming those compliments more at Jenny's ears than mine, perhaps hoping to buy another mile when the time came.

The scent trail led us through some discouragingly thick undergrowth, and followed a tortuous zig-zag pattern. It was impossible for me to keep track of what general direction we were headed. But our dog stayed hard on the path, never confused.

It was the humans who were to be confused, for the trail abruptly ended when we blundered out of dense foliage into a small clearing. On one side of the clearing was a two-wheeled cart. Firmly affixed to it was a large wooden cage, empty, with its door unlatched. Cage and cart had obviously been in place for some time, for a leafy vine had wound itself up the spokes of one wheel. A bedraggled tarp partially draped the cage, apparently for half-hearted protection against rain.

Of primary interest to Tucker and Jenny, however, were a pair of gloves balanced on top of one of the cart wheels.

Tucker picked them up and studied them while he slowly turned them over in the moonlight.

"Can we have another match, Whitney?" he said softly. I quickly obliged. The moment the match light played over the gloves in his hand, Tucker spoke in an eerily flat voice.

"They're *mine*. They're mine aren't they, Jenny?"

She nodded. Clearly there was no doubt. Tucker remained motionless for a long moment, still staring at the gloves. Then he slowly raised them above his head.

"Well — *bless it!*" He threw them violently down, then yelped as his follow-through caused him to slap his injured forearm.

While it was obvious that both Tucker and Jenny were upset, I remained "behind the curve," (as was so often the case in my adventures with these two). It took several moments before the implication of the evidence suddenly came to me.

"Does this mean — that is, do you suspect someone *sent* the wolf after you? Someone in fact controls the animal?"

"Of course that's what it means, man! Bless it!" He stalked round the cage, very like a caged animal himself, full of rage and unable to vent it.

He stopped and looked toward me. His face was a featureless black oval under his moon-rimmed hat, but his tone was positively venomous, "I'll tell you, Whitney, you can look a long time before you'll find any monster as monstrous as *people!*"

Indeed, I believe he was more incensed over the scurrilous corruption and exploitation of a harmless werewolf legend than about the fact that someone had sent out a vicious trained animal to murder him. He was leaning against the cart now, gazing down at his feet. When his head came back up, the burst of anger was spent, and Tucker the Showman had emerged. "All right — all right — they figure to wake up and find me dead. Well, they'll find me. I'm gonna be standin' right in the middle of their little town with their werewolf on a stake. We're going' back right now; hitching up Triumph." He was instantly in motion, plunging away into the forest.

Here I was sure Jenny would protest. But her concern for his injuries seemed to have been swept away, either by outrage that her mate had been targeted for death, or by the sheer energy with which he now set forth.

With Tucker setting a brisk pace, the march back to Sombre Foret took less than half the time of our trip out. Given of the fear the townspeople had of opening doors after sundown, as we strode toward the livery I worried about the methods to which Tucker might resort in order to get our wagon and horses. Fortunately, he wanted no one to know he had survived, and he allowed Jenny to display still another talent: she easily scaled the wall of the livery barn and entered through the hayloft.

We made an absurd amount of noise hitching up Taft and Bronto and rolling out the wagon, but as Tucker predicted, not so much as a candle was lit in the village, so afraid were its inhabitants. While no doubt awakened by the noise, not one would dare show a light to admit to it.

"Probably think the noise is the werewolf takin' out his anger on Crazy Tucker's team," sneered Crazy Tucker.

Before we left, Jenny insisted on cleaning Tucker's arm more thoroughly. This she did by carbide lantern light. Blood seeped still from his deepest wounds, but it seemed all but completely stopped once she rebound the arm with a fresh cloth bandage from her little pouch.

Aboard Triumph, we rode out of town. We again passed Mordia's cabin. Her one window was dark and we saw no sign of her. We stopped at the trail head and trudged once more through the woods to the spot where we'd killed the wolf.

89

The task of carrying the dead animal out fell to me and Jenny, since as she would not hear of Tucker attempting to lift anything. Once the wolf was gutted and dressed, I gallantly volunteered to carry it, holding its forelegs over my shoulders and letting the body hang down my back. But even dressed out it was simply too heavy for me to carry very far. I soon had to give up chivalry to exhaustion, but not before a legion of fleas had deserted the cooling wolf for a warmer home. A pole was cut, the wolf tied to it, and Jenny and I carried it between us for the remaining distance to the road and our waiting wagon.

Back in town, we stopped outside the rooming house. Tucker quietly snuffed out the lantern on the porch. Our carrying pole, sharpened at both ends, now served as his display stake. He mounted his bloody, battered trophy in the center of the street. I half hoped he would then set fire to the building again, so that we might thus gain comfortable sleeping quarters for the night, but he had no such desire.

"I want to be standing right here when these cowards wake up," he whispered. Then he added mysteriously, "Besides, I don't want that old innkeeper to find out anything before the rest of the folks do."

There was only room for two in the wagon, but had there been room for me I would still have had to exile myself due to my newly acquired horde of passengers. The fleas seemed to be having a great deal of trouble selecting comfortable sites on which to settle, and I was sure I would never be able to sleep through such violent activity, but morning found me curled up against a wagon wheel and most difficult to arouse.

Jenny was shaking my shoulder. When I had reestablished where I was, I got up to see three early risers, one of whom was our guide, Ed, gaping at the huge wolf. It was a grisly sight indeed, made all the more so by the dawn light which crept at a low angle down the main street, the rays muted and turned sulfurous by the seemingly perennial mist of this place.

Because of its broken spine, the wolf's lower quarters hung twisted to one side. Its jaw hung open and its swollen tongue was lolled out. One flank was horribly flayed open with exit wounds from the many needless shots Jenny and I had fired. As a result, from rib cage down it was covered with thick, clotted blood.

I looked round to find Tucker, and saw him sitting, arms folded, in a chair next to the rooming house door. More people were coming down the street, and he was waiting to see their reactions to his prize.

But just then the door was unbolted. As it swung cautiously inward, Tucker sprang up, kicked it wide and charged inside. I heard him bellow, "Good morning, old man! Surprised to see me?" Then he came back and beckoned to me and Jenny from the doorway.

We rushed in after him. Indeed, old Tumley seemed astonished, indeed chilled to see us. He scuttled painfully across the lobby and cowered behind his little registration desk, as though it offered some protection. Jenny hurried up the stairs, carrying out some plan to which, as was so often the case, I was not privy.

Tucker, rather an intimidating sight in his muddy clothes, ripped jacket and bloody bandages, stood stiffly in front of the old man, hands clasped behind his back. He was waiting for information. After a moment, he called irritably up the stairs.

"Jenny? Well?"

"Locked," came her reply.

"Not forced open?" he shouted back.

"No," Jenny called down. I realized that they were referring to the door of their room.

Now Tucker advanced on Tumley. "So, sir, someone with a key to our room borrowed a pair of my gloves last night."

Tumley just shook his head mindlessly, endlessly.

Tucker snarled, "Stop it! You look like a windmill lost its tail vane! What'd you do with them gloves? That's all I want to know."

Jenny rushed back down the stairs, hand on her pistol butt. It scared me to see her nearly as overwrought as Tucker.

A tear rolled down the old man's cheek. I felt terrible for him. Tucker's hands twitched behind his back, left gripping the right's wrist, no doubt to keep it from the Le Mat in his holster.

At last, thank God, the old man spoke, "It was only for our own protection. We meant no harm to you."

That seemed to set Tucker back a step. "Your protection? What do you mean by that?"

Tumley stuttered in his characteristic whisper, "Gave them — gave them to Mordia. But only for a spell to protect us, sir! Not to harm you! Your path, we thought, was sure. Your life already undone. 'Twas only to save us from givin' you the rooms. So's it wouldn't come for us after."

Jenny and Tucker glanced at each other with a flash of understanding, which I, of course, did not share.

Jenny said, "The Gypsy woman?"

Tucker slowly nodded. "Finally gettin' a tail-hold on these doings. The wolf was *hers!* Well, don't I feel the fool."

After a moment's reflection, I too got a tail-hold: the wolf had been controlled by Mordia. She had used it to terrorize the community so that she might extract payments for "spells" to protect the locals from the very beast she herself sent on its terrible missions.

Tucker slapped a twenty dollar coin down on Tumley's desk. "Don't you have a care, old fella. That wolf's not coming for you. He's stuck on a stick right outside your door, dead as last year's hay. As for *her* —"

He now turned to me, "Whitney, gather your kit. We are

getting' quit of this place. It is eeevil."

I rushed to my room and threw together my belongings. All the while, I worried that our next stop would be Mordia's cabin — that Tucker would burst in and brutally murder the old woman — that I would be tarred as an accessory to the crime. With these thoughts driving me to a frenzied pace, I flew down the stairs and out into the street.

But there I found Jenny waiting in the wagon, as calm as if we were going to church. To my relief, the horses were pointed north toward Lake Charles, and not south toward Mordia's cabin.

The wolf had been cut down and laid in the wagon bed. Its awful stench notwithstanding, Tucker would not hear of leaving it behind. (Despite being heavily damaged, the animal would be iced in Lake Charles and successfully carted clear to Oklahoma. There it would be painstakingly, expertly restored and mounted by Tucker's talented taxidermist, E.J. Members).

As I climbed aboard Triumph, I saw him talking with Ed, our former guide. Finished with his conversation, he joined Jenny and me on the wagon. Relaxed as could be, he chucked the horses and guided us down the street.

Gaining confidence that I was not to be party to some form of lynching, my indignation at Mordia's apparent actions rose to the surface, and I boldly declared to Tucker and Jenny, "We should report that woman to the authorities, the very moment we reach Lake Charles!"

Tucker glanced at me as though confused, then stared straight ahead, saying quickly, "Indeed we will, Whitney. Indeed we will."

His seeming lack of concern was baffling. The Tucker who would set fire to a rooming house rather than be denied a bed was now leaving without even confronting a woman who had evidently tried to kill him? Was he really content to wait and report her macabre and murderous exploitation in Lake Charles?

At the risk of prodding him to the very action I feared, I had to ask, "Does it not worry you that the Mordia woman may hear of what you've done? That she might escape before someone can get back here to arrest her."

Tucker continued looking straight ahead, but his mustache now twitched with a slight smile, "Oh, I don't think we have to worry about that."

As we trundled on up the street, I noted that only scattered wide-eyed children were watching us. The adults had disappeared. The significance of this escaped me, and I pressed on with my growing sense of outrage.

"Mr. Tucker, frankly, I'm quite astonished at your attitude toward this woman. I mean, she tried to murder you, in effect."

I saw a man come out of a house ahead of us, strapping on a pistol. But I continued, "and she is almost certainly responsible for at least three other deaths in this village."

The man with the pistol was joined by men coming from other houses along the way. One carried a rifle, another a fireplace poker, another a blacksmith's hammer.

Still I continued, "And her wolf might have killed Luddy had it not met with his dogs first —"

I saw more people with weapons — a pick-axe, a bucket of coal oil. The group was now virtual army. And leading it was Ed, himself carrying a pitchfork.

The army passed us, headed in the opposite direction, toward Mordia's. Some of them, including the young blond tough who'd squared off with Tucker in the saloon, now nodded stiffly and respectfully to him. At last the significance of their actions dawned on me.

"You — you told Ed everything?" I whispered to Tucker.

"Told him what I thought he had a right to know. What

all these folks oughta know."

In a flash I imagined the villagers, informed of Mordia's cruel plot, descending on her cabin. "But, those people — she may have murdered their relatives. They might be driven to do anything. Even to —"

"Oh, now you're gonna switch to *her* side, are you?" he flared at me.

"No, no," I stuttered, and looked anxiously back at the crowd of grim-faced villagers. "But there are — proper ways of dealing —"

Tucker interrupted me, "Just on account of you, Whitney, I also told Ed that we *would* report all this to the Lake Charles sheriff, that he'd likely come down here, and that he might not take kindly to vigilante law, no matter how well justified. I made the suggestion it'd probably be best to keep Mordia alive — more or less, 'til he gets here. 'Course, it's up to the townsfolk to decide their course."

His dark glee was chilling. I sat back uncomfortably on Triumph's stiff bench; and as I fixed my eyes on the road ahead, I thought: *Even a real werewolf might do well to avoid the path of Harold B. Tucker.*

CHAPTER SIX

Quiet Times — and One Mummy

I will admit that, as we returned from Louisiana to Oklahoma, I seriously considered resigning my position as ranch "zo-ologist" and scampering back to the more civilized world from which I'd sprung. However, Tucker reverted to less bombastic behavior, and this lulled me into believing that his actions in the episode of the werewolf stemmed primarily from the personal nature of the attack on him.

Had I fully appreciated the extreme lengths to which he would go to achieve his ends, I most certainly *would* have resigned. In the end, of course I did not, and will never be sorry for it. In remaining attached to Tucker's coattails, I would be swept into events outstripping the most uninhibited imagination.

That said, and despite the adventures to come, for a long while life on the DH was "downright unsalted" (Luddy's term for "bland"). Much of 1904 passed without dinosaur reports of significance. Luddy himself went off to Oregon on a posse trip to investigate sightings of some sort of ape-like creature. He returned with the usual: wild accounts by "eyewitnesses" who could offer no proof of any kind.

Tucker organized a jaunt to Oklahoma City to hear a concert conducted by John Philip Sousa who was, he said, "The only genuinely reliable composer of our day." By "reliable" he meant that Sousa's marches were consistently full of verve and of a quick pace. Tucker could not abide slow or solemn music. He also found Beethoven enjoyable, but somewhat less reliable.

I learned more about the diversity of Tucker's expansive world. One afternoon, as Luddy and I were heading out on horseback, we saw a man leaving the main house. Portly, well dressed, sporting elegantly sculpted mutton chops, he was clearly irked, grumbling to himself as he climbed into his buggy. Spotting us, he started his horse and gave a curt nod to Luddy as he rode closer.

Without introduction, he spoke huffily, "Be lucky if he still has his ranch when this is through! Be lucky if I keep him out of jail!" Then his chest swelled as he attempted to stifle a burp.

Luddy just smiled in his easygoing way, "Don't give yourself the gas, there, Winters. He's the best paying client you'll ever have."

"Hah! I'd settle for half the hours and half the heartburn," the man burped. And he continued on his way.

Luddy turned to me, leaning comfortably askew in his saddle, "That there's G. Winters Wayne, high muck-a-muck lawyer comes all the way from Oklahoma City."

I thus discovered that there was a consequence to Tucker's traveling the world kicking in doors, setting fires, pointing firearms, and generally being rude. Mr. Wayne's near full-time job was settling the lawsuits left in that turbulent wake. In this case, he had just reported the progress on suits arising from Sombre Foret. Despite Tucker's having solved a mystery, dispelled a myth, and brought to justice a murderer, several people there (Tumley and his sister among the foremost) were suing for damages, mental distress and the like. For the most part, G. Winters Wayne succeeded in keeping these matters out of the courts, almost always by dispensing more of Tucker's money. This, I correctly surmised, disturbed Tucker not in the least, and only abetted his cynical view of human nature.

One other visitor of note stopped at the ranch during this quiet period, a Mr. Carl Denham. He was of note in that he was not bearing tales of monsters. Instead he was seeking funding for his own explorations. He had with him a motion picture camera and explained that his intention was to tramp the planet's remotest locales, photographing the strange and magnificent, and then exhibit his work in theaters and opera houses. Very enthusiastic, he marched round the library gesticulating as he made his case, "Not only will I be exploring the world in a manner that suits your own ends, I'll be there with the mechanism," he patted his camera, "to capture incontrovertible proof, should I come upon a dinosaur, or a dragon, or Beelzebub himself!"

Tucker was unimpressed, "Not interested in photographs. I'm looking to catch the real article. And I fund enough silly expeditions as it is."

"Say now, look here," said Denham. "My expeditions won't cost you a cent, I mean in the end, of course. And you know why? Because the crowds thronging to see my motion pictures will be paying the tab, see? We're gonna pack'em in like sardines, I tell ya. Why, you'll get my exploring for free and make money in the bargain! There's a gold mine in motion pictures, Mr. Tucker!"

"They say the same thing about the oil they're squeezing out of the ground hereabouts."

"I tell ya, you're going to see my name up in electric lights in the biggest cities — and be cryin' 'cuz you aren't sharing the windfall!"

Tucker was calmly resolute, "I'll keep my money in cattle, Mr. Denham."

Denham pursued his point fervently and eloquently for some time longer, but ultimately was shown the door, unfunded. Once he had left, Tucker mumbled, "Fella reminded me of a sideshow barker."

↔↔↔↔↔↔↔↔↔

In September, 1905, I had been absent from the ranch for three months. The dinosaur hunting had continued so slow that Tucker granted me a leave of absence to work on a publication with one of my former professors.

As was my habit, I returned on horseback, riding from the nearest train station. On my approach to the ranch house, Luddy loped to meet me with the limp which had stayed with him since Louisiana.

"Hey there, Whitney! Good to see ya! Need ya here, you know. Ol' Harold he gets the doldrums worse than normal when you're not around. And anyways, you're just in time. He's out in the main barn. You'll want to take a gander at what's turned up."

I confess I had little genuine interest, having by now absorbed some of Tucker's cynicism regarding any "monster" brought to our door. But I turned my mount over to Luddy and strode toward the open doors of the barn, imagining one of the usual pathetic hoaxes: a fragment of a putrefied giant squid, an alligator with pig's hooves clumsily sewn on, or perhaps another stillborn two-headed calf.

As I entered, I heard an eerie echoing voice droning in an ancient tongue, "Am Ah Tem ho rom. Am Ah Tem tinep rom. Tho thot ke flana Ah Tem rom."

I approached quietly. The voice was Tucker's. As my eyes adjusted to the dark, I saw a massive freight wagon (not unlike Triumph) hitched to a sturdy team. Tucker was standing in the wagon's bed, scowling at a papyrus scroll as he read laboriously from it. Beside him in the wagon was a huge Egyptian stone sarcophagus. It was open, the vault-like lid resting to one side.

A heavy and sickening smell wafted to me. Somewhere between acrid wood smoke and skunk musk, it overpowered the barn's normal hay and manure perfume. I noted an odd wrought-iron tripod at the head of the sarcophagus, supporting an age-old oil lamp which in turn heated a small hand-hammered copper pot. An unseen liquid bubbled softly within.

Now I saw Jenny. She was leaning against the west wall of the barn, quietly smiling. Spying me, she inclined her head, inviting me to enter. I did so, and could then see a swarthy man in flowing Egyptian robes shrunk up against the rear of the wagon, visibly trembling.

He pleaded with Tucker. "Efendi! I beg you. Do not read the words!"

Tucker paused and glanced down at him, "Shut up. I'm trying to do this with feeling." Then he saw me, "Whitney! Welcome back. Come on up. Might find it enjoyable."

He resumed his florid Egyptian oratory. After a moment's queasy hesitation, I tentatively climbed up onto the wagon to peer into the sarcophagus.

I gaped at my first mummy. I was to learn that this one was a particularly well-preserved, not desiccated and blackened like so many, but pale, with leathery skin, wispy black hair, and much definition to the body. He had been a large imposing man in life, and even now seemed to gaze up with a stern countenance made even more imposing by death's grimace.

Tucker completed his reading with a flourish, then leaned down and peered closely at the mummy, almost nose to nose with it.

"Well? What d'you say, friend? Come on, Ah Tem, I'm talking to you. I'm laying eyes right on you, desecrating your rest — not that this other fella didn't already drag you about ten-thousand miles." Here the Egyptian gasped in horror, but Tucker went right on, "I'm doing my best to offend you. Make no mistake."

The Egyptian appeared about to faint. "Efendi — no!"

Tucker ignored him, "I'm waiting," he said to the mummy. There was no response. "Strike me down, or your man here stands to lose a bundle." Still no response. Tucker stood up with a frustrated grunt and casually tossed the ancient papyrus into the sarcophagus.

The Egyptian wilted against the wagon like a dying vine, "The curse *will* strike you! You no longer live!"

Tucker whirled and glared down at the man, "Listen, sandal toes, it'd make my whole day if this dust bunny was to rise up and take a swing at me, or spit some locusts, anything."

At that Tucker got a new thought. He reached over, lifted the simmering copper pot by its handle and waved it above the mummy. "Genuine article, friend. Don't want no one to say I didn't provide all the trimmings."

He noticed my questioning look at the pot and explained, "A brew of tanna leaves. Actually, leaves from the Nile bromiliad, which is the best guess anybody has to what tanna leaves really were. Costs an arm and a leg to import the silly stuff. Got me an for-sure third-century Egyptian pot and lamp, too." He gestured to the lamp. "Burning rendered camel fat, as per the recipe. That's what stinks. The horses hate it. Be acting loco for a week after smelling it."

With typical impulsiveness, Tucker suddenly tilted the pot, letting some of the viscous liquid spill onto the mummy's lips. "Come on, Ah Tem, join me in a drink?"

The Egyptian let out an involuntary shriek. Jenny leapt forward angrily. "Kiyuga! At least *some* respect!"

Tucker was mildly chastened, "Well, bless it, Jenny, I'm trying to rile him. *Somebody's* gotta call the bluff."

The horrified Egyptian now grew bolder, moving toward Tucker, pointing an accusing finger, voice rising to a frightening pitch. "Today you become of the walking dead.

Your heart will burst in your body! Your eyes will boil in your head!"

Tucker roared back, his booming voice considerably more frightening, "Save it for the vaudeville! If Mr. Bones here wants to crumble my cookie, he's gonna have to stand in line! He is number *thirteen*, sir. The thirteenth mummy I have fairly challenged. I've broke their seals, read their curses, said their names out loud, talked boldly about their ancestors, spoke rudely of their gods, and borrowed an amulet here and there. Even learned to read these blessed hieroglyphics myself to make sure they knew who was insulting them. Been at it twenty years this November, and mister I'm still strutting!"

The Egyptian physically staggered under this onslaught, but maintained his resolve, pointing still. "Even so, you are cursed!"

"True enough, but that is only because your mummy is just one more in a long string of let-downs. Now pack him back to the circus!"

The Egyptian sullenly climbed into the wagon, scowling at Tucker. Finally he burst out with what no doubt concerned him at least as much as the mummy's purported post mortem powers, " You — you have cheated me! The mummy is real! The scroll is real!"

"A deal's a deal, mister. I ain't dead. You don't get paid."

"But — it cost much to bring Ah Tem this far to your ranch! Feed for horses. Two days of ticket sales lost!" (It turned out the mummy was in fact a sideshow attraction in a circus.)

"Believe me, I know what it costs to move these blessed things around. That's why I don't foot the bill for it anymore! Now good day, sir!"

The offended Egyptian urged his team forward, invoking new curses in his native tongue — quite creatively, from the sound of it.

Tucker called after him, "By the way, fella, says on

Ah Tem's scroll there's a special punishment just for those who dare to move his sacred body. Your manhood turns black and is eaten by maggots, never again to enter woman from that day on."

The Egyptian went pale and involuntarily clutched his groin, moaning, as he drove his horses faster.

"You oughta read the fine print!" Tucker shouted, "Pfhuh!"

And as the disconcerted, reward-less, and now evidently cursed man rode off, I asked my employer, "What exactly was the bargain with that fellow? Something about your dying?"

"My standard mummy deal. You bring me a mummy. I insult same. Mummy kills me within two hours — in front of witnesses mind you — Jenny pays you a thousand bucks. More than fair."

And Tucker strode off. Needless to say, unlike the rest of the world, he was singularly unimpressed with the discovery of Tutankhamun many years later.

↔↔↔↔↔↔↔↔↔

Occasionally, and often in late November, Tucker and Jenny would disappear into the remote range lands of the ranch, sometimes for as much as three weeks. The official reason was that the restless nature which had helped Tucker build the cattle empire now chafed at its smooth-running, successful operation. But it seemed to me that he was driven to do something physically demanding in advance of each approaching birthday, to help himself deny any impending frailty, real or imagined.

Whatever the real reason, he would leave details to his trusted foremen while he and Jenny went out to enjoy the austere life they had shared in the DH's infancy. This struck me as quite wonderfully romantic, for they had met on those vast plains, and could be said to be reliving their honeymoon with each return. I admit I had to broaden my conceptions of an idyllic honeymoon to include that brutal, wind-blasted country in late fall. But there was no denying Jenny's simple sincerity when she explained, "*U-la-go-hv-s-di* [the fall season] asks only that you show it respect. Then it gives life and even good times."

CHAPTER SEVEN

News From the Posse

It was November 1909. Tucker and Jenny had been away on another of their private sojourns into the "back forty." This particular camping trip carried additional weight for all who worked the ranch, indeed all who knew Tucker personally. For soon, on December 2nd, he would turn fifty years old. Hands, housemaids and friends alike dreaded this calamity almost as much as Tucker himself. It was like an inevitable approaching storm, the ferocity of which could be neither predicted nor avoided. What a great irony that this year Tucker's birthday would pass completely unnoticed, even by himself.[1]

Tucker and Jenny had returned from their sojourn two

---

[1] Readers with a sensitivity to chronology will notice that there is a gap here of several years in Grandpop's writing. The werewolf story took place in 1904. He states that the mummy was brought to the ranch in 1905. Yet his next tale happened near the end of his employment with Tucker. Now, the older grandchildren, myself included, have assumed this simply means that nothing worthy of a Tucker story happened between 1905 and 1909. But youngest sister Jenny (yes, named after Tucker's wife) insists she remembers being frightened half to death by Grandpop's telling of meeting a "scary snowman" in the Far East (and he did travel there with Tucker). She claims it is the reason she became an avid fan of Rudyard Kipling. None of the rest of us recall it; and in any case, it does not appear in this manuscript. Next younger brother, Boyd, vaguely remembers something about Tucker and vampires, but he's seen so many horror films we tend to discount his memory of real-world events.

days before. It was after dinner and he and I were seated in the library, as so often we had been before.

He was haggard, and annoyed to be so. As he stared grimly at the mountain lion and its companion of several years on the boulder, the wolf, he complained to me that he had been back for two days and was still tired. This he took to be yet another sign that old age was fast overtaking him.

I was about to maintain that most people I knew would die if they attempted to live under the conditions which he and Jenny so matter-of-factly endured. But Jenny interrupted by walking swiftly into the room. She was carrying letters which had accumulated in their absence (by this time Tucker had taken to letting letters pile up un-read, since they universally disappointed him). She held one out to Tucker and dropped the rest on their reading table. Then she sat down stiffly in her chair and looked at Tucker with vividly unnerving distress.

The letter was unopened, yet Tucker was motionless from the moment he saw it. He held it as he had taken it, his arm half outstretched, face showing confusion and utter disbelief. Then he slowly he brought it towards him saying under his breath, "What in thunder — what in thunder —?"

As I wondered how an unopened letter could engender such a response, Tucker ripped it open with trembling hands. It contained two sheets of paper. The first he glanced at and cast aside, "That's just the regular one. But here — here he's added something."

He began reading from the second sheet.

"Well, he's up in Vermont, like he said he'd be." He stopped reading, almost as though he didn't want to continue, and looked at Jenny. "You know, all this means is he got delayed somehow, that he didn't get back when he said he would."

But Jenny was sifting through the other envelopes she'd

set on the table. "Where?" she demanded, "Where did you say?"

"Vermont," he answered flatly. She selected one of the other letters and handed it to him, "From a sheriff — in Vermont."

"All right," mumbled Tucker, "Let's see what *he* has to say." He tore open that second letter, read, and then emitted the most horrible little moan — so shocking from this normally taciturn man. He closed his eyes and lowered the letter slowly into his lap.

When he did not speak for some time, Jenny asked very softly, "Kiyuga, please — he is dead?"

Tucker nodded once slowly, keeping his eyes closed. At last, Jenny remembered I was there. She shot me the briefest of glances and spoke bluntly, "It is Luddy Sedlak."

A rush of mental images assaulted me — photographic memories of Tucker's gangly, boisterous, fun-loving, lifelong friend. Such a vibrant, humorous counter-point to Tucker's gloomy determination.

I instantly recalled our most recent meeting. He'd stopped by the Science Building "to bid you adieu, as the French have it." As he gently poked fun at my growing collection of impaled insects, he had, with sudden candor (and I cannot now remember what had turned our conversation this way), explained why he'd remained a bachelor into his 40s. "A woman wants a home," he'd said. "Here I am, high-stepping round the world on ol' Harold's whim. Women don't want that. Oh sure, lotta times I wished I could've found me one like Jenny, who'd just go along whereever I went without a seeming care. But looks like there's only one of her. Only one that's crossed my path anyways. But I've no right to kick, you know? 'Cuz of ol' Harold, I lead a life not a man in a thousand gets to lead."

Moments later, Luddy had indeed bid me adieu. And

now, with life's unforgiving finality, I realized that was our last conversation.

I glanced at Tucker. His eyes were now open, staring blankly at the floor. Suddenly he snatched up the letter from the first envelope and finished reading it, shaking his head with fuming frustration.

"Bless it — bless it!" he hissed. "You just wouldn't quit it would you?" Jenny stood, walked quickly behind her husband and put her hands on his shoulders. He kept staring at the letter.

"He was chasin' more blessed ghosts, Jenny! Always chasin' *ghosts!*"

"I know," she said softly. Tucker now re-read the second letter, the one from the sheriff, his stricken frown hardening into a glare. He began to nod repetitively.

"Well, it better well have been a ghost done him. 'Cause if it was anything living, it'll be a ghost when I catch up with it!" He sprang up, the letters fluttering away from him like startled birds.

He started to walk out, but checked himself and turned to me. "Some fool's killed Luddy Sedlak. I'm gonna find out who, and I'm gonna make him pay. I won't be expectin' you to come along, of course. If anything happens to me, your severance, per our handshake, is provided for in my will." With that foreboding statement, he strode out of the room. Jenny raced after him. I heard her voice in the great hall.

"Kiyuga, it is night."

"What matters that?" Tucker snarled as his footsteps echoed.

Confused, shocked, dismayed, I was left alone. After a moment I leaned forward to peer down at the letters scattered on the floor.

Later I would learn why the first envelope had precipitated such a strong reaction. It contained a form letter carried by each of Tucker's "posse." Since they spent much of their time in remote areas, searching for allegedly dangerous creatures, Tucker felt it was possible, even likely, that they might disappear without a trace. Therefore, on each posse trip he required them to leave a letter in the nearest civilized area with the most trustworthy authority available, to be mailed to Tucker if the operative did not return for it by a specified date. In truth, as the years had worn on, Tucker had assumed that none of his searchers bothered with the formality any longer. It had become abundantly evident that genuine monsters were too scarce to constitute significant danger.

But now we knew that Luddy had steadfastly adhered to the practice. In this case it had proven redundant, because the sheriff with whom he had left his letter was also the one who had learned of his death. Thus we received the form letter and the sheriff's official notice on the same day.

The form letter simply detailed where Luddy was and what he was looking for; in this instance, a ghost which reputedly haunted a local abandoned mansion. But Luddy had added a personal note in the envelope. Had he done this at the start of every mission? Or, had some premonition prompted him to do it this one time? We would never know. In any case, the note reflected the irrepressible, good-natured humor of the man:

> Dear Crazy Harold,
> I am off to New Ocland now to search out the ghost of Castile Obsidia mansion. Stopped first here in Villetownburg Mills.
> If you ever get this, I hope it's because I handed it to you in person. Looking for monsters ages a man. I figure I'll quit you one of these days and demand a pension, so I hope you're setting aside a

good-sized chunk of your fortune. You can keep your d—n smelly cattle.

If you are getting this from anyone else, I hope he's a humdinger of a monster. [Somewhat to Tucker's annoyance, Luddy always referred to their search as being for monsters, rather than dinosaurs]. Harold, honestly I think I'm really truly on to something this time.

Your dear friend,
Luddy

The official notice from the sheriff's office bluntly described the circumstances of Luddy's death. He had been found on a road north of town, having bled to death from a single massive cut apparently inflicted with a large knife or sword. His gun had been fired and was empty. It was assumed that he had been attacked by highway thieves.

I sat back in my chair, giving myself up to sadness. I knew Tucker and Jenny felt a loss greater than mine, but even so, over these seven years Luddy had become a close friend to me as well.

Jenny appeared in the library doorway. While I could see only her shape, shadowy in the lantern light, I could tell she was more upset than I would previously have imagined possible. She was rigid as a post, hands clasping and unclasping undecidedly at her sides. I felt compelled to try to comfort her, and stood as I spoke.

"Jenny, I am terribly sorry to know of this loss. It must be — "

"Will you come?" she suddenly blurted.

"What?"

"Please. He is *very* angry," she rushed on. "I'm afraid he will — will do things without thinking. I'm not sure I can make him think on my own. He respects you very much. Perhaps with both of us there he will think. He is all right

110

when he thinks. But — I don't like to ask you. It will be dangerous. He is *very* angry. And someone *has* murdered Luddy — but — will you come?"

She stepped forward into the light. Instead of the usual cool mystery, there was desperate pleading in her dark eyes. To my credit (I like to think) I did not pause to ponder possible ramifications that might come of my decision, but said immediately, "Jenny, you and Harry — and Luddy — you've become my dearest friends. Of course I will come."

"Thank you!" she whispered, and hurried back out. I followed. We met Tucker already coming from the direction of his study, his Rigby in one hand, the holstered Le Mat slung over his shoulder. He was marching for the back door of the house.

"Mr. Tucker," I called. I don't know why I felt the need to address him so formally in this moment. "I'd like to go with you."

He stopped, turned, and looked at Jenny, who avoided his eyes. It was evident that he suspected some plot already.

I hurried on, "I like to think of myself as a friend as well as an employee. If you feel there may be danger to you, then I might be of assistance." Tucker eyed me for a long moment. Then he said, "You'd best stay clear of this, Whitney. Your methods are not mine."

"I promise not to interfere. Only to assist if need be. I have faith in your — good judgment," I boldly lied.

He again looked at Jenny. She steadfastly looked elsewhere. Then he glanced back at me, grunting, "Suit yourself," and disappeared into the evening gloom.

CHAPTER EIGHT

The Episode of the Ghost

Of the episodes I shared with Tucker, this was in many ways the most unusual. After all, it was not a hunt for a dinosaur, nor for any fantastical creature, since Tucker certainly did not expect to find a ghost. He had not the slightest belief in anything so ephemeral it could not be laid low by a decent-sized gun.

Simply, he was seeking revenge.

Sharing Jenny's fear of what he might do in service of that quest, I hurried to my quarters and flung together such things as I thought I would need for a trip of unknown length to a somewhat vague destination.

In spite of his desire to leave immediately, Tucker took the needed time to load Triumph with his entire array of paraphernalia; trunks, five gallon tins, suitcases, elephant guns and all. He had roused the usual staff to help with this.

Dawn still had not touched the eastern horizon when we were finally ready to leave. It was pitch black, windy, cold and miserable. But Tucker swung up into Triumph. Jenny, wrapped in a buffalo robe, sat beside him. I chose to hunker down against the chill in the wagon bed.

As Tucker snatched up the reins, he called one of his hands over to him, Ebson Truesmark, who had worked with him nearly as long as Luddy.

"Eb," he said, "I want you to take care of Luddy when he gets here. See he gets the best coffin they got, and see they plant him right across from Mam and Pap. And get that Methodist preacher from in town, pay him if you have to, but get him to come out and read. Luddy set store by that kind of stuff and I know he'd want it done."

"We'll see to it. Be done just like you say," said Eb. "And, Mr. Tucker?"

"What?"

"Well, you know — all of us worry about you."

"What is your meaning?"

"Well — just don't go off half-cocked, is all."

"Trigger's been pulled, Eb," said Tucker darkly. "Just waiting to see where the bullet's gonna land."

He sharply slapped the reins across Taft and Bronto's flanks, and the big horses lurched us forward into the night.

Tucker set a pace which the animals obviously could not endure. After interminable minutes of this, Jenny leaned over and shouted above the clatter of hooves and wagon.

"Luddy would not want horses killed in his name!"

Tucker shot her an irate glance. Then his expression softened and he pulled the horses to a stop. In the abrupt silence, our dust caught up and washed over us, cold and clammy like dirty fog. Tucker let out a long sigh, staring down at his hands, clenched tightly on the reins. Then, without looking at her, he reached over and squeezed Jenny's hand. When he started the horses again, he let them walk comfortably.

Tucker remained outwardly calm the whole way to the train station, but spoke hardly at all. This singular change in his usual manner caused a return of my old misgivings about his potential behavior. I realized that, in responding to Jenny's plea, I was ignoring Tucker's old warning. Had he not himself told me that Jenny would be the indicator of his true level of anger? Still, I had known him for years now, and had never seen him act rashly; impatiently of course, but never without some thought. So I set my mind to remain committed to the enterprise, and to the task of helping Jenny control him if necessary. Yet how unfit I felt for that!

For the next several days we were on trains, making our way northeast. Each day, Tucker rose, wolfed a stoic breakfast and settled in the parlor car. He was re-reading the many detailed letters Luddy had sent to him over the years, having brought the whole lot of them from his library file drawers. He eventually selected twenty or twenty-five very long ones which he began to study quite closely, sitting motionless and frowning at the pages for hours at a time. This struck me as unnecessarily morbid, and I suggested to Jenny that it might be wise to try to dissuade Tucker from immersing himself in these strong reminders of his lost friend.

She shook her head. "He is not living in sadness. He is preparing himself for what we may find. He has never hunted ghosts, because they do not interest him. Luddy loved them — I think he believed in them."

It was true. Luddy had hunted ghosts far more often than he had pursued any other phenomena that Tucker's ads turned up. Tucker had patiently indulged and funded the passion, for such was the depth of their friendship.

"But," I pressed, "Harry doesn't believe in ghosts any more than he believes in yetis, vampires or werewolves. What does he hope to learn from Luddy's letters?"

"Simply to know all that Luddy knew of haunted places. Because we may need to know it."

Leaving me with that unsettling thought, Jenny began to work with Tucker on the letters. She seemed to feel that it was good for him to occupy himself this way, and they spent the rest of our train ride sitting close together, reading, exchanging quiet words, making notes.

I passed the time compiling my own neglected notes on my insect collection, or gazing out the frosted train windows at the increasingly bleak and wintry landscape. While winter is no slouch in Oklahoma, it is a different creature altogether in northern Vermont. I grimaced to see the snow growing deeper and the skies grayer — the steam and smoke from our locomotive lending its own undulating wash to the muted black-and-white scene.

It was during this somber, nearly wordless journey that December 2nd, Tucker's fiftieth birthday, came and went unnoticed by all of us. What I did notice was that Tucker ceased shaving twice a day, something he had done as long as I had known him, lest he seem like an old man going to seed.

At last we arrived in Burlington. Triumph was unloaded and rigged for travel. We trundled the remaining forty some miles to the Hog Island area, finally reaching the tiny village of Villetownburg Mills.

It was the Constable (his official title) of that settlement, Adford Diphonia, who had sent the letters. Tucker had telegraphed instructions for the return of Luddy's body to the ranch, but had asked Diphonia to retain Luddy's personal effects.

Diphonia was very pale of complexion, seeming all the more so due to his close-cropped black hair and thin, precisely clipped mustache. Immensely proper and formal, his uniform immaculate, he greeted us cordially and invited us into an office which was so neat and spare it almost seemed as though he was just moving in, or out. His desk was absolutely bare except for a pen, ink bottle, blotter, a stack of note paper, and a small brass plate engraved with his name.

Once we were properly seated, he stepped over to what was easily his most elaborate piece of furniture, a six-drawer oak filing cabinet. From the lowest drawer he withdrew a wooden box. This he set on the corner of his desk.

"Mr. Sedlak's effects," he said. He had a high pitched voice, and spoke in short, precise bursts which reminded me of a chattering squirrel.

He sat and took the contents out one by one, placing them in an orderly fashion on the desk. "You will find everything in order, of course." he said, definitively. "Mr. Sedlak traveled rather light, did he not?"

115

"He did that," said Tucker as he watched the items come out of the box — pocket watch, penknife, a small amount of money. He shook his head slowly with disapproval as Luddy's diminutive .32 caliber revolver joined the collection.

"The rest of his things, clothing mostly, and not much of that, I might add," the constable was saying, "are in his traveling case." He nodded to Luddy's well-worn case, instantly and painfully recognizable to all of us, set beside the door to his office. "You will of course wish to examine it. Then I need your signature on this receipt." From a drawer, he produced the form.

Tucker leaned forward and snatched Diphonia's pen from its holder, sloppily signing the form as he said, "No."

"I beg your pardon?" chirped the constable.

"I mean, no I don't have to examine his clothes. Luddy won't need'em. And they won't fit me."

"Ah, well — very well. I have taken the liberty of making reservations for you at our hotel, as guests of the village. There is little I can say, I'm afraid, which will lighten the burden of this — regrettable occurrence. But if there is anything I can help you with during your stay, please do contact me."

"Well, you can tell me this," Tucker said, as he began listlessly pocketing Luddy's things. "Where'd it happen?"

The constable looked a trifle taken aback by the question. I began to grow tense. Tucker's uncharacteristic quiet and apparent disinterest had been making me uneasy, and now I sensed a confrontation on the rise.

Diphonia stammered, "My letter, I thought, was quite explicit. Traveling alone, he was attacked on the road about two miles from town here."

"Did that road go to New Ocland?" Tucker raised his eyes to meet the Constable's. New Ocland was the village in which Luddy had said the haunted mansion was supposed to be. Diphonia's manner changed slightly. He seemed to grow stiffer.

"As a matter of fact, it did."

"And you say it was robbers, huh?"

"Yes. That is by far the most likely explanation," said the Constable. "I did not meet Mr. Sedlak myself, but all around here who did said he was a most jovial fellow. Not at all prone to pick fights or engender enmity." Then he added, "Ah, perhaps you were wondering why no money was stolen?"

"I *was* wondering that, yes." Tucker kept looking straight at the Constable with a cool, blank expression.

"It seemed probable that Mr. Sedlak wounded his assailants. His pistol was fired, you remember. Wounded them perhaps so severely that they were unable to carry out their robbery. In fact, there was evidence that Mr. Sedlak managed to walk a considerable distance from where he was originally attacked."

Tucker leaned forward, suddenly interested, "Evidence? What, tracks?"

Diphonia became flustered. His eyes flicked from Tucker to Jenny, who was still dressed in the apparel of a docile well-to-do lady. He flicked his eyes toward her repeatedly, as though trying to send Morse code to Tucker while he stammered, "Evidence, sir. Of — of — well, a *graphic* nature."

"Bless it! What are you talking about? Blood?"

Diphonia's eyes jittered more energetically, "Please, sir, in deference to the lady —"

"The lady has tracked her own gut-shot deer by their blood trails. Now please go on."

Diphonia seemed to go a shade more pale, but bowed slightly to Jenny and did as ordered, "Well, yes then. Exactly that. A trail of — of his blood."

117

Tucker nodded thoughtfully, still gazing at him, "You didn't happen to follow the trail back to where it started, did you?"

"Well, no. It was quite indistinct by then. Mr. Sedlak had apparently been dead for two days or more. And there had been a dusting of new snow."

Tucker nodded again, then rose, walked slowly over and picked up Luddy's case. "Well, thank you very much, Constable. We're obliged that you took care of so much for us, sendin' Luddy back and all."

Jenny and I realized Tucker was about to leave and quickly got up to join him. Diphonia shot up from his chair and bowed once again, "It was the least I could do."

As Tucker opened the door, Diphonia hesitantly asked, "Mr. Tucker, might we know when you are planning to leave?"

Tucker paused in the doorway. I could see it was a question he'd hoped to avoid. He spoke softly, almost lethargically, "Oh, not just yet. Thought I might go up and talk to some of the folks in New Ocland."

Diphonia frowned and leaned forward on his fingertips. "Are you perhaps implying that everything that can be done in this matter has *not* been done?"

"No, no," said Tucker, holding up a hand, "Mr. Sedlak worked for me. His job was hunting — ghosts. The letter he left for you to send said he'd found one up that way. I just wanted to talk to some of the people — see if I could find out anything. Ghost hunting is my hobby, you know. I sure meant no disrespect." I was taken aback by this unexpectedly tactful Tucker.

"I see," said the Constable. "Well, whatever your reasons, I would strongly advise against your traveling to New Ocland. The people there are — they keep to themselves. They rarely come here, even to trade. No good, I mean nothing useful, can come of your visiting them I'm sure. I've been told that many of them don't even talk to strangers."

"Well, I'm used to that sort of thing. Thanks for your kindness." Once more we started out, but again Diphonia stopped us, speaking quickly.

"Mr. Tucker. Ah, frankly, I'm not absolutely certain as to your true intentions. We have a good town here, with good people. And the people of New Ocland are law abiding, even if they do lack a certain courtesy. Criminals are everywhere nowadays, and when they strike as they have in this case, tracking them down is nigh impossible. Mr. Sedlak's death was regrettable, but it could have happened anywhere. Unnecessary meddling, and upsetting of people will not help." He was speaking more and more rapidly, the pitch of his voice ever more squirrel-like.

Tucker's voice remained low and calm. "Take it easy, Constable. I'm not gonna try to cause trouble. I'm just gonna ask those folks about their ghost. That's all. It just seems like something I should do after Luddy went to the trouble to find it for me. Like I should do it for his memory, you know?"

"I understand, but I still think it is unwise. I want it clearly understood that I advise against it, officially."

"Understood, absolutely. I always take all the blame for anything I do. Thanks again for everything."

We walked out. I waited until we were well into the street before I lauded Tucker, "I had no idea you were capable of such exemplary behavior."

Tucker's voice was suddenly tight and ominous. The show of calm in Diphonia's office had been as shallow as his usual displays of anger. "The man has his eyes closed. He's got an easy job in a quiet town and he don't want to be looking under rocks. Makin' him mad'd just get him all over us. I don't need a blind man

119

trippin' over himself gettin' in my way."

"Then — you were, uh, understating your plans for the people of New Ocland?"

"I was not. I'm just gonna ask'em where their ghost hangs out. That's what Luddy asked'em and that's what got him killed."

"You don't know that for certain. Can you not at least consider the possibility that he really was attacked by thieves?"

"Could be, could be. And if he was, then askin' the same question will get no response. True?"

"I suppose."

"But if it does get a response, and that ghost, or whatever it is, comes after *me* — that'll be its second and last mistake."

↔↔↔↔↔↔↔↔↔

At dawn, a beautiful clear morning, we were aboard Triumph. It was eerily quiet travel, for the packed snow on the streets of Villetownburg Mills muted Taft and Bronto's heavy stride as well as the normally strident clatter of the wagon's steel tires.

Despite Tucker's resolution, we had no clear destination. While Luddy had indicated that the so-called haunted house was near New Ocland, he had not known its exact location as of writing his last letter.

Tucker had requested of Jenny that she remain in conventional dress until we learned more about the situation in New Ocland. Though this request at first seemed level-headed, it now occurred to me that it could also mean that Tucker's normal sense of humor in dealing with locals had gone by the wayside; and that his dark mood might color all his actions, making him that much more dangerous.

To add to my unease, early risers of Villetownburg spied

us and scuttled off in the direction of Diphonia's office. I hoped the Constable would ignore their reports. But we were not even out of sight of the town before we heard muffled thump of hooves in the snow behind us.

Here came Diphonia, riding flagpole straight on a russet thoroughbred groomed as finely, and strung as tautly, as he. I wondered how he kept his ornate cap on his head as he bounced rigidly toward us.

"Mr. Tucker! Mr. Tucker!" he shrilled in his squirrel voice.

Tucker halted the horses and sat, staring straight ahead. Even from the side, his blank look was terrifying to anyone who knew him. Jenny gripped his arm, as though to retrain him physically, as Diphonia drew alongside, no doubt utterly oblivious to the fact that he approached a seething volcano. I was thankful Tucker had chosen not to wear his gun.

"Mr. Tucker, did I not make my opposition to your further inquiries clear?"

"You did, sir," he said. "And I told you that I take full responsibility for my own actions."

Diphonia, unused to resistance, twisted stiffly in his saddle like some wind-up automaton. "Perhaps you think I spoke in haste. I did not. I know this area. You do not. The people of New Ocland, they are a superstitious sort. They will quite possibly be — upset, perhaps even angered, by your inquisitiveness. I simply hope to avoid any unpleasantness that might result. To maintain the local peace, as is my sworn duty."

Tucker whirled and unleashed a searing glare. The sudden move made Diphonia's nervous horse bridle. It spun in a full circle as he struggled to bring it under control. Meanwhile, Tucker grated, "What you really hope is I don't find something you didn't even look for!"

Not only was all trace of placating good nature gone from

his voice, neither did he display the overly dramatic tremor typical of his mock anger. His right hand gripped the wagon brake, not to secure the vehicle I was sure, but to keep himself in his seat.

When the Constable's horse had stopped dancing, he shot back, voice now stretched thin as cat gut, "That is an outlandish — a slanderous accusation!"

Tucker chucked our horses. We lurched forward. Diphonia verily shrieked now, "I am the authority here! I *forbid* you to make this journey!"

"Why don't you arrest me!" snarled Tucker over his shoulder.

Diphonia again rode up alongside, "Very well! Very well! You are under arrest!"

Tucker gave Taft and Bronto another slap and we speeded up. He shrugged at Diphonia, "Funny, I don't seem to be stopped. Tell you what, polish up that arrest and have it ready for me when I get back."

The Constable was open-mouthed. I worried that he might attempt to block our path, or even draw his sidearm. I glanced at Jenny. There was no hint of the boisterous woman who at other times had joined in Tucker's play-acting. She was as tense as I; fearful that a wrong move by Diphonia would unleash Tucker's anger and invoke utter calamity.

Thankfully, Diphonia did nothing. He simply slowed to a stop and sat on his horse, gaping, until we were no longer in view.

With the cloud of this confrontation hanging over us, we rode in silence for a time. Eventually, prompted by the memory that Jenny had asked me to come precisely to help control Tucker, I timidly asked him, "Was that wise?"

"Nope," he said, "Not if I'm wrong about this." He added after a moment, "Don't worry, Whitney. We'll get you out of it somehow. Tell'em Jenny had a gun on you or somethin'."

"I appreciate the gesture, I suppose, but I am worried about you, too, you know."

"You worry too much. I'm just aimin' to see this thing through, and I won't have that jackass gum up the works. With luck he'll stew in his own juice long enough for me to finish what I'm hoping to start."

Clouds gathered as we passed a road sign pointing down a fork toward New Ocland. Was it my imagination, or did that fork seem overhung with twisted trees much uglier than those lining the other fork? No matter, of course, for we pressed on.

New Ocland itself was a drab little place, with none of the charm of so many New England communities. Buildings were unpainted. Yards were unkempt. Leaves, never raked, lay in wet moldering piles where they had swirled in the fall, half covered by snow left un-shoveled; that same snow blackened by soot from chimneys built too low.

We spied a man on foot, shoulders hunched against the cold. When Tucker hailed him, I was astonished at how he reminded me of the people of Sombre Foret. He had the same beaten-down manner, as of a slave toiling in a hopeless land ruled by some unseen dictator.

"Sir," said Tucker, forcing a jovial tone, "I'm looking for your local ghost house."

The man seemed to blanch, but said only, "Don't know what you mean."

Tucker sighed. "Nobody ever does, nobody ever does. Well then, where can a man get a drink in your fine village?"

The man jerked his head rather indistinctly up the street and hunched away from us. As Tucker drove on I glimpsed pale faces jerk back from several windows in the buildings we passed. Where at first it had seemed there was no one about, in fact we were being furtively spied upon from every shadowy corner of the gray little town.

Ahead, above a doorway in peeling paint, the faded image of a beer pail allowed us to identify the local tavern, itself as unkempt, downtrodden and sad as the rest of New Ocland. Tucker reined up and swung down without hesitation, marching for the door, "Here we go."

As Jenny and I hurried after him, my heart raced. Even though in my travels with Tucker and Jenny I had by now entered many saloons of one sort or another, in one land or another, tension was always our unseen companion. I had accepted the truth of what Tucker had told me all those years ago in Louisiana. The tavern denizens would be sullen, mistrustful and belligerent. They always were. But what gave tension new potency was Tucker himself. In past times, he had sought (in his way) to avoid trouble. Today he looking for it.

It was nearing midday, and there were a quite a number of rough-looking men in the place. (*Don't these people have jobs?* I often asked myself.) They stared at us with the typical sour, suspicious expressions as Tucker strode to the center of the bar and faced the ominous group.

"Howdy," he said, turning on unconvincing grin. "My name's Harold Tucker. Cattle rancher from Oklahoma. Friend of mine told me that there's a haunted house up around here somewheres; place called Castile Obsidia." Soft gasps escaped from several men in the room at the name, but Tucker plowed onward, "And I wondered if one of you gentlemen'd show me where it is. I'll pay you, of course. Say ten dollars, gold?" Some of the men looked down into their drinks.

Behind Tucker, the bartender spoke, "What do you want here?" Tucker's grin faltered, but re-established itself as he faced the man.

"I thought I was clear. I want to see the haunted house. It's a hobby of mine, you know? I'm just interested in things like that." Tucker kept his voice friendly, but his right hand played impatiently back and forth on the edge of the bar.

"There is no such place around here," the barkeep snapped. Tucker's hand stopped moving. A mere trace of his smile remained as he said, "Oh now, come on. I'm sure I haven't made a mistake. See, my friend's name was Luddy Sedlak. You remember Mr. Sedlak comin' up here about a month back, now don't you?"

The bartender now avoided Tucker's gaze as he mumbled, "There has never been anyone here by that name."

Tucker's fist crashed down on the bar. Glasses rattled underneath. Heads jerked up. The bartender flinched backwards.

"Now *look!*" Tucker hissed, "I'll not stand for any of your guff! I'll not play any of your games with you people! I know he was here. I know he talked to you about this Castile place. And I'm here to find out what he found out!" He spun round to face the room again. "Twenty dollars to the man who takes me within sight of the house. Double eagle!"

No reply but angry stares. Despite my years of experience with Tucker, I was again amazed at the remarkable predictability of the fear-ridden people in these lonely, stricken backwater villages.

"*Forty* dollars!" Tucker called out, his eyes jumping from face to face. But each face only looked away.

At last, an old man rose slowly from a table at the rear of the tavern.

Tucker looked at him hopefully, "Ah, do we have *one* man here with some sense?"

But the old man only pleaded, "You must not go there. It is a place of eeev —"

Tucker jerked up his hands as though to cover his ears, "I know, I know, I know!"

" — vil" completed the old man.

"It is no such thing!" Tucker raged. It's nothin' but a spook house for children to be scared of, children and cowards!" My stomach leaped. "Coward" was not a word to be tossed about lightly in small town saloons.

A heavy, bushy-bearded man, two tables from the older fellow, leaned back in his chair, which creaked loudly. "Would you be saying that you see a coward in this room?"

I prayed for the diplomacy Tucker had shown in the Constable's office, but did so in vain.

"*A* coward?!" he shouted. "I see a whole *room* full of 'em! You look around and tell me what you see. Don't you see a bunch of men who are afraid to go near an empty house in broad daylight? Don't you see a bunch of fools who would pass up forty dollars cash money because they'd rather stay in a hole, hiding like rabbits?"

Anger filled the room like a physical thing, like flood water mounting up behind a flimsy dam. Men twitched and flexed and seemed literally to expand in their chairs. Yet Tucker rained still more upon them.

"And how about the *liars?*" He jerked a thumb over his shoulder at the bartender. "How about the liars who say they never heard of Luddy Sedlak? Yep, looks like a room full of cowards, fools, and liars all right!"

The bartender scowled, but Jenny had edged to the end of the bar, and now opened her handbag (for she was still dressed as a lady) to reveal the butt of her Colt. While she always "covered" bartenders in these situations, the sober deliberateness with which she did so now horrified me. She meant business every bit as much as Tucker. Fortunately, unlike some others before him, this bartender needed no further indication of her intent; he remained well away from his bar and whatever dispute-ender he kept there.

The bearded man in the creaky chair lacked this discretion. He rose menacingly and stepped toward Tucker, who halted him with a pointed finger. "Forty dollars, sir! Just to take me within sight of the place. Then you can run back and get under your bed."

That last insult had the opposite of the desired effect. The bearded man flung open his jacket, revealing a sheathed hunting knife easily ten inches long. As his hand fell upon the handle, Tucker's own jacket flew open and, so swiftly I barely saw it happen, he was suddenly holding a derringer aimed at the bearded man's head.

It was a derringer only Tucker would carry. Another of his custom-ordered weapons, at easily fifty caliber it was a "hand cannon" by any definition, with two enormous barrels, side-by-side like a shotgun. In all our years together, this was the first time I'd ever seen it.

Tucker's eyes twitched with anger. His voice was low and excruciatingly ominous as he gestured to the bearded man's knife, "Show me an inch of that steel, mister, and I'm the last cuss you'll ever lay eyes on!"

I glanced at Jenny. She was a trembling mass of nerves. A cat about to spring. And I knew with sickening certainty, *Tucker is not kidding!* I cringed as he drew back the derringer's double hammers.

Jenny spoke in a desperate whisper, "Kiyuga, be sure of the enemy before you strike!"

But, already cowed, the bearded man eased his hand away from his knife. Tucker responded by slowly tipping the derringer's muzzles upward.

The man glared at Tucker, trying to maintain a little face, "You're a fool. You don't know what you're dealing with here."

"Then let me die a fool's death!" Tucker shot back. He glanced round the room at the other men, every one of them unmoving, as if captured in a photographer's tin-type. "One hundred dollars!" Tucker shouted. "And no one has to fight me to get it."

Then, as so many times before, a timid voice came from another part of the room, "I'll take you." A spindly, red-faced man rose unsteadily from his chair.

"Sit down, Dulcek," ordered the bearded man. "You're drunk."

Tucker bellowed, "Shut up! He's not drunk enough to pass up some easy money." Come on, fella, let's go." The thin man, Dulcek, started for the door, but was stopped by another shout, now from the old man in the corner.

"No, Dulcek! The ghost will kill you!"

"Twist off your blathering!" Tucker roared. As the old man choked himself into silence, Tucker then focused on Dulcek, "Don't listen to these idiots, man. Let's get goin.'" Dulcek hesitated an instant, then called to the old man, "It won't get me, Blick! I'll leave! With a hundred dollars I *can* leave. Leave this accursed place and that accursed house. For good!" He walked swiftly outside.

Tucker turned to the stunned group, "It's a question I always ask myself: if life in your neck of the woods is so fearsome frightening, why in Hades *don't* you just leave?!" And he marched out, with Jenny and me tight behind, she going backwards, eyes on the group, gun-hand ready.

We rushed for Triumph, Tucker keeping a firm grip on Dulcek's sleeve lest the man lose courage. I glanced uneasily back at the tavern. The riled men clustered in the doorway, but made no move toward us.

Tucker barked at the horses. As we wheeled about and drove back past the hostile faces, the bearded man condemned us, "You *will* die the death of fools!" Dulcek cringed.

But Jenny stood up, faced the group, threw off her overcoat and began unbuttoning her dress. I guessed that she had her maroon-and-buckskin "work" outfit on underneath, and I was right. However I was unprepared for the piercing battle cry she delivered as she kicked her dress off into the wagon bed. She held her knife aloft with one hand and made a strange hand gesture with the other, rendering the men at the tavern door thoroughly speechless. Then she dropped onto the seat beside us, stone-faced as ever. Tucker saw my confusion and explained her action, "It kind of means, 'my spirits are stronger than your spirits.'"

Never had I seen such a display from her. I could only think it was her own anger coming out at these cowardly, superstitious people and the part they may have played, even unwittingly, in Luddy's death.

The road to the Castile mansion was completely overgrown and of course not cleared of snow. It would have been difficult to find had not Dulcek been there to point it out. Even with his help it was difficult to traverse. Jenny and I spent much of the trip lying down in the wagon to avoid the branches scraping over us. Taft and Bronto labored valiantly to drag Triumph onward.

As we drew closer, Dulcek grew more and more fidgety, and Tucker grew correspondingly more annoyed, until at last he spoke.

"Bless it, man! You don't quit twitching, I'm gonna hog-tie you!"

Dulcek's eyes remained locked on the overgrown path ahead, "Road's easy to see from here on. Anyone can follow it. I'll take my leave."

"You'll stay the course with us," grumbled Tucker.

Poor Dulcek trembled; just like the many other skittish guides we'd encountered over the years; all so remarkably similar.

"Mr. Tucker, sir, you don't know. The Castiles, they were bad terrible people. Turned against the Lord. Made blood pacts with the Evil One himself!"

"Uh-huh," said Tucker with profound disinterest. "And was they sitting on a pile of gold, haystack high, when they departed this earth?"

Dulcek seemed taken aback at Tucker's perspicacity, but answered, "Yes, it's been told they were that. House was packed to the rafters with booty from their evil doings."

Tucker glanced back at me, "You'll find, Whitney, there ain't a ghost worth the name that ain't lording over a fortune he never spent — or avenging some terrible wrong." He turned to Dulcek, "So if they was in tight with Beelzebub, what brung'em down? Who did'em in?"

Dulcek raced on with the details, "Greed. Greed consumed them. Each wanted the fortune to himself. Sisters turned on brothers. Children on parents. But it was the grandfather who won out. Won out in most terrible ways on all the others. And it's he who guards the gold to this day!"

"And how blessed long ago was that? How long's granddaddy been settin' on the pot?"

"Fifty-seven years this Christmas Eve!" whispered Dulcek.

"Fifty —! Before you were *born*, man? You been scared all your life of a ghost story older than you?"

Dulcek finally took offense, saying testily, "It isn't just tales. People around here have seen it with their own eyes, those that dared get close. And people have died. Your Mr. Sedlak — he died!"

Tucker sobered, "Well that little bit of history you got right."

Dulcek mistakenly took this as capitulation on Tucker's part and rose to get off the wagon. "I won't go any closer. Even — even if you don't pay me!"

Tucker grabbed Dulcek's jacket and wrenched him back down with such force that mighty Triumph shuddered when the poor man's buttocks struck the seat.

Tucker snarled venomously, "You will take me within sight of that house, or by the saints, no ghost will ever find enough of you to do harm to!" And, as so often with Tucker, we rode on in uncomfortable silence.

At last we pushed through a final curtain of drooping, snow-covered branches and found the Castile house suddenly before us. What a place it was! Surely no other had greater claim to the title "haunted."

It stood, in classic style, on a hilltop, framed by grotesque twisted trees, everything all the more forbidding on this bleak day. Even the snow, which usually beautifies a desolate scene, seemed the color of ash.

If there had been gardens or landscaping round it, all evidence of them was lost in the matted tangle of brush and vines attempting to overtake the main house. There were signs of outlying buildings, but these had been made of wood and all had apparently burned in some distant time. Here and there, blackened beams with icicle beards jutted from the snow, vaguely marking ruined foundations.

But the main house had been built entirely of stone. It loomed over all, more fortress than mansion, a weird blend of architectures three stories high. Unapologetically square, it had steeply peaked turrets on all four corners. Five huge, cracked Romanesque columns rose from the narrow front porch to the roof. The single most unsettling feature of its exterior, however, was its aggressively asymmetrical windows. On the first floor, those to the right of the porch were long and narrow, with sharp gothic arches, while those to the left were large wide rectangles. Windows on the second floor were all in the shape of inverted crosses, which gave credence to Dulcek's claim that the owners of this place had been less than devout, at least in a conventional sense. The third floor windows were round like a ship's port holes.

All the windows were heavily barred. Long rust stains ran

from the bars down the walls. It made me think of some great animal, bleeding from many wounds; for in an odd way the building, though long-abandoned, nevertheless seemed alive, defiant. It was not nearly ready to surrender to gravity's pull or man's neglect.

Even the normally jaded Tucker was moved by the sight. He gazed up at the mausoleum-like façade for a long moment and, in his way, laughed softly, "Pfhuh." Then he turned to Dulcek, "I'll say this, there's no question you brought us to the right place."

Dulcek was petrified with fear. Tucker thrust the payment into his hands, but he still simply sat shaking. Tucker growled, "Well, you said you wanted to leave. Changed your mind? Want to go in with us?" That broke Dulcek's trance and enabled him to organize himself into a chaotic escape, tumbling off the wagon, floundering monkey-like in the snow, and crashing away through the frozen brush behind us.

Tucker looked after him scornfully, "Believers. You know what's wrong with them, Whitney? Don't care about proof. Don't ask for it. Half the time don't hear it when it's screaming at them. All they do is believe."

We dismounted from Triumph. Tucker strapped on his hulking Le Mat. As I dutifully uncased my Winchester, Jenny, instead of donning her usual holstered Colt, drew a different weapon from our traveling armory — a short, fat, double-barreled Ithaca shotgun with cavernous 10 gauge barrels (a "coach gun," they were called). Ever aware of everything around her, she noted my un-subtle gape, and said simply of it, "I like it indoors, where there is little room and ranges are short." There was no arguing with her matter-of-fact logic.

To his normal regalia Tucker added an additional heavy belt. On it were a hatchet and a crowbar slung in leather loops, and a row of metal canisters about a foot long and an inch in diameter. I had the uneasy feeling they were some type of explosive but had learned by now not to ask.

So, armed to the teeth as Tucker would always wish it, we walked toward the mansion. I confess we went more slowly than one might approach an ordinary domicile. The monolith's towering, glowering walls made even Tucker approach with respect.

The front door was solid iron. Tucker gave it a kick, but found it solidly barred from the inside. One wondered, if truly abandoned for such a long time, had no one tried to enter this place? Have not at least a few fearless teenaged boys, on a dare, spent a night here? Certainly the door made it appear not.

We circled the bleak structure and found it equally well defended on all sides. In the rear, adding to the generally sacrilegious atmosphere, the arches of the gothic church-like windows pointed downwards.

The front door proved to be the *only* door and, as unyielding as it seemed, was the only hope for a point of entry. The lowest windows were ten or twelve feet from the ground and the stone walls had been built to give no hand-hold even should one have presumed that the windows' massive bars would offer less resistance than the door.

Tucker studied the door as he said, "Never gone into one of these places myself. That's why me and Jenny was reading over all Luddy's letters, to learn the tricks of the trade, like they say."

"Luddy found more than one place like *this?*" I asked.

"Not exactly. All different in particulars, but all the same, too, in a lot of ways. Most are dressed up in hogwash tales with nothing to them at all. In a few, people or youngsters was playing tricks to get the laugh on their neighbors. All were disappointments in the end. Luddy wanted to find him a ghost as much as I want to find a dinosaur." Then, softly, "He was kind of a believer himself, in that way."

133

Jenny flicked him one of her piercing looks, "Kiyuga, don't talk badly of spirits."

"Not speaking of spirits, Dickens. Just people."

He returned to Triumph and obtained a sledgehammer and some heavy steel wedges from his seemingly limitless stock of supplies. He surveyed the door for a point at which to begin his assault — and then scowled with a hint of uncharacteristic doubt. "Don't see a scratch on it. You suppose Luddy never got this far? He'd have tried to get in for sure."

Jenny and I shrugged. Luddy's body had been found miles from here. Had he reached the house? Did he discover something that caused his murder? Or, had his mere questions brought about his death before he reached it? Or had he, as the Sheriff suggested, simply run afoul of highwaymen wholly unrelated to his quest? There was no way to know.

Such questions did not lessen Tucker's resolve. He worked one of his wedges between door and frame just above the top hinge.

"Stand clear," he said, picking up his sledge and taking a wide, solid stance. He swung the hammer back, intending to strike a shattering blow. But just as he reached the end of his back swing, we heard a loud click from the door, and it suddenly opened *by itself*, its rusted hinges screeching in disharmony. Jenny instantly leapt to the left of the doorway. Tucker stumbled awkwardly in stopping his swing, but quickly dropped the hammer and flattened against the wall to the right of the door. As he drew his Le Mat, I was left standing in front of the open doorway for a long inactive moment, gaping at it like a fool, until at last I sprung over to join Tucker. He shook his head at me with disdain, "Bless it, Whitney, you've gotta think quicker than that. Be *ready*."

"Sorry," I whispered, embarrassed, and then annoyed that

I should feel embarrassed. It was my first haunted house, after all.

"Hello the house!" shouted Tucker, his bellow making me jump. "We just want to talk. But know this, too, we go armed!"

Silence was the only reply. We waited perhaps a full two minutes for any further activity from the house. There was none. Finally, Tucker looked at Jenny. She nodded to him in the cryptic visual code I'd grown used to, but still rarely understood. Then he turned to me, speaking low.

"We're playing somebody else's game by his rules, here. I'm not asking you to go in with us. You want to follow our friend Dulcek, I'll not think ill of you."

To this day, I cannot say what drove me to answer as I did. Pride? Curiosity? Loyalty? Whatever it was, I, who utterly lacked the instincts, quick reflexes and "savvy" of my compatriots, now shook my head with histrionic resolve and said, "I'm with you."

A complex look flickered across Tucker's face. It was like that of a father: proud of a son's bravery, yet fearful of the danger it will bring. I was pleased to have received that look.

"All right," he said, "but keep your eyes open and your wits about you."

He eyed the doorway for a moment, in some way monitoring for unseen threats, then suddenly bounded through it, landing in a tense crouch just inside. Jenny followed him, springing through to the opposite side. After a moment, when nothing had attacked, they slowly straightened. Tucker whispered, "All right, Whitney, come on. Oh, and hand me the sledge."

I snatched up the sledgehammer he had dropped, stepped through the doorway, and handed it to him.

It was appallingly dark inside. What little light bled through the high narrow windows was instantly swallowed by

135

the stone walls within. I could just make out that we were in a towering entrance hall with large open rooms to the right and left, perhaps parlors or sitting rooms. These were richly furnished with fine pieces. Dust was thick. Cobwebs were abundant. There was no sign of the vandalism one would expect in a place so long abandoned. It seemed that the ghost had protected the house well.

Dead ahead of us was a stone staircase. To the left of it was a hallway leading back into an infinity of blackness.

Tucker motioned Jenny and me to go ahead. As we edged forward, he hung back. I heard his boots grate on the gritty stone floor. But then there was another sound, the screech of the front door's hinges. Without a breath of wind, the door suddenly, impossibly, was swinging shut! Tucker leapt back, thrusting the handle of his sledge into the jamb. The handle was crushed and half splintered, but it kept the door from closing completely. As though alive, the door reopened part way and slammed again, but Tucker moved the handle so that the door fell on an undamaged section and again the door could not close. It made one more attempt, failed, and then seemed to go lifeless, rebounding to a half-open position. Tucker nodded knowingly and whispered, "Just like Luddy said."

Jenny nodded. Utterly confused, I whispered, "What did Luddy say?"

Tucker jerked his head toward the door, "Standard haunted house trick. Door closes by itself. Locks you in."

I was incredulous, "This is something that happens *frequently?*"

Tucker shrugged, "It's what he said."

Keeping his sledge handle in place, Tucker glared into the darkness and addressed the house. "Ghost, we know all your tricks! You ain't getting' shed of us! All we want is to talk, so let's get to it!" Still there was no answer.

Tucker sighed, "All right." He turned to me. "Whitney, take the sledge and keep the door from closing." He pointed to the inside of the door. "See how it's built?" Indeed, I now noticed there was no knob on the inside of the door; and that the deadbolt somehow operated from within the door itself. Had it swung all the way shut, we'd have been trapped with no way to open it.

"But why would anyone make a door you can't open from — ?" I began, but Tucker interrupted.

"To throw the scare into us. That's all it is."

Unwilling to admit that something of a scare had already been thrown into me, I gripped the sledge handle and held it firmly in place to prevent any further shenanigans on the part of the door.

Tucker pulled another steel wedge from his belt-load of implements. Using his ax as a hammer, he began pounding the wedge into door frame behind the strike plate.

As he worked, I studied the mysterious door more closely. How had it tried to close by itself? There were no ropes or wires attached to it. But then I saw that the large center hinge was recessed deep into the stone wall. If there were a lever attached to the hinge on the other side of the wall, perhaps someone pulling the lever would be able to make the door open and close at will. This was my best theory at the moment. And I used it to reassure myself that the door's behavior had a logical, rather than metaphysical, explanation.

Tucker had damaged the strike plate to his satisfaction, bending it out so that the door could not possibly be latched. "There! Now let's go see what other trouble we can get into."

He stepped up beside Jenny. All this time she had remained rigid, glancing swiftly from point to point in the house, watching for danger from any quarter.

Tucker bellowed again into the blackness, "We're coming

on in, ghost! We'll not be persuaded otherwise!"

"Look!" Jenny suddenly whispered, pointing ahead. My stomach wrenched as I saw a flickering lantern at the far end of the long hallway to the left of the stairs. The lantern floated, eerily disembodied, then disappeared off to the right, clearly beckoning us onward.

The eerie sight seemed only to energize Tucker. His mustache curled up in a sneer. "Well, they're dealing another hand." He glanced at Jenny and me, "Mind your weapons and your flanks. They might get rougher when they see we ain't scarin'."

Tucker in the lead, we tiptoed down the long hall. As we moved farther from the ajar front door, farther from that lone slit of light, the encroaching darkness literally seemed to become tactile. It pushed against my eyes, my temples, on my eardrums. I silently cursed my hands, which in spite of the cold, were making my rifle's stock slippery with sweat. Nervously, repeatedly, I rubbed first one hand then the other on my overcoat.

Reaching the point where the lantern had disappeared, we turned right, first Tucker, then Jenny, then I. We now faced an open door, through which we could see only more disheartening opacity. There was no sign of the lantern.

But then a faint orange glow began to fill the room beyond the door. The light came from oil lamp wall sconces, whose flames were being turned up as though by invisible hands.

I could see that even Tucker was impressed. But he was determined not to entertain thoughts of spirits, and muttered, "Quite a show they put on. But ain't it odd that ghosts would bother to keep oil in the lamps?"

We remained tensely in the doorway. As the lantern light grew brighter, my gaze swept round the room. It was huge, perhaps at one time a ballroom; and it was as opulent as the outside of the house was austere. The walls were of lustrously lacquered maple. The ceiling was a magnificent white dome in which hung an enormous scintillating brass chandelier with dozens of polished reflectors.

Despite its size, the room was incongruously furnished with a sparse arrangement of two huge, velvet-covered couches, attendant end-tables, and one overstuffed chair, upholstered in luxurious red leather, brilliant even under the decades of dust which dulled everything. These were placed in the center of the otherwise empty space.

Tucker scowled as he glanced nervously round the room. "Don't like being led by the nose," he whispered. He paused to size up the door. It was of wood, not like the armored front door. Even so, he took a moment to chop out the latch with a few artful blows of his hatchet, lest the door get any ideas.

"Okay, now keep a little ways apart."

He entered first, keeping close to the right wall. Jenny moved in along the left. So I crept slowly forward toward the center of the room, toward the little island of furniture.

It was unearthly quiet. Each step we took seemed as loud as hooves on a wooden bridge. But now a curious tinkling came to my ears, like tiny Christmas bells. Then I felt a soft patter on my hat, like sand dropping from above.

As I was about to glance up, Tucker suddenly hissed in alarm, "Oh, bless it!"

With swiftness that belied his stocky frame, he leapt toward me and grabbed the back of my overcoat, yanking me bodily backward. As we both tumbled to the floor, the immense chandelier suddenly tore free of its ancient mounting and crashed down exactly where I'd stood!

I scrambled up and backed further away, as though the chandelier might rise up and attack again.

"Bless it! Bless it!" Tucker cursed himself. "Forgot all

about that."

Jenny rushed over, whispering, "I didn't think of it either. Whitney, are you all right?!"

"Yes — yes," I stammered, then asked, utterly confused, "Think of what?"

Tucker pointed his Le Mat at the crumpled remains of the chandelier. "Gotta watch them things. They make a regular a habit of trying to fall on folks."

"But — but surely *that* can't be a common occurrence!"

Jenny shrugged, "It was in Luddy's letters."

Shaken as I was, I was determined to argue the point that every haunted house couldn't have a chandelier that just happened to fall when you walked under it. But that's when the lanterns began to go out.

One by one, clockwise round the room, their flames sucked down until only a single lantern's tenuous flicker remained. Then that, too, blinked out.

Utter darkness rushed over us in a cold silent wave. It is strange to think that so many of nature's creatures revel in and covet darkness, while fainthearted man does all he can to keep it at bay. I was instantly disoriented, dizzy; could feel myself reeling and had to kneel down to steady myself. Even as I did I realized I now had only the vaguest idea where the hallway door was — somewhere behind me. If I crawled that way, how long would it take to find it? Panic fluttered round me, snatching at my thoughts. Even now I'm embarrassed to admit I imagined nameless un-seeable things moving toward me. Things from under a child's bed.

"Hold still," Tucker barked. I froze. I could hear rattling and clicking as he worked at something. Then I heard a short, rasping sound and a small pop like a firecracker.

With a sputtering hiss, we were lit up in a blinding white glare. I squinted, shaded my eyes, and could barely make out Tucker holding a magnesium flare. I now realized that's what the cylinders on his belt were.

An electric arc lamp could not have been brighter. The flare transformed the room into a black-and-white world of the harshest light and shadow, all of it shifting and reeling crazily with each move of Tucker's hand. Everything round us that had seemed mysterious and ominous was suddenly drab and ordinary — and I was much relieved to have it that way.

We drew into a circle, backs to each other, watching in all directions. I jumped as Tucker bellowed, "Come on, ghost! Another old trick. Ain't gonna stop us. You'll have to do better."

I whispered, "Luddy predicted lanterns going out, too?"

"That he did," Tucker whispered back. "Told you, he must've run down a hundred or more of these places." Then he shouted again, "Well, ghost, you coming out?" His voice echoed round the room and down the hall outside.

This time he finally he got a reply. But it was not one that settled my frayed nerves. It came in the form of a distant, hollow laugh. It started low and then built to a maniacal pitch, echoing differently from the way Tucker's voice had, as though from a tunnel or from inside a barrel. The laughter came from the direction of a closed door now visible on the opposite side of the large room.

I glanced at Jenny. She had her shotgun leveled at the door, her blank expression one of profound concentration. If one had taken a photograph of her in this instant, she would have looked as calm as if shooting trap at the village gun club. One absolutely could not tell if the maniacal laughter affected her not. But it was certainly taking its toll on me, and I envied her, feeling that my own face must be betraying all manner of fear and doubt. I aimed at the door as well. At least it was a slight relief to have a definite direction from which to expect danger.

For Tucker, the ghostly sound was more success than threat. He grumbled, "About time," then threw back his shoulders and shouted, "Ghost! I'm a busy man! I've got no time for your blessed games. I'm lookin' for the killer of Luddy Sedlak. If it's you, get out here and face me. If you know who it is, get out here and tell me. But you'd best get out here!"

The ghost obliged by beginning another long trill of evil, cackling hysterics. A scowl twisted Harold Tucker's face in the pulsing light of the flare. The ghost was trying his patience (unaware that he had none!); and it was little comfort to realize I had no idea what either of them would do next.

"Not gonna play at this all day," Tucker muttered. Then he roared, "Ghost! I'm gonna set fire to your place here unless you come out and start talkin'.

Ah, Tucker's tried-and-true solution, I thought. *If it resists thee, burn it down!*

Tucker tossed his flare onto one of the velvet sofas. Smoke swirled up chaotically in the intense heat of the flare as the old tinder-dry cloth instantly caught fire.

Tucker struck the friction igniter on a second flare. This one he flung toward the door from behind which the laughter had seemed to come. He lit a third flare and heaved it out into the hallway down which we'd come. Hissing, sputtering, smoking light was now all around us.

"Your place is burning!" he thundered. "You'll have one blessed time scarin' people away from a pile of ashes!"

The laughter stopped. Only the sibilant flares filled the silence. I dearly hoped the ghost was taken aback by Tucker's challenge. I thought I heard a distant rasping intake of breath, and hurriedly reassured myself that a real ghost shouldn't have to breathe. But then the cackling welled up again, more hollow and echoing than before. It rose to an awful, diabolical screeching. For the hundredth time I vainly rubbed my sweat-slick palms on my coat.

Now we heard footsteps. Heavy. Plodding. Like those of an imagined giant. And with the steps, bizarre metallic *clanking*. Did this giant wear steel boots? Was the ghost indeed draped in rattling chains?

Tucker and Jenny spaced themselves further apart, bracketing the closed door. I felt woefully out of touch with their unspoken, intuitive teamwork, and it did not help when Tucker snapped at me, "Be ready."

"Ready for *what?*" I hissed back.

"Anything! Watch our backs — the hallway, man!"

Ah! The hall! Yes, someone *could* come from that way, I realized. I dutifully spun round and aimed my weapon at the door through which we had entered.

The ominous clanking footsteps were louder. They were coming closer, yet it was hard to tell *where* they were coming from, for the sound echoed round the room and off the high domed ceiling.

Tucker moved nearer the closed door. Jenny did the same on the side opposite him. I stayed in my position at the hall door, head boggling back and forth between guarding my post and watching them.

Then, with a shattering crash, the closed door burst open. Inexplicably, there was no one beyond it. The light from Tucker's flares revealed only a small empty anteroom. Yet, from somewhere, the footsteps continued, loud, heavy.

I forced my head back to the hall door. My finger tightened on my rifle's trigger. My eyes twitched in anticipation of firing a shot, but nothing came into view here either. I thought, *Why didn't I accept Tucker's invitation to leave? I'm not meant for this sort of campaign! Foolish pride!*

Unexpectedly the footsteps now seemed to recede. The awful, hollow laughter continued, derisive and taunting. Yet still the steps seemed to move away from us.

While this was fine with me, it naturally angered Tucker. "Come back here, you coward!" he barked. He moved toward the anteroom door, then paused, his senses warning him not to continue. The footsteps continued to grow fainter. Tucker shot Jenny a questioning look. She shot back the slightest shrug, keeping her shotgun leveled at the doorway. I presumed that, in their code, she meant, "I have no idea what to suggest."

I became aware of the soft crackling of the now busily burning sofa, which added an orange flicker to the vivid white light of the hissing flares. Smoke was filling the great dome above us. I thought, *We must not remain here long or we'll surely perish in this old tinderbox!*

Suddenly the fading footsteps stopped. The three of us glanced at one another, as though needing to verify that we all heard the same thing. I focused on my doorway, and drew some confidence in the assumption that anyone attempting to enter the room would have to come either through the brightly lit hall or the now open anteroom door. Had Luddy been there, he no doubt would have taken issue with my assumption.

For, with a heart-stopping BANG, a section of the maple wall *behind Tucker* suddenly flew up. It was nothing less than a classic secret panel.

With the reflexes of an animal, Tucker sprang away from the opening, whirled and crouched, his Le Mat ready.

Jenny's shotgun swung swiftly toward the source of the noise. My rifle, I must honestly report, bobbled indecisively, for I could not comprehend what I saw.

Standing in the heretofore concealed doorway was an immense figure in full sixteenth century armor. At first I thought it was a knight, then realized the armor was Spanish, like that of a Conquistador. At least seven feet tall, the figure's broad steel breastplate and chain mail gleamed fantastically in the flame-tinged flare light. It carried a long, tapered broadsword in its glittering metallic hand.

The awful laughter burst forth, ferocious and painfully loud, yet still with that inhuman echoing hollowness. I looked for the mouth that could produce such a horrid sound, and saw instead the naked teeth of a skull, a filthy skull with bits of flesh clinging to it, half hidden by the a metal rim of its battle helmet. And, glaring at us from beneath the helmet's visor were livid, madly glowing red eyes, set deep in the black sockets.

I like to think that, for at least an instant, Tucker was as startled and alarmed as I. Certainly, he scrambled further back from where he'd landed, then sidestepped so that the red leather chair was between him and the huge creature.

It took a clanking step into the room, brandishing its sword, twisting stiffly at the waist to look first at Jenny and then me. Seeming to sense that Tucker was the primary threat, it faced him squarely, taking another step. Tucker raised his pistol. If at first taken by surprise, he was now as doubting as ever, his voice easily as menacing as the hideous laughter.

"Now you just hold it. I ain't firing any warning shots." The thing responded with another peal of high-pitched laughter, yet now I saw the skull's jaw did not move. The sword rose higher and the Conquistador took another step toward Tucker. He jerked back the hammer of his handgun, aiming lethally at the creature's metal chest. At that instant, I noticed there were already several small holes in the breastplate — *bullet holes*?

The thing raised its sword higher. In one more step, it would be within striking distance of Tucker. His lips drew back from his teeth in a feral snarl and he fired. The Le Mat's blast was unexpectedly loud within the confining room. My ears sang against the abuse. Black powder sparks flew like fireworks. The plume of gun smoke billowed round the Conquistador, splitting into diverging puffs, revealing a new and larger hole in the breastplate. The creature paused for an instant. Then its crazed laughter exploded in a triumphant shriek. It seemed utterly unharmed!

Tucker's face showed signs of a mind struggling with disbelief and confusion, and surely it was instinct alone which launched him backwards in time to avoid the vicious downward cut of the massive blade. Missing him, it sliced deep into the back of the sturdy chair, throwing up an explosive cloud of dust. The sword went in so far it got stuck. The ghost-Conquistador worked to wrestle it free of the chair.

The velocity of Tucker's leap had caused him to trip, but he gracefully rolled into a kneeling position. He was in shadow, out of direct light from the flares, but then was lit in vivid staccato gunpowder-orange as the room rocked again with concussion from his pistol.

This time he went for the ghost's decayed head. With his first shot one of the sunken glowing eyes disappeared. Pieces of shattered bone rattled across the floor. Tucker fired again and again, emptying his gun. His last shot sent the ghost's helmet spinning away to carom off the wall, ringing like an ill-tuned gong. The whole top of the ghost's skull had been blasted away, but still the frightful giant seemed invulnerable! Nothing would stop its gasping, demented, infuriating, peals of laughter.

It tore the sword free, leaving a livid gash in the leather chair, trailing stuffing in an upward arc. The creature advanced on Tucker, and I was horrified to see he was wholly indecisive. His gun arm drooped as though deflated. He stepped back, at a loss what to do, yet unwilling to fully retreat. But Jenny was moving in behind her husband, and now called for a clear shot simply by saying, in a remarkably even tone, "Kiyuga."

Tucker knew in a split second what she intended and instantly dropped to one side.

Where Tucker's Le Mat was a deafening roar, Jenny's 10 gauge blast was like a naval broadside. While a sharp pulse of pain stabbed my ears, flame and smoke fully enveloped the giant and, to my relief, it stumbled backward with the impact of the buckshot, its hideous laughter choked off.

Through the roiling smoke I could see she'd made a huge jagged hole in the center of the giant's breastplate, but Jenny did not wait to judge the effect. Leaning forward against the recoil of her stocky coach gun, she fired her second barrel. The balls struck to one side of the first hole, literally spinning the ghost a quarter turn. It wobbled as though about to fall. Its sword arm sagged, and sword point dipped down to clang against the floor.

At this moment, the flares were spent. They sputtered and went out, leaving only the dull flickering glow of the burning sofa. In the sudden comparative darkness, I could barely see at all. But what I did see gave rise to despair which was rapidly building to blind panic. The creature steadied itself, straightened up, and faced Tucker and Jenny.

The horrid laughter began yet again, first as a silly giggle, then a bellow, and finally the agonizing screech which combined with the ringing in my ears to produce a painful sensation more like pressure than sound. I confess my skepticism was losing its grip. Surely no living thing could survive those shots!

The ghost took a clanking step toward my friends, waving the sword overhead in threatening circles. Smoldering wadding from Jenny's shot-shells, embedded in the mangled metal of the breastplate, sent web-thin curls of smoke snaking round the advancing creature.

Jenny frantically threw open her shotgun's breach,

ejecting the spent shells and digging in her pocket for fresh ones. Tucker was reloading his Le Mat.

From my position across the room, I thought I must fire, too! But I knew that I carried the least powerful weapon among us and, stupidly, I hesitated, as though my rifle might somehow protect me as long as I did not make the mistake of proving it was useless.

As these equally useless thoughts paralyzed me, the hulking thing took another step toward Tucker and Jenny. Its remaining eye still glowed in the one black socket in its lopsided skull.

Tucker and Jenny were backed to the opposite wall, he still seemingly undecided about what to do, and she resolutely waiting for his decision. The gap narrowed between them and the ghost. In another step it would surely cut them down. I was horrified that Tucker seemed unable to comprehend the futility of battling this un-killable thing.

"Run!" I called, but could not even hear myself above the demon's cackling. So I yelled again, now with fear's volume, "RUN!" But Tucker did not run. He suddenly dropped down on one knee, thumbed his pistol's lever, switching to its shotgun barrel and fired — not at the giant's body or head, but at its right foot.

The utter futility of Tucker's choice spurred me to action. I jerked my rifle to my shoulder, but before I could pull the trigger I realized Tucker's shot had in fact had an effect.

The ghost's laughter changed to a piercing, agonized moan. It lurched to one side, throwing its weight on its left foot. The sword fell and rang on the floor as the monster bent over stiffly, vainly reaching for its right foot. The moaning lessened to pain-hissed sobs, and the ghost simply stood in this bent-over position for moment, tottering on one leg. Then it lost its balance and toppled, crashing down on its back in a cacophony of chiming iron.

On impact, the remainder of the skull snapped off at the neck and bounded erratically toward me like a grisly football. I sprang aside to avoid it.

Even though the prostrate body was headless, heavy breathing, alternating with grunts of pain, could still be heard coming from it. Jenny and I were statues, our weapons trained on the fallen enemy, trigger fingers trembling.

Tucker flicked open the Le Mat, loading a fresh shotgun shell as he rushed forward, grabbed the fallen broadsword and flung it across the room to clang resoundingly among the remains of the chandelier. Next he aimed his pistol at the Conquistador's uninjured foot.

"Ghost, you best lay real still." His voice was chilling. "I got another load of buckshot pointed at your good foot."

And suddenly we heard an utterly incongruous whimper wheedle from the headless being's ragged throat hole.

"No — no — please!"

With those pathetic syllables, the spring-tight nervous tension which had gripped us all suddenly dissipated.

"Pfhuh!" Tucker's snorted, and glanced at us. "You two hold down his arms."

Jenny quickly knelt and took a firm grip on one of the ghost's heavy mailed wrists. I hurried over and grabbed the other, placing my knee on the arm for good measure. Near me was a section of the ghost's fragmented skull. In the eye socket I could see an ingenious metal clip which held a small glowing ember of coal. I'd discovered the source of the glowing "eyes" which had so rattled me moments earlier.

Tucker holstered his pistol, drew his hunting knife and leaned over our captured, rather less-ghostly being.

"No!" it whimpered hollowly again.

"Shut up," snarled Tucker. With his knife he began slitting the leather straps which held the front half of the breast plate armor to the rear half. He freed the plate and tossed it aside. Beneath the armor was a garment made of many layers of silk (a "bullet proof" vest of the time), and under that was a sort of clam shell of iron covering the giant's chest from neck to waist. Jenny's shotgun blasts had torn through the silk, but had only dented the iron. The interior shell was hinged on one side and had two latches on the other. Tucker flipped these and opened the shell.

We saw the head and upper chest of a small, very pale, very frightened man. Thin and angular, his face was heavily freckled. Even his glistening bald head was freckled, and ringed with sweat-matted, scraggly gray hair.

The top of his head barely reached the base of his ghost contraption's neck. Concealed in the neck was a periscope through which he could peer out over the top of his armor shell.

"Don't kill me! Please! Please! I'll make you rich! Split it all with you!" He spoke with desperate speed, looking wildly from one to the other of us. I recognized the reedy voice that had made the raucous laughter, but it was far less intimidating when not emanating from within his metal shell.

Tucker gripped the man by his wispy hair, making him wince. "Did you kill Luddy Sedlak?"

"No! No!"

With his free hand, Tucker snatched up the outer chest armor he'd flung aside, pointing out the five small bullet holes which had already been there when we first encountered the ghost.

Tucker's voice rasped with an anger I'd never heard in all our adventures. "Five rounds. Looks to be about 32 caliber, which is what Luddy carried. He fired on you, and you cut him down!"

"No!"

He yelped as Tucker viciously slammed his head down against the armor back plate. Tucker's bellow seemed to rattle the very walls.

"Tell me true or tell it to the devil!"

"It — it was an accident!" the little man cried. "I didn't want to! I didn't mean it! He — he wouldn't run! All the others ran! I — I swung at him, yes. But I thought he would duck or run. Anyone would, wouldn't they? But he never moved! Only after I struck did he even shoot! I never meant to kill him!"

It seemed to me a preposterous lie, but Tucker sagged a little hearing the words, deeply affected by them.

Perhaps seeing he'd won a small point, the ghost man keened again, "I was sure he'd run, don't you see?"

Tucker glared at him, "He thought you were *real*, you dirty little weasel!"

"But — but then wouldn't he run?" wheezed the man. He seemed genuinely perplexed.

Tucker just shook his head. Finally he mumbled bleakly, "All his life he wanted to see a real ghost."

He stood and paced round our prisoner. Jenny and I kept a firm grip on the man's arms, though I doubted he could even get up without help. Indeed I wondered how he got in and out of his creation.

Tucker was growing agitated again, Luddy's death preying on him. He whirled on the man again, "What then? How'd he end up some six miles from here? You cart him him out of here? Leave him to die?"

"No, no, no!" hurried the man. "He left on his own. Wounded, yes. But walking. I couldn't of catched him if I wanted, not in all this," he nodded to his cumbersome costume.

"Not that you tried, did you? You scum-swimming excuse for a man!"

I flinched as Tucker suddenly drew his pistol. Pointing it at the ceiling, he cocked it, the multiple clicks seeming

151

excessively crisp and sharp as the hammer came back. Then he slowly began to lower it in the direction the man on the floor. Tucker's face was a dreadful gray mask.

"No!" the poor fellow shrieked, jerking his head wildly from side to side. Seeing no mercy in Tucker's vengeful visage, he glanced desperately at Jenny and me.

Jenny jumped up, mouth opened as though to speak. Tucker froze her with a single cold glance.

"Not a word, Jenny. Knew Luddy seven years longer than I've known even you."

Jenny said nothing. Instead, she looked right at me. It was with that same pleading expression she'd had back in Oklahoma when she'd asked me to come with them. In that instant I knew this was the moment she'd anticipated. The moment where she thought I might have more sway than she. I had to say something! Do something!

And so it was, with painful banality, that I blurted in a cracked voice, "Mr. Tucker, two wrongs don't make a right!"

Tucker jerked as though he'd been jabbed with a pin. He twisted his head round to look at me, blinking as though he didn't recognize me. I'm sure he'd quite forgotten I was there at all. Then he glowered as the meaning of my ridiculous proverb sank in.

"You got no say, Whitney. No say at all."

He aimed the gun at the whimpering little man's head. The man shrieked pitifully and squeezed his eyes shut in anticipation of death.

I feverishly spoke again, "I do have a say, sir! Any rational human being does. This is the twentieth century, we are in a civilized land, and — and you are not a vigilante!"

Tucker still peered malevolently down his gun barrel. Jenny's body twitched like a cat about to spring, wild eyes locked on his revolver as though, should his bullet be loosed, she would somehow snatch it from the air.

But then Tucker's head went back. His chin jutted out. He made a sound, a single short grunt. It wasn't even "pfhuh," but it would pass for a laugh under the circumstances.

He raised his gun, de-cocked it and, with a baleful look at me, said, "I don't believe I hired you to preach law and manners."

"Even so," I said.

He holstered the Le Mat, spun round and stood with his back to us. Jenny uncoiled from her cat-stance, glanced at me and gave the briefest nod. I had won the moment.

Tucker walked stiffly in a semicircle, coming to a stop in front of the red leather chair. He sat down heavily and a cloud of dust welled up around him. Jenny walked behind the chair and placed her hands on Tucker's forehead, pulling his head back against the chair back, massaging lightly.

"I'm too blessed old," Tucker said.

"Your age brings you wisdom," Jenny answered.

"Yeah, well — wisdom brings me a headache."

As my pulse slowly returned to normal, I suddenly realized the great dome above us was full of sickly yellow smoke, undulating like a stormy sky. The sofa, forgotten in the grander drama, was now fully aflame, the beautiful old hardwood floor around it catching as well.

"Oh my!" I called. "We'd better see to this quickly or it will get away from us!"

Tucker and Jenny looked over. He rose, but said only, "Leave it."

"What? Don't be ridiculous. The whole building will burn!" I proclaimed righteously.

"I said leave it!" he roared back. And I saw in his eyes that, while I may have won the ghost's life, the ghost's house was not to be bargained for.

He strode over to the prostrate little man, grabbed one of

153

his armored arms and gave it a tug. When the ghost didn't budge, Tucker mumbled, "Lord, how do you move in this get-up?" (It was later determined that the elaborate rig weighed over one hundred pounds on top of the wiry little fellow's one hundred thirty).

Tucker turned to me. "Better lend a hand, Whitney, you're so bent on keeping him this side of the Devil's house."

I quickly handed my rifle to Jenny and grabbed the man's other arm. With considerable effort, we dragged him, clanking and scraping, out of the ballroom, down the long hall, and finally out into daylight.

Once we had heaved him into Triumph, Jenny worked to bandage his wounded foot. The armor had partially protected it from Tucker's Le Mat shotgun blast, but it was a bloody mess all the same. Even as he whimpered and winced, he tried to bargain.

"There's a hundred thousand Spanish gold coins buried somewhere on this property."

"There always is," said Tucker tiredly. "That, or a wagon load of Aztec gold, or some queen's jewels, or some train robbers' loot."

"I tell you it's there. Help me in my search. I'll split it with you!"

"Not interested."

Meanwhile, with shocking speed, the fire spread through the old mansion. By the time we left, flames were shooting from the windows and jetting thirty feet above the roof as they pierced through the black oily smoke. I thought of the lost antiques, lost architecture, lost history, but dared not raise such trivialities to my simmering employer.

We rode wordless all the way to New Ocland. As we approached the outskirts of that town, Tucker threw a blanket over the little man, still lying in his armor in the wagon bed. "You keep quiet," he ordered him. I couldn't guess Tucker's reasons for doing this, but was certain it was unwise to ask what they might be, given his mood.

Our reappearance caused quite a stir. The normal route for the rare visitor to the Castile mansion was straight away from the area at the highest possible speed, so our leisurely return was an anomaly. Word spread faster than our wagon's pace and a small crowd of dour-faced villagers quickly collected along the dingy main street.

To our surprise, as we approached the saloon where we had hired Mr. Dulcek, Constable Diphonia stepped from inside, stiff and officious as ever. With him were two nervous young men, armed with rifles. Behind them came the bearded man Tucker had confronted, arms folded smugly, the law now on his side.

Diphonia marched out in front of the wagon, halting the horses, "Mr. Harold Tucker. I have a warrant for your arrest."

Idiot! I thought, *must I now save another man from being shot today?*

But Tucker answered calmly, "Do you now?"

"I do!"

"What for? Not following your travel advice?"

Diphonia spluttered, "For disturbing the peace and for making armed threats upon a citizen." Then he added quickly, as though it were not obvious, "I have two deputies to ensure said warrant is properly served."

"You'd arrest the man who's gone and caught your ghost?"

Gasps and mumbled excitement rippled though the crowd. But Diphonia was not to be deterred, "I'll brook no more nonsense from you, sir!" he bleated, "Now step down from your wagon!"

"No nonsense to it. I've got the ghost right here."

More gasps as mumbles as Tucker slowly reached back and gripped the corner of the blanket covering the prostrate figure in the wagon bed. With deliberate theatricality, he hesitated before pulling it off, scanning the townsfolk with disapproving eyes. Tension mounted. Constable Diphonia stiffened even more and nervously cleared his throat.

Now I saw the reason for the blanket: sheer showmanship. Something in Tucker relished exposing as groundless the superstitions he so detested. Repeatedly disappointed in the quest for his own dream, he drew a perverse pleasure from rubbing people's noses in their delusions.

He whipped the blanket aside with a flourish. People literally shrank back from the wagon in fear of what horror they might see. Then, one by one, they inched forward to peer inside; and finally stared in confusion at our captive in his incriminating Halloween costume.

After an almost comically long silence, one of the townsfolk said, "Jeffrey?"

We would learn that the mortal interior of the "ghost in armor" was named Jeffrey Meadows, and that he was a local wheelwright. In recent years he had been taking long absences from his shop due, he had claimed, to recurring illness. Now it became clear that in fact he had spent the time searching for the supposed Castile treasure, and scaring off others who might have similar desires.

There were several among the onlookers who had, at different times, been personally petrified by Jeffrey's apparition. As animated discussion rippled through the crowd, they confirmed that this was indeed the ghost they'd seen. Confusion and shock evolved into anger. Suggestions for appropriate punishments for Meadows' swiftly became more and more creative.

Tucker leapt down to join befuddled Diphonia and his deputies. "You might want to get your boys to haul this ghost someplace where you can keep him from getting lynched."

Diphonia agreed and directed his men to extract Meadows from Triumph. As they did this, Tucker pulled the Constable aside.

"Now, as to my arrest, you should do what you feel is correct and necessary in your capacity as law officer in this country. Personally I'd prefer to avoid any trial where I was forced to jaw-wag about the quality of the investigation into Luddy Sedlak's killing."

Diphonia gave Tucker a frosty look, but clearly understood the advantage of following his suggestion. So, once Meadows had been lugged into the tavern, we were on our way out of the dreary town.

Within a day, treasure seekers from New Ocland and many other surrounding villages descended upon the burned-out Castile mansion, even while its timbers still smoldered. Beneath the foundation and the grounds they found over two miles of tunnels Meadows had laboriously hand-dug in his search for the lost Spanish gold. The treasure itself forever avoided capture.

CHAPTER NINE

Change

The episode of the ghost drastically altered life on the DH. For one thing, the influence of easy-going Luddy was sorely missed. He was not only much revered among the hands, he was well-known and admired throughout the county. His passing at the hands of a "dirty little weasel" aroused a long-lasting rancor that pervaded the place.

It was in this grim time Tucker concluded that the pursuit of his dream had cost the life of his dearest friend. Gone was the rough humor that had tempered his cynicism. He spent long days alone in the library, reading science fiction in a fruitless attempt to escape a relentless depression. Twice Jenny was able to lure him into going on their rugged camping trips. But he returned from these outings as melancholy as before.

Two months passed during which I saw little of Tucker. I busied myself with a description of the scissor-tailed flycatcher (*Muscivoria forficate*), whose exotic mating flights I'd first witnessed the year before.

G. Winters Wayne had more legal work dealing with a lawsuit arising from the ghost episode. It was filed not by Constable Diphonia (who remained scrupulously silent), but by the bearded man at whom Tucker had aimed his derringer in the New Ocland tavern. Co-plaintiff in his suit, curiously, was one of the men Diphonia had hastily deputized in the ill-considered attempt to arrest Tucker. (I could only assume the "deputy" sought to share in the bearded man's hoped-for financial windfall.) This suit Tucker fought with uncharacteristic vigor, traveling with Wayne all the way back to New Ocland to successfully trounce the opportunists in court. He seemed to glean a sort of dark delight in the victory.

A bright spot arrived with word from one of Tucker's posse that dinosaur-like "land crocodiles" had been discovered on the island of Komodo. The spark of the hunt was briefly ignited and, in less than a month, Tucker had arranged to have a live one captured and sent all the way to the ranch. (This was well ahead of the notoriety these "Komodo dragons" would enjoy later, by around 1912). When the lizard arrived, Tucker looked at it for less than a minute, summarizing: "Nothing but an overgrown horny toad." With that he slipped back into his hapless torpor.

Soon after, I was dismayed to learn that, one by one, Tucker was dismissing the members of the posse. He also ceased placing the advertisements offering rewards for unusual creatures.

Some weeks later, on a fiercely cold March night, with the Oklahoma wind once again trying to tear shingles from the house, Jenny came to me and asked that I speak to Tucker directly. It was always astonishing to me that she felt my opinion carried weight with Harry Tucker. My opinion of that opinion was that every third word I said to him fell on deaf ears. Nonetheless, I agreed to add my arguments to those already given by others in attempts to raise him from his sunken state.

I entered the library to find him gazing into a roaring fire, his well-worn copy of *20,000 Leagues Under the Sea* open in his lap (he could recite the battle with the giant squid verbatim).

The wind was driving smoke backward down the chimney. It billowed from under the mantle and rolled along the massive wooden rafters above us like ominous clouds. Tucker gave me a look to suit the setting.

"You another emissary from Jenny?"

"We are all worried about this turn you have taken."

He looked back into the fire. "Folks are supposed to rejoice when a man comes to his senses."

"It is neither sensible nor appropriate that you blame yourself for what happened to Luddy. He, like you, was —" I hesitated, then plunged onward, "was a bull in a china shop, bound for trouble. Indeed, looking under every rock, as you say, for trouble!"

"He looked under'em at my bidding and with my blessing."

"Yes and no. You said yourself he followed his own whims."

Tucker leaned back in his chair, eyes still on the fire, clearly not swayed by, nor even particularly interested in my arguments.

"Whitney, am I going to find a dinosaur?"

I was taken aback by the question and fumbled for an answer. "That has no bearing on the point I'm trying —"

Tucker interrupted by abruptly turning his grim gaze on me, asking very deliberately, "As a graduate of college, a zoologist, a reader of scientific literature and follower of the scientific method, in your learned opinion, am I ever going to find a live dinosaur?"

It was significant, I realized, that in all the time since hiring me to help identify trickery, Tucker had deliberately avoided asking me this question. And in all that time, now was when I least wanted to answer it.

So I countered, "And if I say 'no,' your self-condemnation will be complete and justified?"

"Nobody wants to be on a fool's errand, Whitney."

"There is nothing foolish about what you have accomplished. Your tireless research has resulted in amassing huge amounts of valuable data. Your trips up the Amazon and Orinoco. Our travels to Egypt, Nepal and elsewhere. And what of your discovery of the sunken Revolutionary War ship in Lake Champlain?"

"I was looking for Champ!" (Tucker was referring to the

lake's legendary monster.)

"That does not matter! The find in itself had value. Science is the search for answers, whatever they may be."

"Oh, so all this while I've been engaged in science?"

"In — in your boisterous way, yes. The very fact that you recognized the need to hire me is more proof of the same. You cannot say that nothing has been accomplished simply because one goal has not been met."

Tucker's eyes flashed beneath those dark cloud-like brows, "*One goal!?* Never mind that little thing, eh?"

I had overstepped, besmirched the Holy Grail. I quickly tried to recover, "I don't mean to suggest that wasn't important — isn't important. I only wish to stress that you mustn't overlook what's been achieved with this remarkable worldwide network you've created, which even now you are dismantling. And to say that it is painful to see someone with your drive just suddenly stop moving."

His momentary anger evaporated. His gaze returned to the fire. "Well, I won't have to keep moving much longer. I'm fifty y — "

For once, I interrupted him, "Fifty years old! Dear Lord we know, Harry. How could any of us forget?"

I was immediately sorry for speaking sharply, but he just nodded slowly.

"All right. You've made your speech. You've done Jenny's bidding. Good night."

I left thoroughly dejected, positive that I had utterly failed to reach him. I could not know that, quite the contrary, I had planted the seed which was to grow into our ultimate, wholly unexpected "success."

↔↔↔↔↔↔↔↔↔

The seed would not sprout until spring. Prior to that, life was more or less routine, albeit tinged with the uneasiness engendered by Tucker's constant malaise. I catalogued the previous summer's collected arthropods. Evenings were passed in civil conversation. Now and then Tucker and Jenny entertained friends. The necessities of the ranch were seen to. Tucker devoted his free time to reading, but not science fiction. Instead he had turned to various scientific journals, not all of them of the best reputation. This new interest was a direct result of our earlier conversation.

A beautiful day in late May found me at my old prairie dog haunt. I had taken an interest in the black-footed ferrets which preyed upon the prairie dogs. Encamped some five miles from the main house, I was surprised to hear horses approaching at the gallop. Upon them were Tucker and Jenny.

Tucker fairly vaulted from his mount, landing before me in a swirl of red dust as he blurted: "Whitney, could you thaw out one of them mammoths and bring it to life?"

Tucker was of course aware that mammoths had been found frozen in Siberian ice at least as far back as 1799. In 1886 he had traveled to Russia to see the remains of one for himself. (Its skeleton is still in the St. Petersburg museum.) His summation at the time was, "Nothin' but a hairy elephant." Further, the mammoths' vast separation from dinosaurs in geologic time made them of minor interest to him. Thus, his current question was surprising and baffling. I answered it flatly.

"No."

"Pfhuh! I have word from a fella says maybe you could." Doctor, scientist, college fella like you. Doctor Martin Penny-smith. Know him?"

"I'm afraid not."

Tucker rushed on, "Says here you can," and he read from a letter hastily pulled from his jacket, "'revitalize dead tissue through the controlled scientific application of electrical energy.'"

"Well, I believe it's true," I said cautiously, "that there are electrical signals traveling in the nervous system, but I don't know of any credible research indicating —"

"The point is, if he thinks he could do it do a frozen mammoth, maybe he can do it to other things."

I wasn't following him at all, and it obviously showed on my face.

"Bless it, Whitney!" he shouted. "Don't you see the possibility? We're gonna take my ichthyosaur fossil down to him; see what he can cook up with it, eh?"

Now, with dismay, I understood what had happened. In encouraging Tucker to think of his quest as at least quasi-scientific, I had opened his mind to this decidedly unscientific possibility. I hardly knew where to begin my response.

"Harry, surely you realize there's a vast difference between 'frozen' and 'fossilized.' In a fossil, the original animal tissue has been replaced by minerals. There's no actual flesh remaining —"

But over Tucker's shoulder I saw Jenny sending me a look of entreaty that would have given a Hun pause. And it burst upon me that I was about to quash the first hint of animation we had seen in Tucker for many months. I quickly changed course and desperately tried to climb from the hole I'd begun digging: "But of course I shouldn't speak hastily. Perhaps I should correspond with this fellow. Seek to understand the true nature of his claims."

"*Correspond?* And me five months past fifty? You'll talk to him in person. We leave in two days. Much to do!"

"Very well — of course. And we're leaving for — ?"

"Venezuela!"

CHAPTER TEN

Venezuela

By wagon, by train, by ship; it seemed we fairly flew the thousands of miles to Florida and then across the Gulf of Mexico. I rather enjoyed our first Venezuelan stop, the unexpectedly modern city of Maracaibo, perched at the end of the strait leading in from the Gulf. Tucker had procured rooms in an excellent hotel, and I'd spent a pleasant two days perusing the markets and sampling the local food while he sought passage further south.

He settled on a dismal-looking lake steamer, more because she was available than that she was acceptable. However, when I strode down to the harbor on the third morning, I found our kit still piled on the dock, and the dockhands pointedly ignoring it.

Tucker was in a discussion with the disheveled, unshaven captain of the steamer. As the captain waved his arms and nattered in Spanish, I didn't need to follow every word to get the gist: that our mountain of supplies, our horses, our large freight wagon were, "Too much! Too much!" While his ship was indeed crowded with passengers, animals and trade goods, I knew he'd been clearly informed how much we carried. It was obvious that, by threatening to strand us in port, he was simply making a show for more money.

In the past, to attempt such open-faced coercion on my employer would have been to invite swift and likely violent retribution. In the past, to travel with Harold B. Tucker was to ride a skittish horse in snake country — you must always be ready to find yourself suddenly flying through the air or hanging on for dear life.

But today, Tucker simply dug into his money belt and offered the required gold Bolivars to the boorish captain. The man grabbed them, and the dock hands, with nothing more than a smug nod from him, went to work.

Nothing could have a pointed up more sharply what was most different about this, the last of our journeys — Tucker himself.

I confess I was disappointed. I missed the guilty pleasure of seeing that captain instantaneously reduced to terror when the well-to-do, impeccably dressed rancher suddenly exploded in wild-eyed, seemingly uncontrollable rage. I glanced at Jenny. I could not read anything in her immobile features, but I fancied she was disappointed, too.

With this cloud over us, we boarded the old steamer and she commenced to flop her laborious way across one of the world's largest lakes. The wind was at our backs, kicking up a chop which caused the ship to roll most queasily. First one side-wheel then the other rose entirely clear of the water to flail futilely and spatter brackish mist over us. Worse, the tailwind whorled the smoke from her stack round us in an incessant sulfurous, eye-burning fog. Taft and Bronto, hobbled and on short leads tied to the stern winch, snorted unhappily and tossed their heads, scattering oats from the feed bags that did little to comfort them. Retreating into the lounge cabin was pointless, as the stifling heat and crowd of sweaty humans (many transporting assorted animals) made the atmosphere in there even worse than that on deck.

Ironically, our lumbering, odiferous conveyance was christened *Triunfo*, Spanish for "Triumph." I should have noted this as a good omen, for surely it proved to be. But the coincidence went un-remarked. I merely clung to the arms of my deck chair and mentally condemned the country's humidity. (Never again would I complain of Oklahoma's summers!)

After a grueling day and night's steaming, we were at last within sight of our next stop, La Ceiba, a tiny fishing village on the southeastern shore. The wind had turned full round and was now against us, slowing our pace considerably. I appreciated the smoother ride and the smokeless air; and I even enjoyed the further delay, for I alone knew a dark secret about our destination, and I dreaded our ultimate arrival.

My secret tension had been mounting since we'd left Miami by freighter. On the very afternoon we had set sail, literally as I had walked up the gangplank, a messenger boy had overtaken me to deliver a bundle of mail. This had come about because, before leaving Oklahoma, I had telegraphed several scientific societies asking for information on our host-to-be, Doctor Martin Pennysmith. Here at last were some replies.

Telling neither Tucker nor Jenny, I'd sequestered myself in my cabin and pored over the information in the first hours of the voyage. To my dismay, the reports on Pennysmith were universally cautionary, and in some cases were outright condemnation.

He was all but expelled from the medical school he attended. and had not in fact even obtained his doctorate. Both Thomas Edison and Nikola Tesla had rejected his applications to join their competing companies in electrical research. A Boston medical association included in their reply to me a copy of a paper he had published. In it, his description of restoring life to dead tissue seemed to owe more to Mary Shelley than the study of medicine.

Yet I was bound to say nothing. To voice my concern that we were about to meet an utter charlatan was to snuff out the hope so newly rekindled in Tucker's heart. Let that happen in its own time. Or, God willing, let Pennysmith somehow surprise me with unexpected genius.

So instead, I spoke only of my eagerness to catalogue new animal species in the remote district where "Doctor" Penny-smith chose, or more likely was forced, to reside.

Trinufo slammed into the small dock at La Ceiba with enough force to confirm my suspicions that our captain was a drinker. We disembarked, relieved to be on solid footing. As the long process of unloading our kit began, I was surprised to see a large Case steam traction engine huffing its way up the little town's main street, headed for the farms to the south. Modern methods and machinery were finding their way to the most remote spots on earth.

In the meantime, Tucker asked about for a man named Ximen, whom Doctor Pennysmith's letters had indicated would meet us on his behalf. Unnervingly, the questions were met with that curious local reticence we encountered on many another journey. Townsfolk reacted to Pennysmith's name with nervous shrugs, sidelong glances, even winces. This unsettled Tucker more than it might have otherwise. He grumbled: "They're acting like folks who think there's a werewolf or yeti on the loose." It was disturbing to him because there was no such local legend, and in his estimation we were merely on our way to meet a noted scientist. It was disturbing to *me* because I knew that we weren't.

Unable to find Pennysmith's emissary, we ambled about the town and decided to procure lunch in a quaint lakeside café. We sat at an outside table, for the heat was even more miserable inside, and sampled a dubious stew of indeterminate ingredients and the much more appetizing local round bread called "arepa."

As we ate, I noticed a man across the street. One could not help but notice him, because he was appallingly deformed — one-eyed, hunched over, with one twisted leg much shorter than the other. And he was staring intently at us. I also noticed that he carried slung on his malformed hip a knife of disturbing proportions. It was more miniature sword than conventional knife, hanging bare in a crude leather loop. After a moment he approached our waiter and asked a question. The waiter pointed us out, and the man began lurching toward us.

Tucker now saw him and, assuming him to be a beggar, rose to shoo him away. But the man explained, in barely decipherable English, that he was in fact Pennysmith's envoy, Ximen.

Lunch instantly forgotten, Tucker of course urged that we leave immediately. So, in less than an hour we were on our way, with Ximen in the lead, riding a small burro on which he seemed very precarious.

If the heat on Lake Maracaibo had been impressively oppressive, the heat in the forested lowlands we now entered was nigh unbearable. I wished our horses could pull Triumph fast enough to generate a breeze, but the steep twisting track made this impossible. Though we wore our lightest cotton garments, they were damp with sweat in minutes.

Onward we pushed. The road forked and forked again; and each time Ximen took the less-traveled path. Thus, to the heat was added the worry that perhaps our supposed guide was leading us into ambush for a robbery. I pushed the thought aside, chastising myself for succumbing to unfounded fears. But then my eye fell again on that outsized knife he carried. And *then* I noticed Tucker unsnap the holster strap over his Le Mat and Jenny rest her hand on the butt of her double rifle. The fact that they seemed to share my thoughts gave little comfort. We rode on uneasily, eyes flitting to the dense foliage on all sides, ears straining to discern any potentially sinister sounds masked by the raucous squawks of the Rose Headed Parakeets which abounded in the area.

Suspicions of Ximen having some ulterior motive were allayed when we arrived at last in a large village on the bank of a pleasant stream. Many small huts of sod and thatching were scattered helter-skelter round a clearing in the towering trees. The inhabitants were mostly local Indians, the Timoto-Cuica. Ximen suggested we stop to refresh ourselves, as Doctor Pennysmith's outpost, he assured us, was still yet more remote. He also explained that Pennysmith relied upon this village for local foodstuffs.

These were a poor, but not a savage people. Their culture had evolved artists of considerable talent, and they carved excellent jewelry, statues, and masks from stone. Domination by the Spanish, followed by literal decades of revolution and counter-revolution had left them, like indigenous peoples round the world, trapped between their past and an uncertain future. In addition to subsistence farming, this group dabbled at growing coffee on the slopes near the village, though harvests were meager.

Serving now as interpreter with two village hunters, our guide helped Tucker haggle over a price for providing us with fresh meat during our stay, Tucker being unfond of our tinned supplies. Meanwhile, I slowly circled the village, trying not to gape too openly at what to me were a most exotic people.

Some of the women were grinding corn on stones in a manner quite similar to that used by our own American Indians. A far stranger sight was two men working beside cages crowded with bird chicks that were grotesquely fat. Several of these they dumped unceremoniously, alive, into a large pot of boiling water. Watching this I immediately began to hope Tucker failed in his efforts to procure food from these people. Later I would learn that the chicks were "oil birds" (*Steatornis caripensis*), their fat-rich bodies being rendered for lamp oil rather than culinary pleasure.

Tucker's negotiating done to his satisfaction, he immediately demanded we press onward to Doctor Pennysmith's facilities. But when the villagers heard the name, there were more sidelong glances and scowls. Then, without warning, an old woman hobbled forward from the onlookers and squared off with startled Tucker. She was something of a sight, with dark, deeply wrinkled skin, missing front teeth and one clouded eye. She pointed a crooked finger and shook her head, speaking rapid Spanish in a raspy voice. It was clearly a warning or a threat, but the only phrase I could grasp was the oft repeated, "*Pansmit es malvado!*"

Ximen hurried over and glared at her menacingly. She lowered her finger, but stood her ground and glared back, single eye for single eye. He turned to Tucker, "Just stupid woman. We go."

But Tucker asked, "Was she saying something about Pennysmith? '*Pansmit es malvado?*'" What's that?"

Ximen shrugged, "She don't like. Just stupid. '*Malvado*' it's mean —" he squinted his eye as he mentally scanned his diminutive English thesaurus "— uh, bad — worse bad — what is word? Eee —?" he faltered.

"Eee-vil?" prompted Tucker.

Ximen nodded, "Is word."

"Why on earth would she say that?"

Ximen was getting impatient, "Is stupid, I say already. "No *entiendo* doctor's job."

Tucker nodded, partially satisfied. But Jenny and I shared an uncomfortable glance of our own, while I privately worried, *What has Pennysmith done to engender such reactions among these people?*

But of course we pressed on. Again following Ximen, tottering on his burro, we drove our team further east up a track that followed the stream into the mountains. Cut often now by rain gullies, it was even more tortuous than the road which had preceded it. I knew I'd be sore for a full day as a result of the jolting I was receiving from Triumph's unfor-

170

giving steel wheels.

Some three miles beyond the village, we struggled up a steep grade toward a stunning waterfall that spilled over a natural stone dam. The track zig-zagged higher and brought us into view of the small lake behind the dam, its turgid water flecked with clots of dull green algae.

The dam served also as a ford, and Ximen led us across through the shallow water flowing over it. Continuing now along the lake shore, we had to duck often under huge brooding trees drooping low across the trail and far out over the water. Gray cumulous clouds gathered, blotting out the sun and giving everything a most depressing aspect.

"We must be close," Tucker said, his voice startling after the long wordless ride. "He wrote that his laboratory is on the west end of a lake."

I sighed to myself, dreading our arrival, knowing that it could only be the location of Tucker's next big disappointment.

CHAPTER ELEVEN

The Laboratory

Our first view of Pennysmith's "laboratory" could not have been more dramatic. As we rounded the last bend, lightning crackled and thunder shook the air, sliding along the Andean mountainsides in seemingly endless peals.

On top of that, where we had expected a modest building of modern construction, we instead faced an enormous, ancient, rambling structure of native stone, its once-plastered walls having long since given up their adornment. I assumed that it was of Spanish Colonial origin, most likely built as mission. (I was unable to confirm this, however, as my later research found no record of the Spanish having attempted to build this far from the coast.)

The gray walls towered against the stormy sky. Slipshod repairs had been made to a mostly collapsed roof, original tiles replaced with coarse lumber, native thatching, and broad sheets of canvas. The canvas flapped incongruously in the increasing wind, giving the building the aspect of a derelict ship with tattered sails flying.

Ximen led us round the building. On the way we passed the astonishing anachronism of a huge Corliss engine, its flywheel not less than ten feet in diameter. It was silent, the boiler cool, but was new, in good repair, and clearly saw frequent use. The engine's drive shaft thrust through a hole breached in the building's south wall; thus we could not see what was powered thereby. Tucker was impressed and noted, "Must've brought that up in pieces. Quite a project, I'd bet."

The entrance to the lab was on the side opposite the lake — a weedy courtyard spread before a pair of massive doors. They were of new wood, reinforced with iron already rusting in the perpetually damp environment. Here Ximen executed a slow, painful dismount from his steed, then took the unexpected step of drawing a uniquely shaped horn from his pocket. It was hammered from brass (or perhaps discolored copper) and curved like a ram's horn. On this instrument, he blew a single, long, melancholy note.

We waited. Ximen repeated his fanfare. And we waited.

Tucker was growing impatient. His breathing was becoming deep, chest swelling. But just as he was about to rise from the wagon seat, a rattling of chains was heard from within the building. Then the sound of a bar being removed. At last, the doors swung open with a groan.

A tall, thin man wearing a much-stained laboratory smock rushed out. His wild shock of unkempt wispy gray hair fluttered in the wind as he stepped briskly to our wagon with hand outstretched toward Tucker.

"You are Harold B. Tucker, please say so!"

"I am" said Tucker as he leaned down to shake the hand.

"Delighted! Delighted! I am Doctor Martin Pennysmith!" Utterly ignoring Jenny and myself, he gestured grandly to the building, "Come, come! Into the house! Out of this beastly weather! Ximen! Put the wagon in the south room. See to their creatures!"

Anxiously waiting for us to disembark, he rose on tiptoe and twirled in a full circle. I was immediately reminded of a passage from one of the letters I had received in Florida advising me about Doctor Pennysmith: "You will find him a most energetic fellow, the bulk of that energy bent toward strange and unprovable pseudo-science." But I kept these thoughts to myself as Tucker eagerly followed the doctor to the "house," and Jenny and I less eagerly followed.

The moment we passed through the imposing entrance, we were smitten by an odor, faint yet distinct, and unmistakable to anyone who has hunted or raised animals for slaughter. It was death — the smell of flesh left too long uncooked or uncured.

We stood in an unexpectedly claustrophobic entryway, made so by a wall of newer construction. Built of rough-hewn timbers and sloppily mortared stone, the wall sealed off the now-cramped entry from what was obviously the original nave of the mission. Set in this wall were doors of outlandish thickness and strength. They were wood, but clad in so much iron as to be worthy of a bank vault.

We were not to enter the chamber behind the doors. Instead, our host veered aside into a small anteroom. There a hodgepodge of furniture had been hastily assembled to mimic a sitting room. I say hastily because the legs of the mismatched chairs, end tables and a settee had left streaks in the thick dust coating the floor. Local fruit was presented in bowls. Wine glasses had been set out. Three champagne bottles were nestled a large bucket full of *ice*, an unexpected sight to say the least.

Pennysmith swooped down on a bottle and plucked it up proudly. "Ice, you see! I am far from civilization and near the equator, but do not suffer all deprivations, not so? Amongst my equipment is an ice-making machine of the most modern type." He poured a glass full to overflowing. "A drink! A drink to drown the memories of your beastly journey!" He downed the entire glass. Then, catching himself, he quickly poured glasses for the rest of us. "Forgive me! Forgive me! Too along alone among the savages! Price paid for daring to expand the limits of knowledge, not so?"

We accepted our drinks and sat. Pennysmith sat, or more perched, then instantly rose again as Ximan passed by the doorway. "Ximen! Are their beds ready? Did you procure mosquito netting? Have they water and towels?"

Ximen started to reply; but, brusque as always, Tucker spoke to the doctor, "Never mind all that, Doctor. We're used to rough travel. Now, I have on my wagon my fossil ichthyosaurus that I wrote you about. As you know, I'm hoping you can — "

"No, no, no! Not yet! First a demonstration of my procedures! It's a must! I've gone to great lengths to prepare same!"

"A demonstration is not necessary. All I want is — "

"But I insist! You think I am not aware you've come these two thousand miles to divine whether I am charlatan or changer of worlds?"

At the term "charlatan," both Tucker and Jenny shot glances at me. I cringed, flustered, for I felt I surely had kept my opinions to myself. But Tucker let the moment pass, continuing to the doctor, "I've not come to divine, Pennysmith. I've come only in hope, the hope that you can help me in my own quest."

"And I shall apply myself scrupulously to that end, dear Mr. Tucker!" Pennysmith threw back his second glass of sparkling wine, a pink glow already flushing his cheeks. "But first, on the morrow, or the day after at the latest — there is much to prepare — you shall see an example of the primary work, the great work, your financial aid will sustain!"

To my amazement, Tucker nodded and sat back in his chair, accepting the delay. With some sadness I saw that Harold Tucker was in fact intimidated by Pennysmith, and I knew that this was merely because "Doctor" preceded the name. Despite all Tucker's achievements, and the impressive breadth of his self-acquired education, he would never consider himself the equal of someone who was "college weaned."

And so we were to wait. Ximen led us down a twisting hallway to our rooms. They were bare stone with rude cots, but were thankfully dry, albeit with walls filmed in a patina of mildew that I felt must cover most of the country.

Three days passed. Pennysmith's deadline came and went as he worked behind the massive locked doors guarding the laboratory portion of the building, joining us for neither

175

meals nor socialization. When briefly glimpsed, he was nervously guarded about the cause of the delay, saying only that Ximen needed to obtain additional supplies.

We had carefully uncrated Tucker's fossil ichthyosaur, but it remained unexamined, leaning against the wall in the sitting room. Tucker battled his frustration by reading and availing himself of Pennysmith's extensive wine cellar.

I, on the other hand, had an overwhelming number of opportunities to occupy myself. I needed go no further than the edge of the clearing in which the laboratory sat to find exotic fauna, seemingly on every branch and under every bush.

On only the second day I spent an hour watching a brilliant yellow eyelash pitviper (*Bothriechis schlegelii*) stalk a tree frog. As I leafed through a book on South American amphibians attempting to identify the frog before it was consumed, I heard a rattling on the trail. It was Ximen in a creaking two-wheeled cart pulled by his struggling little burro. Protruding from the rear of the cart, only half covered by a tarp, was a long wooden box which could only be described as a coffin. When he saw me, he gave me a look which was both embarrassed and yet oddly defiant; and he said nothing as he guided the burro round to the lake side of the laboratory and out of sight. The moment only added to the sense of foreboding I had about this whole trip.

At the end of the fifth day, Tucker, Jenny and I sat eating in the sitting room which, we had discovered, was the only furnished room in the rambling estate other than the bedrooms. Tucker was sullen. Jenny was watchful, silent, uncomfortable.

He tossed a chicken bone onto his plate and leaned back, glancing at me, "Well, at least in all this wasted time young Whitney's getting an eyeful of rare critters, eh?"

I swiftly attempted to take advantage of the overture to

liven the mood. "Oh my, there's no end of exotic animals! Insects that defy counting! I hardly know where to begin. Why, just today —" But at that moment, Pennysmith burst in upon us. He was clearly exhausted, wild eyes deep-set in purple sockets, hair more askew, if that were possible. Had he been awake and working this whole time? Disconcertingly, his already filthy lab coat was smeared with fresh blood stains.

He grandly waved his arm in a sort of lopsided salute, "I am ready! All is in readiness!" And he weaved unsteadily into the room, snatched up a full bottle of wine, and weaved right out again. "Tomorrow!"

Tucker seemed un-dismayed by the oddness of the moment. He threw down his napkin and rose from the table, "Tomorrow then — at last!" He marched out. Jenny sat for a moment, staring at her food. Finally she glanced up at me. "Is he a fool, this doctor?"

I struggled for a politic answer, "I — I hope not a fool. His credentials are not exactly what one might hope for, but he has studied the sciences at some fine institutions."

She looked off, "I don't want him to be hurt," meaning Tucker, of course. "His dream is dying. I'm afraid if his dream dies — of what will happen to him."

"It would not have been my advice to come all this way based on —"

"I know. I kept you from speaking. Now all I can do is hope with him."

CHAPTER TWELVE

Pennysmith's "Science"

I was jolted awake by the smell of wood smoke. At first alarmed that our ramshackle lodging might be ablaze, I threw on my robe and raced into the hallway. Tucker and Jenny were already dressed and striding by my door. Full of energy, Tucker boomed, "No alarm, Whitney. He's got Ximen stoking the Corliss, and I'm passing curious what he powers with it."

I hurried into my clothes and raced down the twisting hallways to the laboratory entrance. Even as I did so, the building began to thrum with the steady, breathy pulse of the Corliss engine.

Tucker and Jenny were waiting at the vault-like doors we had never yet seen open. Tucker impatiently tried them. Still locked. Meanwhile, to the chuff of the steam engine outside was added an extraordinary hum. Almost imperceptible at first, it rose in volume and pitch until the very walls around us seemed to vibrate in harmony. It was quite an uncanny sound. Tucker and Jenny looked to me with questioning faces. But I could only shrug my ignorance in return.

Just then we heard locks undone. The doors swung open and Pennysmith stood before us. Looking somewhat less ravaged than the evening before, and thankfully now wearing a clean laboratory coat, he was positively trembling with nervous energy. He beckoned to us, backing away from the door, "Come! Come!" With Tucker bulling eagerly ahead of us, we stepped into the room beyond.

As I passed through the doors, I noted that they could be held secure on the inside by hefty wooden cross bar, as though the doctor feared assault by barbarians with battering rams. I hoped we would not find that the nature of his

178

"work" somehow justified such fear.

We stood in what was indeed the huge nave of the ancient church. Even with the early morning sun streaming through high narrow windows, the ceiling vaulted into night-like darkness far above, supported on great wooden beams.

More striking, however (in those early years of the century) was that the center of the room was brilliantly lit by at least twenty electrical lights on tall masts, powered by an enormous bank of glass wet-cell storage batteries. It was far more light than one needed to navigate the chamber, and I immediately suspected Pennysmith had arranged this for dramatic effect alone. Certainly it had the desired impact on Tucker and Jenny. Their eyes swept over the dazzling landscape like those of wonderstruck children.

And "landscape" it was, for filling every available square foot of the expansive space was a mind-numbing jumble of equipment, most of it piled helter-skelter. The effect was more scrap yard than laboratory, for many items were covered with dust and mildew, suggesting they'd been cast aside over time, replaced with newer devices. Even so, I admit that I, too, was impressed by the sheer grandness of the collection, though my appreciation was muted by the fact that the smell of death was even stronger here than in the rest of the building.

Pennysmith led us forward. Narrow paths wound through the piles in maze-like fashion. As we followed him down twists and branches and forks, he spun full round every few steps to look back and smile eagerly, as though fearful that we might disappear if unwatched too long.

We passed a long row of shelves tottering with large specimen jars. Here the smell of formaldehyde overwhelmed the odor of decayed flesh. The jars held mostly animals, but a few human body parts were mixed in. If Tucker saw this, he gave no indication.

Rising above the general clutter, like buildings from a twisted urban landscape, were several different remarkable contraptions. Only one did I recognize. It was an immense Tesla coil, capable of creating powerful electrical charges. Noting the haphazard network of copper wires linking it and the other devices, I assumed them to be electrical in nature as well, though the science of electricity remains as much a mystery to me now as it was then.

The electrical machines gave rise to the explanation for the shuddering hum that filled the air. The Corliss engine's great drive shaft came through the breach in the old mission's wall to power a tremendous dynamo, albeit largely hidden by the piled paraphernalia. Pennysmith paused and gestured to it theatrically, "The largest dynamo in all of South America! Electrical power unmatched by any other laboratory on the continent!"

At last, we came to a circular area clear of mechanical debris. At its center, gleaming white against the generally gray backdrop, was a porcelain operating table. I mentally grimaced to see that it had been recently used, judging from the bucket of pink-tinged water and cleaning rags beside it. Pennysmith strode round the table and leaned on it as though it were a lectern, fixing us with his intense gaze.

"You are familiar with my views on the restorative power of electricity." It was a statement, not a question. Such was the man's ego.

Tucker was immediately defensive, "I'm not a learned man, Doctor. I'm just here to see if —"

But Pennysmith interrupted Tucker, as he had already done numerous times earlier. I was amazed at the man's gall, and at the fact that Tucker quietly endured it.

"And you are no doubt aware that there are detractors to my work. Some who have gone so far to call me mad!"

Tucker was uncomfortable: "I assure you that is not my

concern, sir."

But Pennysmith railed on, "That is why I insisted upon this demonstration, so that you may set aside all doubt as to the veracity of my research." And he suddenly shouted, "Ximen!"

At this command, Ximen entered from the main doors, shoving a small cart before him. What was clearly a rehearsed entrance was made somewhat less dramatic by his painfully slow gait and the fact that he had to navigate the circuitous junk paths to reach us. Too, I thought I sensed in him a distaste for his task.

When he finally did arrive, we saw on his cart a glass lab dish on which rested a pair of severed frog legs, still joined at the hips. I took them to be of the curious local horned frog Sapo Cuaima (*Ceratophrys calcarata*). Electrical wires rested beside the dish, attached to a glass battery.

Pennysmith jostled Ximen aside and took up the wires. "The nerves in our bodies, which control our every movement and maintain our very life, are nothing more than fleshly wires, conduits for electrical energy. The proof of this has long been known. When death has overtaken the organism, electricity no longer flows through the nerves. However, we have but to restore that lost force — and life returns!"

He touched his wires to the frog legs and, of course, they twitched in response. Both Tucker and Jenny were startled at the hoary old medical school demonstration, having never seen anything like it.

Pennysmith shoved away the cart, "But alas, the effect is fleeting. To date we have not succeeded in causing the flesh to regenerate its own electrical force, to recharge — to re-stimulate that part of the brain which sends forth the life giving signals."

He spun on tiptoe, an increasingly annoying habit, arms

outstretched as though to encompass the whole chamber. "But here you see the greatest assembly of electrical devices quite possibly in the world! Here I can create flows of any magnitude and amplitude! And here I search for that one burst, that one discrete shock, which starts life on its way!"

He rushed off down one of the winding paths, disappearing deeper into the jungle of machinery. "Come!"

Now accompanied by sullen Ximen, we followed Pennysmith to another clearing. Here was a towering metal panel mounted with electrical switches and manipulators of every description — rheostats, gauges, vacuum tubes — and many others I could not name. Wires ran everywhere — up and down the panel, over makeshift wooden lattices and across the floor in tangled masses reminding me of a spring swarm of Manitoba's red-sided garter snakes (*Thamnophis sirtalis*).

But the centerpiece of this arena immediately demanded our attention. It was a steel table with large electrodes fashioned on either end. The wire chaos around us culminated in two thick cables attached to them. On the table was a bloodstained sheet, the outline of a human body beneath. I saw Jenny grip Tucker's arm in alarm. He placed his hand over hers.

Pennysmith was clearly nervous about this part of the tour. He stepped in front of the table and faced us, somewhat defiantly.

"Yes. My work is with the human vessel, because my goal is nothing less than the preservation, the re-instigation where possible, of human life. The timid would have me while away years in experimentation on animals. Time wasted, I say, as the electrical life force of an animal can in no way approximate that of we higher beings. But superstition, short-sighted scientific convention, and the rigid thinking of religion — and here I don't mean to offend — have prevailed against me in all so-called civilized environs. Thus I am driven to this forsaken outpost."

He swung round the table, running his hand along the edge. I feared he would pull back the sheet, but he did not. "Know this. My subjects are legally obtained. Death is no stranger to this troubled country, and many meet a premature end. I have notices posted in western towns that I will compensate well for suitable — material. When a subject has outlived its usefulness, Ximen performs a full and appropriate burial."

I could see that Jenny was appalled. I was at best nonplussed. And at last the Tucker we knew resurfaced, "For Lord's sake, Doctor, I must tell you again that I came here for one reason only."

"And I shall commence work upon it immediately, as soon as I have completed this series of tests. Surely you must have at least a glimmer of wonderment to be present, not so? Today could be the very day on which I achieve my breakthrough. You might bear witness to the greatest achievement in the history of science!"

Once again, Tucker was silenced by Pennysmith's bluster. In the pause, Pennysmith stepped hurriedly to his panel and threw a switch.

With a resounding crack, a blue bolt of electricity arced between copper rods at the top of the panel, writhing and twisting like something alive. The dynamo's hum dipped in pitch, and outside the Corliss engine huffed loudly as it was put under load.

A clipboard hung beside the switch panel. On it was a sheet of paper filled with scrawled notes. Pennysmith consulted these as he threw the next series of switches. Scattered on the floor were many more sheets of paper, which I supposed were discarded records of past experiments.

One by one he brought to life the electrical devices around us. One sizzled with tendrils of electricity crawling over its surface. Another began to spin, firing white-hot lightning flashes to stationary rods ringing it. Everywhere machines crackled, buzzed and hissed. The noise was deafening. My hair stood up and my skin tingled with the terrific energy filling the air. The pungence of ozone stung my nostrils. Jenny and Tucker stood close together, mesmerized. It was undeniably an impressive display.

Pennysmith was as energetic as his machinery, hands flitting from switch to knob, eyes darting from gauge to dial. His unkempt hair stuck out at all directions, giving him an even more crazed aspect than usual. He turned to his large rheostats, pausing to shout above the din, "With each attempt I change the power's route through the machines, each time seeking to modify the charge until I discover the one that will mimic our own."

He pulled out a stopwatch, clicked it on, and then threw one final switch — a large knife switch. Sparks shot from it but, Pennysmith was oblivious to the danger, wild eyes riveted on the steel table. The "subject" beneath the sheet convulsed violently, midsection forced upward as the back arched. Pennysmith whirled back to his panel, throwing another lever. "Reversing polarity!" he shouted. The sheet twitched and jerked horribly.

Jenny was altogether horrified. I shall never forget the look on her normally impassive face. Tucker just scowled, clearly wishing the doctor would get it over with.

In contrast, Pennysmith seemed transported by the ghastly show. He giddily adjusted his controls. The body jerked even more violently. "See! See how the flesh aches to live!"

The body now contorted in a way that one arm thrust out from under the sheet. I was prepared for the pallid skin of a cadaver, but not for the sight of large, crude stitches encircling the arm above the elbow. It appeared that the arm had required reattachment to the body. Why I could not imagine.

Pennysmith now applied so much voltage that the body began to smoke. The acrid smell of burning flesh fused with the already overpowering ozone. This was enough for Jenny. She glared at Tucker, "I will not watch this!" And raced off down one of the meandering paths toward the distant exit.

It was well that she did, for seconds later the sheet slid entirely off the table and Tucker and I saw the true nature of Pennysmith's subject. It was an unthinkably ghoulish assemblage of different bodies cobbled together like some nightmarish Raggedy Andy doll. I could discern at least three different skin tones. The torso was that of a young man. The head looked as though it was from an older person, though the burns on the face and the smoke swirling from the singed hair made it hard to be sure.

Pennysmith eyed his stopwatch, evidently waiting for some predetermined moment, and at last yanked open the main switch, stopping power to the wretched thing on the table.

"Ximen! The dynamo!" he shouted. Unnoticed during the grisly spectacle, Ximen had hobbled his way to the whirring dynamo and was standing ready there. At Pennysmith's command, he disengaged the drive shaft clutch and the machine wound down with an eerie moan, ending the rest of the electrical fireworks. Silence swept across the room like a ghostly wave.

Pennysmith snatched up a stethoscope and raced to the smoldering corpse, listening intently for a heartbeat. He poked and prodded and pressed. His shoulders sagged as he heard nothing. Then he opened one of the dead thing's eyes, presumably to check the pupils. But white liquid spurted out of the socket.

"Damn! The eyes have exploded again." He shook his head, pondering. "An unfortunate effect of the higher amperages. I've begun to question whether heavy charges are the correct route. Yet lower ones seem to have no effect whatsoever."

Unexpectedly, he turned to me, "You're a man of science. Have you any thoughts?"

Tucker and I surely wore expressions of abject disgust, but Pennysmith seemed completely oblivious. Taken aback, I stammered with foolish politeness, "None, sir. I'm sorry."

He nodded, resigned, and leaned against the table, suddenly looking as tired as if he'd run a race. Absently wiping his hands on his lab coat, he sighed deeply. Then he finally seemed to sense that perhaps we were not the most ardent admirers of his work. He straightened and addressed Tucker, "You understand of course that in science any result, however disappointing, is still science, not so? Learning. My work is a steady, relentless, tireless process of — of improvement — refinement."

Oh! How I longed for the Tucker who cursed mummies and burned down haunted houses! But he said only, "To be honest, Doctor, I don't know what to make of your work."

Pennysmith nodded again, "Yes, at first blush it's — it's disconcerting, even shocking I suppose. Society has in it deeply rooted fears and beliefs about death and the treatment of the vessel. But you must look beyond convention to my goal. Imagine that a man shot down on the battlefield might be carried from that field dead, and yet then be returned to life! Imagine that a surgeon might practice his art without fear that his patient will die in the process! Imagine that a loved one struck down by fever might be allowed to pass, only to be revived after the vile pestilence has run its course!"

At last Tucker spoke, slow and measured. He seemed suddenly tired — and old. "These are all wonderful things if

186

they were made to happen. But I've told you and told you again that I came here, and will consider contributing to your financial support, for one reason only."

"Yes, yes! The examination of the fossil! Of course, of course! Bring it to me! I shall begin at once!"

"It's been propped up in your front room for days now, just waiting."

"So? Well, marvelous! I shall begin at once!" He started off, then remembered the "vessel" on the steel table and shouted, "Ximen! I will need a new head!" He scanned the corpse's extremities, "— and left leg. Return the rest to the cooler! Quickly, quickly!"

It was thus that we learned the primary reason for Pennysmith's ice-making machine.

↔↔↔↔↔↔↔↔↔↔

Jenny was livid, her eyes narrowed, brow contorted as she marched toward Tucker. "You will not give that terrible man any of our money!"

Tucker and I had returned from the laboratory to their private room. He sank onto their bed and stared at the floor, "No, I don't reckon I will. But I'll let him look over my ichthyosaur first."

"Let him do *nothing!* I want to *leave* here! As soon as the sun lights the trail!"

I too now felt free to speak my mind, "Jenny is right. We should leave. Surely you appreciate that the likelihood of his being able to —"

"I know, Whitney, I know," Tucker interrupted. "He ain't gonna bring my fossil to life." He looked up at me, and a brief uncharacteristic smile came and went in a blink. "I knew you thought he was a — what'd he call himself?"

"A charlatan."

187

"Yeah. It was kinda funny, you working so hard to keep it under your hat. But I knew. And your opinion on any matter is important to me. That's why I hired you. But I come down here anyways, because, bless it, at my age, even a snowball's chance is a chance. I'll tell you what, though, the other thing pushing me to take this last trip was I felt I owed you."

"Owed *me?*"

"Sure. You've spent how many years now in my employ? Most of'em passed puttering around the ranch writing about prairie dogs and bugs. When you signed on I said we'd be going all over the world and you'd get to study all them exotic species. Didn't work out that way. You caught up with me too late in my life."

I protested, "But we *have* traveled — extensively. To Egypt. The Himalayas —"

"Aw, nothing like I used to — when I had real hope. Anyways, when this come up I figured, what the heck, at least Whitney'll get a look at some different prairie dogs and bugs."

I was very touched. I, and Jenny too, I believe, had been wholly convinced of Tucker's complete enthusiasm for this expedition. It was shocking to learn that in some measure he had made the trip for my benefit. I said softly, "The zoological portion of our travels has been perfectly delightful. Thank you."

His smile blinked on and off, this time aimed at Jenny. "But we're done here now for sure, right, Dickens?"

"Yes. Oh yes," she nodded.

"At first light it is then!" said Tucker.

CHAPTER THIRTEEN

Despair

Most of our kit had remained stowed on Triumph during our stay. There was little to do in the predawn other than hitch up the horses. Shockingly, Tucker decided to leave his prized ichthyosaur fossil and send for it later, another indication of how far his hopes had fallen.

Tucker also considered leaving without telling Pennysmith, who normally slept till late morning, no doubt due the quantities of champagne he consumed on any given evening. But social convention won that internal argument and Tucker went back inside to wake him and tell him of our intentions.

In a matter of moments we heard Pennysmith's agitated voice. In robe and slippers he pursued resolute Tucker right out of the building to the wagon. "I do not accept this decision! We have a verbal contract!"

"We have nothing of the kind."

"But you are in debt to me even now! For — for my hospitality! For the great expense of my special demonstration!"

"I never asked for that. I come two thousand miles and spent two months of precious time. We're square."

"I — I have your fossil! I'll not return it!"

"Keep it. It's just a rock."

Pennysmith was pathetically desperate. His financial situation was evidently worse than we had imagined. He actually shouted, "I will pursue you in the courts! We have a binding verbal contact!" Here he grabbed Tucker's arm; and here, for the first time, he met the Tucker with whom I was familiar.

Tucker whirled, flinging off Pennysmith's hand with force that nearly knocked the thin man down, and roared with a volume that sent birds shrieking from the underbrush, "Now look! You can spit your venom and send your lawyers, if you really got any, but you keep your skinny-boned, blood stained hands off of me!"

Pennysmith withered like a flower in fire. He backed away, hands clutched together. When he was near the doorway, he finally spoke in a small voice, "Please. Funding is so difficult to find."

"Pfhuh! I don't doubt that," Tucker grumbled as he swung himself up into the wagon. He chucked the horses and we rattled forward.

I glanced back once to see Pennysmith, shoulders hunched, slink forlornly back inside the building. But Tucker had already put it all behind him, "Once we get back across the lake, I'm of a mind to stop a month or so in Maracaibo. What do you think?"

"If your aim is simply to give me more time with the local fauna, please don't feel an obligation," I offered.

He shrugged, "Nothing to rush back to."

Jenny glanced at him, concern in her eyes. "There is plenty of work at the ranch. We have been gone a very long time."

Tucker sighed, "Yeah, there's always work at the ranch."

We were following the rutted trail back along the lake shore toward the ford over the natural dam. But as we rounded a turn, jouncing over the roots of the massive trees, we found our way blocked by Ximen's cart and burro. Tucker reined up and we looked around. Not far away, Ximen was loading a cloth sack into a native dugout canoe. It was oozing blood, so it was not hard to guess what was in it.

I would have been most happy to push on, wishing to learn no more of Dr. Pennysmith's grotesque business. But something in the sight goaded Tucker's sense of decency. Instantly suspicious, he asked the question that would change our lives forever.

"Ximen, what are you about there?"

The man avoided Tucker's gaze, "Is — my work." He limped back to his cart and withdrew two more bloody sacks.

"Your boss man said you give these poor folks, or at least the pieces of'em, a decent burial. That what you're doing? You got a proper graveyard over there across the lake, do you?"

Ximen bristled with unexpected anger, "I work hard. That is more hard. Too hard."

"So you just chuck'em in the lake? That ain't right. Ain't Christian, you know? And I'll tell you what, sometime one of'em's gonna swell up and come floating back on you. Your boss man's gonna be plenty mad when he sees'em washing up outside his door."

Ximen grinned in a most unsettling lopsided way, baring stained teeth as gnarled as the rest of him. "Don't come back. Be eat. By *Lagarto Feo!* Bone, meat, everything, all gone!"

Tucker looked to me, "*Lagarto?*"

I had picked up only a few Spanish words, but this happened to be one of them. "Lizard," I translated.

"Lizard? A crocodile? He's feeding them to crocodiles?"

Ximen seemed to be enjoying our confusion. "Not crocodile! *Lagarto Feo! Monstruoso!* Bigger three times than your fat wagon!"

Tucker reflexively glanced at Triumph and scowled, turning back to Ximen, "Bigger? You must mean longer. You're talking about a snake, a python or — "

"Not snake! *Lagarto Feo!* You don't know. You don't see. You never see like it."

And Tucker was hooked, "That so?"

Jenny fumed, "Kiyuga! We are going *home.*"

"Hang on, hang on, Dickens. Lizard bigger than Triumph? Be a bangsite bigger'n one of them puny Komodo

191

dragons. Bet Whitney'd like to see it too, wouldn't you, boy?"

I shrunk down, "I'll not cast a tie-breaking vote."

"Coward," said Tucker.

Jenny jerked her head at Ximen, lowering her voice to a whisper, "He's crazy. Like his crazy doctor owner."

Tucker whispered back, "Now, Jenny, why would he make up a tale like that?" He turned to the twisted man, "Ximen, how far is it to lagarto?"

Ximen pointed vaguely east up the lake, "Short paddle."

"Will you take me to see it?"

"You pay?"

"Pfhuh," Tucker snorted. "Here's my offer. If he really is bigger than this wagon, I'll pay you sixty dollars just for the sight. If he ain't, I'm telling Pennysmith what you really do with his cast-offs."

Ximen blanched at that, but was also struggling to envision the staggering sum. Finally he said, "Sixty? Gold?"

Tucker habitually patted his money belt, "Full of Bolivars." Ximen cast a furtive glance in the direction of Pennysmith's laboratory. Greed won, and he nodded with a single jerk.

Tucker pressed him further, "Now you're sure the animal will be there, that I'll see it?"

Ximen gestured to his bloody sacks, "It come always for the — for what I am bring."

Tucker nudged Jenny, "See, he's on the square. Must be pretty sure we'll see something, whatever it is."

Jenny sighed, relenting. She could not deny Tucker anything when his boyish side surfaced. But she added, arms folded, "I'll wait here."

Tucker leapt down and strode to the rifle cases, which were always stowed ready on the outside of our gear, and withdrew his beloved 600 Rigby NE.

"You don't shoot!" exclaimed Ximen.

"I don't shoot unless lagarto tries to eat me," grinned Tucker. Then he looked up at me, "Well, grab a firearm, Whitney. Surely you're not just gonna sit in the wagon when there's fauna to look at!"

He was right about that, of course. While I couldn't imagine what Ximen had tried to describe in his limited English, I was quite curious. I took my Winchester from its case.

Tucker grinned again, "Sure you don't want Jenny's express rifle? I hear this lagarto's bigger'n Triumph." I certainly didn't feel like lugging Jenny's heavy rifle in the oppressive heat. "If you don't mind, I'll stick with my Winchester. Your own Rigby will safely dispatch anything living in this hemisphere."

Tucker smiled. But we would soon sorely regret my off-handed decision.

CHAPTER FOURTEEN

A Revelation

Tucker sat in the bow of the dugout. I squatted uncomfortably in the center. Ximen paddled from the stern.

The lake was oblong, running west to east. Watching Ximen struggle to paddle the boat was more painful than watching him walk, but he drove us steadily eastward over the glassy, syrupy waters. Flies hummed round his blood-sodden sacks of "cargo." I prayed for a breeze to carry the smell away, but none came.

We were nearing the eastern shore, having gone nearly the length of the lake. I could see Tucker was growing displeased with Ximen's definition of a "short paddle." But just as it appeared Tucker was about to mount a complaint, we had a curious experience. A jet of water suddenly welled up beneath us, carrying the canoe strongly sideways. Tucker and I both gripped the sides to steady ourselves.

"What in thunder!" Tucker exclaimed.

I asked Ximen, "Is there a spring down there?" But the man only shrugged, neither amazed nor interested, "It happen sometime."

He turned us now and paddled into a narrow inlet on the southern shore. We followed this a short distance and came to a wide pool where the mountain stream that fed the lake flowed in. The water here was fairly clear and for the first time I could see bottom, which was comforting after crossing the black, stagnant, algae-infested lake itself.

Ximen stopped paddling and we coasted to about the center of the pool. With an anticipatory grin, he began to rap his paddle on the side of the dugout in a rhythmic way. Tap-tap-tap. Tap-tap-tap. Then he grabbed one of his morbid sacks, lowered it into the water, and shook it, tinting the water pink.

Tucker and I were somewhat confused. He said, "When he said 'lizard' I was thinking of a land animal."

"As was I," I whispered. I chided myself for being nervous. After all, the nation had been colonized, explored, and developed for nearly four hundred years and certainly no animal approaching the size Ximen claimed had ever been reported.

Tucker performed his age-old drill, opening the Rigby, running his thumb over the loaded rounds, locking it shut, and pulling two more cartridges from his belt. He frowned at the green tinge on their cases, "Bless this cursed climate. Verdigris on my brass already."

As he reflexively rubbed the cases on his pants I saw something behind him — a large black shape moving under us beneath the water, briefly blotting out the bottom of the pool.

"Oh my!" was all I could blurt. Tucker followed my stare, but now there was nothing.

"What'd you see?" he whispered.

I immediately felt foolish. Surely it was merely some anomaly of water reflections. "Just shadows," I said.

How wrong I was.

Tap-tap-tap continued Ximen.

To one side of us the water suddenly roiled. There are few things as eerie as something large and unseen rippling water's surface. Our crude little craft immediately seemed very inadequate and unstable to me. Meanwhile, Ximen made a bizarre sound, a sort of combination cheer and laugh, and gurgled, "He come now!"

Tucker leaned out eagerly to peer down. We tipped dangerously.

"Careful, man!" My voice cracked embarrassingly.

The shape passed beneath us again. This time Tucker saw it, too. He twisted round and leaned precariously the other

195

way as he tried to follow it, "Bless me! It's big all right!"

Ximen was still dangling the sack in the water, grinning like a lunatic, expectant.

Suddenly, the water erupted right beside us, and I saw jaws much larger than those of a hippopotamus snatch the sack from Ximen's grasp and submerge.

The animal had been visible for but a second, yet several exotic details leapt to my attention. In the mouth was something that looked like coarse white hair — perhaps baleen as seen in a filter-feeding whale's mouth? Along the edges of the jaws were alternating plates, (too large, I thought, to be scales) of brilliant red and green, giving the mouth a most stunning jeweled appearance. The rest of the head, that portion I glimpsed, was a deep luminescent blue. My mind raced to search out any non-bird creature in memory bearing such exotic colors. The Gila monster came to mind, giving Ximen's designation of "lizard" some validity. But the size — the stupendous size!

As I stared quite immobile at the water, Tucker prodded me, whispering, "Whitney! Great Heavens! Did you see that? What is it? Crocodile?" I could only shake my head. Certainly it was not that.

The thing lay directly beneath us. Even through the rippling water we could see it was eagerly gobbling the sack. Muted popping sounds came to the surface — bones being crushed, I presumed.

Tucker called softly to our guide, "Ximen, what *is* the thing?! Does it ever come out of the water?" Ximen just shrugged stupidly. Tucker raced on, "Does it have legs, fins?" Ximen shrugged again. Tucker was incredulous, "Bless it, man! Have you no curiosity in you at all?"

But Ximen's mind had room for one thought only, "You see now already. You pay me sixty."

"I'll pay you a *hundred* and sixty for a better look!" Tucker shot right back.

Ximen's eye went wide for a moment. His curiosity was definitely for sale. He jerk-nodded, "Sometime he follow, like big fish dog!" Evidently, feeding the animal had become something of a sport for the lonely, disfigured man. He pointed toward shore, "We move boat to water not deep! Maybe he come out."

Ximen began laboriously paddling. But Tucker was charged with fervor I'd not seen in years. "Right! Coax him to the shallows! But you handle your bait bags! Give me the paddle, man! The paddle!"

Infected with Tucker's enthusiasm, Ximen literally flung the paddle over my head to Tucker, who caught it one-handed, laid his Rigby at his feet, and began paddling the canoe backward toward shore.

Ximen grabbed a second sack of "bait" and leaned off the stern, splashing it noisily up and down in the water. He was actually laughing! I sat rigid, trying to add no additional movement to our already gyrating craft.

The water bulged up in front of Ximen and exploded in white spray as the creature lunged for his sack. He yanked it high and the jaws missed, snapping together with an ominous POP. The head splashed back down into the water, creating a large wave that lifted us and sent us scudding along like the surfers I would see years later in Hawaii.

The water surged and foamed as the thing followed us. Tucker paddled hard, trying to keep ahead, unleashing his own maniacal laugh as he shouted to Ximen, "Hah! Good! Good! Keep him coming!"

I had madmen fore and aft. Clutching my Winchester 45-75, which now seemed wholly inadequate, I turned to the one I hoped was more sane.

"You really think it wise to provoke this animal?"

"Not provoking him. We're just feeding him. Besides,

197

don't seem too ornery."

"Oh? Setting aside that it's been taught to enjoy human flesh!"

"Well then, be at the ready, Whitney! These are the times! These are the times! Take the Rigby!"

Had I been quicker to follow his suggestion, again so much that later transpired might not have come to pass. As I tried to keep my balance in the wobbling, bobbing dugout and reached for the double rifle at Tucker's feet, I heard another rush of water and knew the animal was breaching again. The canoe bucked up and I fell forward on hands and knees, twisting quickly round to look over my shoulder.

It rose high, jaws gaping. Giggling like a child, Ximen stood, weaving precariously, to keep the sack out of reach. The animal missed again, but this time its massive head came down on our stern. Such was the beast's weight that the stern was driven quite under water. Peripherally, I glimpsed Tucker catapulted skyward from the bow as from a playground teeter-totter, sailing somewhere above my head.

I did not see where he landed because the lake now swallowed me as the canoe continued its downward plunge. Oddly, I was first surprised at how warm the water was, having expected icy cold. Stupidly, I remained kneeling in the canoe, clinging to the gunwales, letting myself be dragged deeper and deeper for interminable seconds, hearing no sound but the chaotic blithering of bubbles. Something struck me a painful blow on the back of my head. I knew it could only be Tucker's rifle on its even swifter descent. But the blow forced Reason to intrude at last and inform me that safety was no longer to be found aboard ship. As I released my death grip on the canoe, I felt my Winchester slide against my knees along the bottom. I grabbed it and desperately struggled for the surface.

When I found air, a most awful shrieking filled it — an

almost inhuman sound. I knew it was poor Ximen. Daring not even a glance back, I flailed for the shore, making horrendously slow progress, so determined was I to keep my grip on the Winchester. But we'd been closer to shore than I realized and in reality it was mere seconds before my pumping feet found bottom. I floundered onto dry land and whirled round, frantically shaking water from my rifle, fearing the weapon would explode if fired with the barrel plugged, even while hoping the ammunition was not too wet to fire at all.

A new rush of images now assaulted me. Ximen being flung from side to side in the water in the jaws of the animal. Tucker swimming powerfully, determinedly toward me.

I raised the rifle, but could see only Ximen himself in the frothing water. I held my sights hard on the scene, praying for a clear shot.

Suddenly there was the most curious pause. The creature stopped thrashing. Ximen stopped screaming. But it was clear the beast still held him, for I could see him pushing down mightily with his arms.

In spite of Ximen's plight, I confess every detail of the animal clamored for my attention. I could now see the top of its head. Its eyes, like its mouth, were ringed by the shockingly brilliant, nearly glowing, colored plates. And the eyes! Could I be wrong? Were there not *three?!* More utter surprises — the animal's breathing, as loud as the Corliss engine — stirred the water on either *side* of its head, rather than in front, where one would expect nostrils to be. Even in this brief observation I knew the thing could not be catalogued with any other known life form (and I still believe that today).

The lull continued. While Ximen struggled, I saw that perhaps two feet to the right of them floated the blood-soaked sack with which he had taunted the animal. I will never know, but it truly seemed the animal was trying to decide if it wanted Ximen or the sack. A thought flashed through my mind: *Is it a dedicated scavenger, startled to find live food in its mouth?*

To the reader who exclaims, "Why did you not shoot?" I say again that that mere seconds elapsed during these observations. Indeed, I now drew a bead on the visible portion of the animal's head.

But even as I squeezed my trigger, Ximen was using the lull in activity to draw his oversized knife. At the very instant the Winchester belched blue smoke and bucked against my shoulder, Ximen plunged his blade directly into the leftmost of the animal's three eyes. I have always felt that this act, far more than any effect my puny lead pellet might have had, caused the following violence.

With a deafening peal that sounded more like a chorus of French horns than an animal's bleat, the creature breached up and backward. Ximen was flung high into the air, spinning like some ill-trained acrobat, to land far out in the center of the pool. No trace of the unfortunate man was ever found.

The animal landed on its back, sending huge waves left and right — and as it submerged I noted short flailing legs, not fins. So it was amphibious. This revelation was totally eclipsed by another fleeting image — I was sure I'd seen *more than four.*

Tucker, who had been swimming madly toward me, now reached shore and staggered forward to my side. Of the many things he might have said (for example expressing concern for Ximen or myself) he blurted, "Whitney, my God! It's wonderful! *Beautiful!*"

I admit that a disparaging retort was well beyond my ability, but I would have had no time to make it, for again the water bulged up, and the brute surged into the shallows, headed straight for us, emitting its crushingly loud French horn sound; clearly a very angry sound. Its labored breaths were vast and hollow, like wind belching from a large cave.

As it churned toward us, I confirmed what I thought I must have merely imagined earlier — *it had eight legs*, packed closely along its flanks like those of some Olympian millipede, propelling it forward with deadly speed.

I worked the Winchester's lever in earnest, firing round after round. I could not have missed, for the creature fairly filled my entire field of view, yet the big 45 slugs had no noticeable effect (hence my lament at having left Jenny's much more powerful double rifle behind).

Tucker saw the futility of my efforts before I, grabbing my arm and dragging me backward toward the thick foliage behind us, "It's our legs or nothing, Whitney!"

And so we ran. I have no doubt I would have died within my first few steps but for Tucker's remarkable instincts when in a "worrisome spot." He immediately led us between two narrowly spaced trees. Just as I leapt through, I felt a hot blast of breath envelop me and glanced back in terror. The enraged creature had tried to follow directly; its head fit through but its body became wedged between the tree trunks, bringing it up short. Its fearsome jaws snapped shut mere feet behind me, but it then had to back up to go round the trees. This purchased us precious seconds.

Surely no mouse or rabbit ever felt more desperate than we two as we pushed, kicked, dove and crawled through the undergrowth. While the thickness of the vegetation hindered us, it also probably saved us. The much larger beast had to bull its way through, slowing it enough to let us keep a small lead. But always close behind was the awful, relentless sound of branches snapping, roots uprooting.

"Ain't quitting! He's plumb angry!" shouted Tucker, unnecessarily. I very much wanted to point out that I had voted against provoking it, but could not spare the breath.

We struggled on, gasping and wheezing, heading back west, paralleling the lake shore. At last we burst out of the foliage onto the dirt track. Here it curved round a narrow inlet, and on the other side of that, not fifty yards distant, was Triumph. Jenny was standing on the seat, scanning the lake, her Rigby already unlimbered.

"Bravo, Jenny!" rasped Tucker approvingly as we tottered along the shore toward her.

Behind us, unseen but still loudly ripping through the forest, the creature emitted another of its cacophonous bellows. Taft and Bronto's ears twitched, and they snorted their extreme disapproval.

"What *is* that?" Jenny cried as she leapt from the wagon and handed her rifle to Tucker. As he automatically snapped open the gun to double-check the chambers, he swung to me, his face alive with joy, pleading wordlessly for the answer to Jenny's question. I was winded, frightened, overwhelmed at the thought of the thing that pursued us; and I was wholly unable to discern what he wanted. After interminable seconds of my confusion, Tucker thundered, "It's a dinosaur! We've done it, Dickens! Eh, Whitney? Haven't we?"

I was certain even then, and believe more firmly now, that it was most certainly not a dinosaur. It was far, far removed from any taxa I could imagine. I stammered in reply: "It's more of a dragon, I'd say."

"What do you mean?" Tucker scowled. "They ain't no such things as dragons. It's a dinosaur!"

I leaned against the wagon, catching my breath, and relented, "That's accurate enough for now." Tucker beamed at Jenny, and she flung her arms round him in the most impulsive expression of love I ever saw between them.

Interrupting the triumphal moment, a tree cracked like thunder not a hundred yards away. The "dinosaur" had divined our whereabouts and was smashing its way through the forest toward us.

"Still coming!" exclaimed Tucker.

Our horses were now quite sure they did not like whatever was coming. They lurched in their traces and Jenny leapt to the reins to steady them. But Tucker squared himself in the middle of the trail, cocking the double rifle.

My God, I suddenly realized, *he means to stand and face the thing!*

I hope the reader will grant me some understanding that it was only now that my sense of duty to science returned (albeit prompted by a heavy dose of fear). Clinging mindlessly to one great wheel of Triumph as though it might anchor me in a violent sea, I cried, "Tucker! You must not shoot this animal!"

"I feel this animal gives me no choice, Whitney! And did you not let fly at it yourself but a moment ago?"

That was true, and my only defense is that in my subconscious I was reasonably sure my shots would have no effect. Of Jenny's mighty express rifle I was not so sure.

I waved urgently toward the distant laboratory. "Let's race to Pennysmith's! Surely the walls of his building would be proof against it!"

Without looking back at me, Tucker snarled in return, "Running is never the first choice!"

Though still unseen, the "*lagarto's*" approach was louder and louder, its bizarre eight-legged gait sounding like a herd of elephants rather than a single animal. Tucker shouldered the rifle.

Jenny heaved on the reins, convincing Taft and Bronto to stand their ground while keeping one eye on Tucker. Of course she feared for him, but I knew she would not challenge him in this of all moments. She would not support me. I feverishly grasped for an argument.

"Tucker, please! Isn't a — a dinosaur worth inestimably more *alive?*"

The head tilted. The chin jutted. I like to think that his years of association with me changed him from a man who would have been satisfied to shoot and mount a dinosaur to one who appreciated the scientific value of any rare creature. Then again, how much simpler things might have turned out had I kept my mouth shut!

As it was, Tucker lowered the rifle and set the safety, "So be it! We run! Turn the horses!"

Jenny yanked on the reins. I ran to the head of the team and grabbed the traces, leaning for all I was worth to pull the disconcerted animals round.

Even as we did so the maniacal beast burst from the trees. It had come out further back along the trail, across the narrow inlet. Spotting us, it plunged headlong into the water, swimming powerfully, coming straight for us like a living torpedo.

Taft and Bronto jolted as if struck by lighting, wrestling and bucking, dragging me helplessly. Tucker coolly stood his ground, ready to shoot if need be. "Turn'em! *Turn'em!*"

The trail was narrow and the horses swung wide into the water. I was flung off as they completed the turn. It was horrid to again be in the preferred element of the pursuing behemoth, even if in only three feet of it. I sloshed wildly back to shore, vaguely aware of Tucker swinging up beside Jenny as he shouted, "Be quick, Whitney! He's right on your backside!"

He leaned down, holding out his hand. I grabbed it and he yanked me bodily up into the cargo bed. As Tucker straddled the wagon seat, still ready to shoot, Jenny slapped the reins and shouted to the horses, but Taft and Bronto needed no encouragement. They were well ready to depart.

As we vaulted forward I heard rushing water. Hunkered in wagon bed, I looked back to see the animal catapult itself out of the lake like some stupendous sea lion, pushing a small tidal wave ahead of it, crashing down where Triumph had just stood.

Our stout team charged ahead. Triumph's unforgiving wheels transmitted every shock of the rough trail. Boxes, cases and sacks leapt under me like living things. Tie-downs snapped and our kit was strewn piecemeal behind us. But far worse, the lake "dinosaur" *still* gave chase, lumbering down the track behind us with an unyielding sense of purpose. But the horses, no doubt as frightened as we, gained a good lead and our pursuer soon fell from view.

Reaching the laboratory, we made a harrowing turn, Triumph going up on two wheels! I felt sure we would overturn, but the wagon righted herself and we jounced on into the courtyard.

Jenny manhandled the frantic team to a stop. We listened. The French horn chorus signaled that the creature still pursued.

"Cut the horses loose!" ordered Tucker as we leapt down.

Jenny pulled her knife and swiftly freed Taft and Bronto. They proved most cooperative in fleeing straight away into the forest.

Jenny and I ran for the outer doors of Pennysmith's building — much relieved to find them still open! Tucker followed us at a walk. He would not run. We entered the outer doors into the cramped entryway — only to find the massive laboratory doors locked from the outside!

Tucker veered into the anteroom in which we had first conversed with Pennysmith. There was the doctor, unconscious on the tattered settee, surrounded by champagne bottles. In the mere hour or so since our departure he had apparently drunk himself into a stupor. It flashed through my mind that this was for the best. A time-wasting argument with him at this point might well have cost all our lives. Tucker handed Jenny the Rigby, knelt and tore Pennysmith's key chain from his trousers. The keys he also tossed to Jenny; then he bodily scooped the limp scientist up and threw him over one shoulder.

I stood in the entryway, watching for the creature's arrival in the courtyard. I could now hear its cave-wind breathing and its elephantine stride. And arrive it did, crashing headlong into Triumph, butting the wagon forward as though struck by a locomotive. My mind reeled all over again at the sight of our dragon. Eight legs! Those miraculous rainbow colors!

The animal paused, sniffed the air, and turned its head unerringly toward us. Its remaining two eyes rolled wildly, flashing white like a those of a crazed horse. It charged forward. I stumbled back, announcing unnecessarily, "Here it comes!"

With her usual expressionless precision, Jenny swiftly found the key to work the padlock on the laboratory doors. I helped her shove them open and we stumbled inside. Tucker was right behind, waddling between us with Pennysmith. Jenny and I pushed the doors closed. Just before they met, I glimpsed the creature galloping through the outer doorway toward us. I madly slammed the doors' locking bar in place.

The very building shook with the leviathan's impact. Horrifyingly, the doors cracked on this very first blow. One of the iron straps popped outward, some of its rivets sundered; they ricocheted round the room like bullets. It was woefully clear that the doors would not hold if the creature continued with such fury. Tucker tossed limp Pennysmith aside like a sack of grain and grabbed the Rigby from Jenny.

"Never seen an animal so bent on a chase," he scowled.

"Not merely a chase. Revenge," I said grimly.

The creature attacked the doors. From the sound, I imagined it must be rearing back and butting them with its head or striking with its forelegs. The tremendous blows echoed like cannon fire through the cavernous room.

We moved away along one of the paths through Penny-smith's debris. As the building shook, centuries old dust drifted down from the great wooden beams above us, glinting gold in the shafts of sunlight from the high windows.

At the far end of the laboratory was a raised area, no doubt the original altar of the church. We rushed up its ancient stone steps. "See if there's another door out of here!" Tucker commanded. We ran left, right and center, but discovered a dismaying truth. There were two small exit doors but —

"He's bricked them all up!" I yelled to Tucker.

"Fear-ridden son-of-a-gun," he growled.

We faced the entrance doors. The stout crossbar still held firm. But it was an upper hinge in the poorly mortared new wall which finally gave. The creature battered at the gap, and soon both doors swung aside as one unit, still held by the crossbar.

The thing spotted us instantly and charged. I was sure Pennysmith, whom we'd left by the doors, had been crushed by its first steps. Tucker raised the double rifle, two extra cartridges held between the fingers of his left hand.

Our position gave us a commanding view of Penny-smith's domain. The monster plowed toward us like some hell-bent warship, throwing aside Pennysmith's collected detritus in a veritable bow wave. The Tesla coil toppled. Specimen jars were catapulted from their shelves, formalde-hyde splashing everywhere.

I confess I was thoroughly terrified. I looked wildly for some escape, but the only path out was to clamber over the junk mounds in a panicked dash back to the shattered entrance doors. And if I reached them — what? Run outside? To where? Would I have time to climb a tree? Would that help?

While I was succumbing to these thoughts, Tucker was, in his unique way, living a moment of which he had dreamed for a lifetime. He was motionless, peering down the double barrels with both eyes open. Now my mind screamed, *Science be damned! Why does he not fire?!*

Then, to my absolute horror, he took the time to make a joke at my expense.

"*Now* have I permission to shoot, Whitney?"

"In Heaven's name, Tucker!" I screeched. Jenny, yelped something at him in Cherokee that no doubt meant the same thing.

With the slightest demonic smile, Tucker fired. The rifle belched a three-foot flame and a whirling ball of blue smoke. The creature did not slow. Tucker unleashed his second barrel. The creature's head jerked up and it lurched sideways, colliding with Pennysmith's large panel of switches. But then it regained its footing and surged forward again. Tucker had snapped open his breach, ejecting his spent cases, and reloaded even before the second shot's reverberations died down. Even so, the creature was at the base of the steps, not fifteen feet from us, by the time Tucker fired both barrels. The recoil nearly knocked him over.

As I planned a hopeless leap to one side, the beast's forelegs buckled. It pitched forward, slamming down with a wet crunching sound, coming to rest with its head literally at Tucker's feet. His last double shot had blown a gaping hole between its remaining eyes.

Sudden silence engulfed us, save for a long sibilant sigh — the creature's last exhalation of breath. I realized I wasn't breathing either, and took a sudden rasping gasp of air.

Tucker, ever the pragmatist, swiftly loaded two more rounds and fired them point blank into the dead animal's head. It remained just as dead.

"Well, good thing its brain is where you'd expect," Tucker said.

Jenny stepped close to him with one barely audible

breathless word, "Kiyuga." He hugged her tight to his side.

Blood now trickled from Tucker's nose. Jenny reached up and wiped it away, showing him her hand. He was mystified for a moment, then realized it was the result of the rifle's brutal recoil. "Pfhuh," he said. "Teach me not to let loose with both barrels."

I felt dizzy, clammy, nauseous. I sank down on the bare stone, trembling. "Thank God — thank God —"

Tucker had no trouble accepting that he was still alive, and certainly wasn't about to attribute it to any power other than his own. It was a fact and there was no sense getting emotional about it. Instead he pulled a handkerchief with which to dab at his nose as he proceeded with a hunter's typical post mortem, pointing to a bullet hole in the front left foreleg, then to an oozing gash on the right side of the animal's head, where a white streak of bone was exposed. Tucker shook his head with self-recrimination, "First shot was plain low. Second was wide. Skipped off the skull."

I could only smile at his seeming disregard for the world-shaking enormity of the thing that lay before us. But his manner brought me back to myself, and I began to focus. My eyes danced over our fallen foe. So much detail to try to catalogue, now that I was not running for my life. Nostrils — three on each side of the head. The feet — not like those of an elephant or hippopotamus, but rather webbed and clawed, something like an alligator's. Oh, and look, a tail! I hadn't seen it earlier. It was a lighter blue than the rest of the smooth skin. And what of the skin? Was it reptilian? Amphibian? Mammalian?

I was just warming to the sheer joy of discovery when Jenny shouted, "Fire!" The spilled formaldehyde had some-how found a spark, perhaps in shorting one of Pennysmith's batteries, perhaps struck on the stone floor by one of Tucker's first bullets.

In seconds flame erupted over a shockingly large area. In seconds more, thick black smoke was billowing from the miles of rubber-insulated wire.

Tucker pointed to the south wall, where flames had not yet spread. "That's our way if we have any!" We ran along it, or rather navigated, climbing precariously over discarded equipment, tripping, barking shins and elbows, making our way as fast as possible toward the only exit. The acrid fumes of the flaming formaldehyde burned our eyes and choked our lungs.

Coughing and retching spasmodically, we tumbled down the last slope. As we made for the door, we were surprised to see Pennysmith lying where Tucker had dropped him, quite un-trampled and still blissfully unconscious. Tucker and I grabbed his arms and drug him with us.

Outside, we stopped when we reached Triumph; and turned to gaze at the conflagration. Many things conspired here to create a loss of catastrophic proportion. Pennysmith had stored many other flammable liquids haphazardly round the lab. (One muffled explosion inexplicably sent up a cloud of green smoke.) In addition, due to the frequent rainfall, Ximen had maintained his large supply of firewood for the Corliss inside. Taken altogether, the blaze grew fast, burned hot, and lasted long. The tremendous updraft carried whole sections of the oiled roofing canvas flaming into the sky.

Tucker's face was lit orange by the inferno, yet still seemed dark as night. "There will be nothing left," he said softly. "Not a bone. Not a tooth." He would be proved right. He sat down on the ground. Jenny and I sat beside him. And we watched.

The big wooden ceiling beams withstood the blaze for over an hour, but finally they, too, surrendered. The old building collapsed inward with a roar that shook the earth and an explosion of sparks that looked like an erupting volcano.

Pennysmith's laboratory was a mound of glowing stone and molten metal. Of course, neither Jenny nor I bothered to ask whether or not we would wait there until we could sift through the rubble. Of course we would. It was a full thirty hours before we could approach close enough to confirm Tucker's prediction.

During the wait, Pennysmith regained consciousness. Undergoing pronounced agony in the aftermath of imbibing an alcoholic deluge, he had difficulty comprehending the destruction of his laboratory. We explained, of course, but, barely able to sit up, eyes watering, nose running, he simply stared at the ruins mumbling over and over, "But, what happened?"

I knew Tucker assumed no blame for the events. So I was surprised when he eventually kneeled at Pennysmith's side and said, "Doctor, I was much amazed by those wonderful lights in your laboratory. It would do me great honor if you'd accept the task of electrifying my ranch in that manner."

Jenny was shocked, as well. Her eyes flashed anger. Tucker's eyes flashed right back: *Be silent!* And she was.

Pennysmith's wandering, bleary gaze settled on Tucker, "Lights? But they are mere electrical toys. My work is — is —"

"Your work is nigh important to you, I know well," Tucker broke in. But, seeing the loss you have suffered, if you would do me this favor, then we might discuss how I could aid in the continuing of your work."

"Ah! Ah!" managed Pennysmith. But before he could continue he was overtaken by nausea. He twisted round and clung to the spokes of Triumph's wheel, vomiting. Tucker used the interruption to pull Jenny and me aside, whispering vehemently, "If this butcher has, by any chance, some legal claim to this property, I need unfettered access." He looked out a the lake, "Where there's one, there's got to be more."

And I knew we would not soon be leaving Venezuela.

CHAPTER FIFTEEEN

The Search

Doctor Pennysmith was duly packed off to Oklahoma. We would later receive reports that he was industriously carrying out Tucker's directive. The ranch soon rivaled Oklahoma City in lighting up the night sky. This was of no interest to Tucker. Deprived of even the slightest scrap to prove the existence of his find, he had become obsessed in a new way.

A substantial camp swiftly rose where Pennysmith's laboratory had stood. In addition to tents, two cabins appeared, one for me, and one for Tucker and Jenny. Fishing boats were purchased in Maracaibo and laboriously trundled up the mountain. Locals were hired to troll the lake, towing chunks of fresh meat. This was done even at night, by lantern. While it made me quite nervous to see men in flimsy boats out on that water, the fishermen had no concern and were delighted to collect the relatively exorbitant salary Tucker was paying. Somewhat surprisingly, there was no local legend equivalent to the supposed Lake Champlain creature for which Tucker had searched years before. No one outside of Ximen seemed to know of the animal we'd found. We could only surmise that he discovered it by accident when he decided to streamline his burial duties.

Corrals were built. Animals were maintained and slaughtered almost daily to provide a steady supply of bait. A bunkhouse was built for the fisherman, lest they waste any time traveling to and from the search site.

Another team of men worked constantly at hacking the forest back from the lake in the hope that, should a creature somehow emerge from the water undetected, we might discover its tracks on the exposed shoreline.

The fishing was disappointing. Except for leeches and the occasional turtle (unidentified), there seemed virtually no life in the lake at all. We learned that locals called it the "dead water," and that, at least in tribal memory, it had never been a good lake for fishing. One old gentleman from the village on the stream below told us that his ancestors blamed the Spanish for the lake's demise. His family's version was that the mission (that's what he confirmed it was, despite there being no official record) had never been used. A native god had struck back at the Spanish, sending down a flaming star that drove the invaders away and killed all the fish in the lake.

Throughout the first month, I worked closely with Tucker. And be sure that I was never without all twelve pounds of my new personal double rifle — a Holland and Holland of .577 caliber. Bruising my shoulder in frequent practice sessions, I became almost as swift as Tucker at firing two barrels, then loading shots three and four in his manner.

Tucker, of course, frequently insisted that I venture onto the water with him. As much as I dreaded being in a small boat on that black forbidding liquid, I consented. We rowed the lake's length and breadth (about a mile long and a half-mile wide). We explored every inlet. We took soundings; the deepest section we found was sixty-seven feet. We also noted a unique shallow area on the east end near the mouth of the incoming stream. I first supposed it to be a sandbar deposited by the stream, but its sides were so steeply sloped that I discarded those ideas in favor of the supposition that it was simply some natural feature which would have been an island were the lake less deep.

It was in this same shallow area that the lake's surface bulged and undulated with the strange water jet which had startled us on our canoe trip ·with Ximen. The logical explanation was an artesian spring, but the irregularity of the flow made me consider other possibilities. One day, I thought to compare the temperature there with that of the rest of the lake; and found it to be several degrees warmer. I then theorized that the source was geothermal — an underwater geyser, surging and ebbing with Earth's mysterious rhythms.

On land we repeatedly scoured the shore for tracks. We hiked the forest all round and followed the stream above the lake. Unexpectedly, we found a healthy fish population there. If fish were upstream, why not in the lake? I expanded on my geyser theory, postulating that the warm water was carrying noxious dissolved minerals into the water, driving most aquatic creatures away.

The search went on and on. Tucker desperately tried every imaginable bait — pig, sheep, goat, cow, horse, dog, cat, bird. I dreaded that he might resort to Ximen's preferred attractant, but he did not, at least as far as I know. Regardless, in the end, nothing was found. No tracks were left. Nothing of significance was tempted by any bait. Tucker even sent fishermen to nearby bodies of water on my thought that, given the creature's size, a single one might stake out an entire lake as its territory. But these men, too, fished to no avail.

Tucker remained inflexibly dedicated to his mission. He berated and chastised the workers for the slightest infraction of his protocols. He paced up and down the shore like an incarcerated asylum dweller.

It became simple grinding routine, and there was less and less for me to contribute. I was merely on retainer to provide scientific observation should Tucker suddenly succeed. I had unlimited time to continue cataloguing the local fauna, and had turned my attention to tree frogs.

While I enjoyed this time immensely, uneasiness permeated the atmosphere, for Tucker's determination was taking a physical toll. Every day he drove himself to exhaustion. When too tired to continue, he often simply threw down an oil cloth and slept fitfully on the lake shore, lest he miss the slightest hint that something had been found. His beard grew long, his hair dirty and matted, his mustache unkempt. He was losing weight. His eyes were sunken with fatigue, yet bright and wild with unhealthy passion.

Jenny endured this phase as she had every other, with quiet stoicism and unflagging support. Some days she spent with Tucker. More often she sat in a rocking chair on their cabin's porch, reading.

One afternoon I was returning to camp with a jar holding my latest prize, a specimen of the tree frog *Hyla crepitans* (which until then I'd been confusing with the similar-looking *Hyla pugnax*). My way took me past Tucker's cabin. Jenny was there in her rocker; so I nodded to her, and would have gone on without speaking, but it was she who suddenly spoke.

"I am worried now."

I stopped, and we had one of our rare, but always significant, private conversations.

"Worried about Harry, you mean?" I asked needlessly.

"I think he will not find another lake dinosaur."

"I think that is correct."

"I can't say this to him."

I mentally blanched, "And you think I can?"

She gave me a disparaging look, for she knew I knew the answer.

"He's tired. He'll get sick," she went on. "He'll die in this ugly place." She looked off toward the lake, "I want to take him home."

With a sigh, I set *H. crepitans* down on the porch. It was the same with Jenny as with Tucker himself: once something was decided it was to be done immediately.

❀❀❀❀❀❀❀❀❀❀

I found him about a half mile up the south shore, where the deforestation team was currently at work. Some days he wielded an ax with them, hoping to uncover sign or tracks in the process. At the moment, he was seated on a tree stump, eating cold beans from a tin with his fingers. One hand was wrapped in a dirty bandage. I saw well-established, infected blisters on his palm, and was embarrassed I had not noticed them earlier.

He glanced up at me, apparently not noticing, or choosing not to notice, the tension I brought with me. "Whitney, how goes the frog hunting?"

"Better than your hunt, I'm afraid."

"Hmm."

"Anything new from the fishermen?" I asked, clumsily making conversation. He shook his head. I took a stump across from him. He gave me a wary look from under his bushy eyebrows.

"It's been almost three months," I began cautiously. "Isn't it inconceivable, with men on the lake day and night, that any animal, especially something so large, could have escaped notice for this long?

"You're not a hunter. Animals go unseen all the time."

"But it would have to surface to breathe."

"Might have gills."

"We heard it breathing. It breathed *on* us, or on me, at least."

"Might have gills anyway. You don't know nothing about it. Could be like a lung fish. Might stay down long as it wants. Might not have to eat but every few months, like them blessed pythons they got down here." Tucker's knowledge of exotic animals surpassed that of many more educated people. I tried a different tack.

"Have you considered my postulate that it was large enough to need the lake all to itself? That there might be only one in a very large area? And that one we have already killed?"

"It's gotta have a mate. It's gotta breed sometime."

"I don't think we can assume that."

"Of course we can assume it!" He was getting riled already. "That's how all life works."

I tried to sound calm — and educated. "Tucker, I have no idea what the thing was. And that should tell you something. I've read thousands of taxonomic descriptions, studied specimens and photographs of animals from the world over. I know you fervently wish it to be a dinosaur but —"

"That's what it is!"

"For heaven's sake! Eight legs? Three eyes? There is nothing else even remotely like it, living or dead!"

"You don't know that! You don't! And you *do* know, better than me, they've dug up the only tiniest fraction of the fossils there are to find. There's dinosaurs of every shape and size — *and* number of legs — nobody knows about yet."

"I don't think so. Even dinosaurs seem to follow basic anatomical conventions."

"What are you trying to say? It's some kind of miracle animal? That there was only one?"

"That has to be considered. Some sort of freak. A mutation. It was so *very* strange."

My words were having an impact, if only because he'd been wrestling with the same thoughts himself. Even so, he stood and glared at me, "It's a living thing. It can get shot and die and be burned up just like anything else on this earth. And by Heaven, someplace here there's more of them!"

His own murky logic must have bothered him (he was normally so unforgiving of illogic in others), because he then ended the discussion, snatching up his ax and striding off to

217

attack a tree with grim ferocity.

I returned to camp and reported to Jenny that I had failed in my initial foray. Together we lamented that Luddy was dead, feeling that he might have been more persuasive than either of us. We had no inkling that my words had already precipitated a major change of course.

↔↔↔↔↔↔↔↔↔↔

I was not to witness the first phase. The following day I was back to my normal habits, on another forage for tree frogs. I spotted one on a leaf near the ground, at the edge of dense foliage. At my approach, it leapt for cover, and I stupidly made a grab for it deep into the brush, hoping to catch it by blind luck. Instead I felt instantaneous searing pain. I had been bitten by something. I yanked back my hand, but forced myself to remain calm, grab a stick and push aside the foliage, for I knew it was crucial to find out what had bitten me. I hoped it was not one of the country's deadly snakes, but what I saw almost made me wish it had been. It was a tarantula (*Theraphos blondi*), the goliath bird eater. Body raised in classic threat posture, it stood fully ten inches tall. Its fangs had found the side of my palm.

Frightened as a child, I wildly clubbed the thing to death, picked it up gingerly by a hairy hind leg, and carried it back to camp. By now my hand was terribly swollen, and I'd noticed the spider had also fired a broadside of its irritant urticating hairs into my skin like some venomous porcupine.

Our Venezuelan workers were of divided opinion as to my fate. Some shook their heads and said the bite was guranteed fatal. Others said they knew of people who had survived.

I was becoming feverish and faint (probably more from revulsion and shock than any real effect of the venom, which later research would show is not terribly dangerous unless one is allergic to it). Tucker was not to be found, off as always somewhere on or near the lake. But Jenny acted with characteristic swiftness and decisiveness. Inside of ten minutes she had me loaded aboard Triumph and was driving me down to La Ceiba.

There was no doctor in the small town. The lake steamer to Maracaibo wasn't due until the next day. So Jenny found a local midwife whose ministrations included painfully squeezing my hand to force the wound to bleed. I spent a miserable sleepless night in her small house.

The following day, Jenny packed us off to Maracaibo. There she found a doctor who lanced the now ulcerated wound and provided a topical remedy to ease the pain.

I encouraged Jenny to return to camp and watch over Tucker as best she could. She gratefully accepted and left the same day. I remained in the city to recuperate. After two days, the swelling around the bite subsided. A painful rash on the back of my hand, raised by the urticating hairs, became more uncomfortable than the bite itself, but it was clear that I would survive. At the end of a week, with no signs of infection appearing, I deemed it safe to trek back to Tucker's search site.

I journeyed back across the mighty lake, hired a horse in La Ceiba, and began the climb up to the camp. When I reached the village on the creek some miles below Pennysmith's lake, I was surprised to find the people loading their belongings into carts and wagons. It appeared some sort of mass exodus was in progress.

As I dismounted and looked around, mystified, the same old woman who had reproached us on our first arrival spied me and stalked over, railing heatedly in Spanish. I attempted to ask her what was happening, but we were limited to pantomime. She pointed to the creek, made a sweeping gesture at the village, and pointed east toward Pennysmith's, but I could not grasp her meaning. However, one word, hurled repeatedly, was unmistakable: "*Malvado!*" It was clearly aimed at me and, presumably, an imaginary Tucker. Nodding my apologies for whatever *malvado* was afoot, I retreated to my horse and hurriedly continued up the track.

More mystery awaited me. As I neared the steep portion of the trail that led to the natural dam, I came upon Triumph. She was loaded to beyond capacity with barrel upon barrel of blasting powder! What on Earth was Tucker planning? As I rode on I heard men's voices, rattling equipment, and the clanging of sledges on steel.

The dam came into view — and I was stunned to see the whole area transformed. Scaffolds had been erected. Ropes and pulleys dangled from booms along the top. Some twenty men were working feverishly on the dam's face, boring into it with sledge driven drills. Dozens of lanterns mounted on poles gave evidence they'd been at their task round the clock. Seeing that Tucker was not among the workers, I put my horse to the gallop and rode on to camp.

There were big changes here, too. Gone were the fishing boats and the fishermen. Gone were the animals being maintained for bait. But the forest-clearing crew had been tripled; the fifty-foot-wide swath they'd been clearing now extended eastward out of sight on either side of the lake. Also on the cleared shoreline, men were working at stringing sections of strong netting between stout poles driven into the mud.

I rushed to Tucker and Jenny's cabin, expecting to find only her. The door was open. Jenny was seated at their small table, and there was Tucker himself, hair neatly trimmed, shaving himself. He heard my step on the porch and turned.

"Whitney! You've missed much, you spider baiter!"

"So it would seem. You would appear to have a new plan."

"Indeed! Indeed I do!" While it was heartening to see Tucker seemingly in better spirits, he still put forth the frenzied aura which had marked this whole period. "You passed the miners, eh? You must have seen them."

"At the dam, you mean. Yes — miners?"

"Copper miners. Brought them in overland from the state of Lara to the north."

It seems somewhat absurd to admit it now, but I still had no idea what Tucker was thinking. I stammered, "So, the plan entails — what, exactly?"

"We're dynamiting the dam! Blasting powder, that is. Best I could get in this Godforsaken country. But it'll do. I'll drain every ounce of foul-smelling water from that cursed lake. By Hades, I'll see every living thing in it or know the reason why! If there's dinosaurs, we'll have men about to run them into the nets, and rifles ready!"

The scale of this new enterprise quite overwhelmed me. My mind stumbled over consequences, "But, but — "

"But, but, but what?"

"Well for one thing, you'll unleash a deluge! The village below us —!"

"I own it. Bought it lock, stock and barrel. They're packed and headed for better pasture with more money than they ever dreamed of. When we do the deed, I'm sending men all the way to Lake Maracaibo to warn people away from the creek banks. No other habitation along its way. I'm not irresponsible, no matter your opinion all these years."

"All right, all right. But what of my thought that the lake, this lake I mean, might have supported only one creature."

"Well it was exactly your lecture on that what got me thinking," he said, clearly intending to praise me. "Could well be wasting months on an empty lake! So, in one bold stroke, we get the answer we need. If there's nothing there, then we move on to the next lake, and the next!"

"What?! And this course does not strike you as — somewhat *excessive?*"

Tucker frowned, "You know, at times you're a negative influence, Whitney. Fearful and negative. I'm off to the dam to make sure them boys are minding the pace."

He stalked out. I turned to Jenny. But in one glance I could see that she was pleased to have back the Tucker she had married, however chaotic his pursuits.

I was angered by the precipitous nature of Tucker's plan, but truthfully I wasn't quite sure why. Rather than act rashly, I unsaddled my horse, turned her into the corral, and marched to my cabin, determined to give myself over to analysis.

As I pushed open the door, I heard an abnormally busy buzzing of flies and was met by an odd, unpleasant odor. Someone, Jenny perhaps, had thoughtfully left the dead tarantula on my table, knowing that I often collected such things. But of course no attempt had been made at preservation, and maggots were now crawling through it. As I scraped the unappetizing mess onto a scrap shingle and disposed of it outside, I found myself thinking, *What an exotic land where an arachnid can grow so large as to be carrion.* And in that moment, the reason for my anger also became clear: this was an exotic land. I set off to confront Tucker on the matter.

I walked the half mile or so to the dam. Tucker was in waders, striding back and forth through the water flowing over it. He was barking instructions to the workers; but the scene was somewhat amusing, as he had to do so through an interpreter he had hired, Ernesto Mendoza.

Ernesto was a white-haired older man with an elegant white mustache. A school teacher in Cabimas, he had been imported by Tucker along with the miners. I immediately felt sorry for him, since he was wearing a rather formal white cotton suit and stylish broad-rimmed hat. He had taken the job thinking he would be interpreting for some sort of American dignitary. Now, with pants rolled up and suit mud-stained beyond reclamation, he sloshed back and forth in his street shoes, struggling to keep up with Tucker's stride.

A young worker walked past carrying a heavy load of fresh drill bits. Evidently he wasn't moving fast enough, because Tucker charged after him, bellowing, "You there! You think I have time to wait for you? I don't. I live on borrowed time every day! Mam gone at forty-seven! Pap at fifty-three! Move yourself accordingly or you'll be gone *today!*"

Ernesto dutifully attempted to translate the tirade to the frightened worker, who gamely waddled faster under his load. Meanwhile, I waited at the water's edge. Tucker eventually spotted me and approached, immediately sizing up my countenance, "You look like a man overstuffed with words."

"I am disturbed by this course of action."

"Well, un-disturb yourself. It's no concern of yours."

Frankly, I had little faith in my primary argument, so I began with a secondary one: "Man, what of your finances? What must all this be costing? What of your future security, your responsibility to Jenny?"

"I'll gladly die penniless if it achieves my goal."

So much for the secondary route. I straightened myself and looked him in the eye, "Very well, then let me put it bluntly, in my capacity as your adviser in matters of science. I object to this grossly destructive plan."

"Destructive? Of what? There ain't nothing out here."

"Not true. There is an untouched natural lake and essentially untouched primeval forest."

"A what and a what? What are you on about?"

"And the man-made flood you envision will irrevocably alter the whole course and nature of the stream. Even further, it will scour untold tons of debris off the land and carry that into Lake Maracaibo."

Tucker gaped at me, "Why should any of this concern me?"

I gestured round us, "This is pristine wilderness."

Tucker glared, "Pfhuh! Whole blessed country — whole blessed *continent* — is pristine, and they can have it. I'll tell you what else: I'm fifty years old!" Oh! His dreaded age again! "I could drain a lake a day for the rest of my days and the world would be no different."

"Not true again, Harry! Not true. In your own lifetime the American Bison has been hunted to near extinction. The billions of passenger pigeons have been reduced to one lone bird!"[2]

"I had no hand in any of that! Well, a buffalo here and there, but only for food. Anyway, there's no similarity to this situation. You'll not sway me from my path, Whitney. You'll only anger me."

Acutely aware of that possibility, I nevertheless fairly shouted, "Must you be so obstinate? Must you overcome every obstacle by burning it down, blowing it up, or shooting it to pieces?"

"I'll hear no more," he warned, more harshly.

But I pressed on, "Have you not read the works, listened to the words, of a man you say you admire, Theodore Roosevelt? He long ago recognized that man now has the power to destroy the natural world, indeed is in danger of doing so. The fact that this land does not fly the banner 'National Park' makes it no less precious. Would you plug the geysers of Yellowstone? Fill in the Grand Canyon if it suited your purpose?"

---

[2] Well known among zoologists of the time, this last known passenger pigeon died only four years later, in 1914. [Amusingly, this is Grandpop's only footnote.]

Tucker came near to striking me. I flinched at the jerk of his shoulder and the clench of his fist. But he caught himself, and only fumed, "You're talking about America, a civilized land with civilized problems. You've said your piece, and I now free from your duties as my advisor. Get out."

He turned stiffly away. Ernesto had been watching our argument uncomfortably, and the nearest miners had paused to watch as well. Spotting them, Tucker bellowed, "Back to work!" They were moving well before the old man could shout, *"Vuelve al trabajo!"*

I would win no chin-jut from Tucker today. And I felt cold for the first time since landing in Maracaibo.

↔↔↔↔↔↔↔↔↔↔

So I prepared to leave the employ of Harold B. Tucker. It took the better part of a day to box my specimens for travel. My intention was to go to La Ceiba and arrange for a wagon to come back to Pennysmith's lake for my collection. But Jenny came to my cabin on the morning of the second day.

"Kiyuga says you can have Triumph and our team, to take your things."

"That's civil of him. Tell him I appreciate the savings in effort that will afford me."

She nodded, but did not leave. Her unblinking gaze made me uncomfortable. At last she said, "You are stupid. He doesn't want you to go. Not really."

"I believe he does. And I believe I should. He no longer values my judgment."

"Ah. Stupid and proud."

"I'll not apologize, nor change my opinion, if that's what you are suggesting."

She nodded again. And this time she left.

Later, one of the miners brought Triumph to my cabin. I

loaded her myself, as Tucker felt he could spare no one from the work of preparing the dam's destruction. Knowing the going would be slow in the heavy wagon, and not wishing to travel at night, I decided to leave early the next morning.

I hitched up Taft and Bronto before sunrise. The eastern clouds were just beginning to glow as I guided Triumph toward the dam. Lanterns shone everywhere, but something was different. I stopped the horses, and realized that there was no clanging of steel drills, no sound of work at all.

Tucker's unmistakable silhouette loomed in front of the lanterns, marching toward me. "Whitney! You're timing is remarkable! The charges are set! Today's the day!" Surprisingly, and somewhat annoyingly, he seemed to have forgotten the unpleasantness of our last conversation.

I hadn't. "I've not come to watch. I'm leaving."

He was genuinely surprised, filled as he was with the childlike eagerness that possessed him whenever he was on the hunt. "You don't even want to see it? Gonna be stupendous!"

"I've explained my feelings on the matter. Goodbye."

"Hold on. You're not going now, in any case. I've already dispatched the men to warn folks downstream. The track follows the stream near six miles. You'll be more than half the day before you're clear of the flood. I'll not have your drowning on my conscience. It already bears the weight of destroying the wilderness."

"I'm ready to leave. You can't wait half a day?" I asked. I then instantly remembered who I was talking to and added, "I'm sorry. That was an absurd question."

"Indeed it was. Now turn Triumph round and come enjoy the biggest blast since Petersburg! Had the forest boys clear a hilltop about a quarter mile down stream. Perfect spot to watch from. That's where Jenny and me will be. Or go sulk in your cabin if you must."

Later I would wonder if Tucker somehow engineered events to make it inevitable that I would be on hand for this spectacle. But I never asked him.

With Triumph returned to camp, I wrestled with my emotions. Of course I was curious to see a man-made cataclysm. Yet I hated to give Tucker the enjoyment of my admitting to that curiosity. The reader may already have presumed which emotion won out.

The hilltop was crowded — not only with the miners and forest workers, but with citizens from the soon-to-be-obliterated village downstream, and even people from distant towns who had got wind of the event.

Tucker was at the forefront of the crowd, the electric detonator arranged ceremonially on a table before him. Jenny's rocker had been transported from the cabins and she sat in it as though the "show" was going to last more than a few moments.

As I approached I saw Tucker was in an argument with (I would later learn) the miners' foreman. The two men were shouting in their respective tongues, and harried old Ernesto was earnestly endeavoring to keep up with the translations. I caught only the last words, which were, of course, Tucker's: "Well *you* don't get to say what's too much! You ain't at your mine, this ain't your powder, ain't your dam, ain't your money paying for it all!" I assumed they were arguing over wages, though I knew that Tucker was paying, by local standards, princely sums to everyone involved. I would soon find out my assumption was incorrect.

The foreman threw up his arms in frustration and marched past me down the hill. I thought it odd that he broke into a run, but imagined that he was retreating from embarrassment. Again, I was quite wrong.

With the foreman summarily dismissed, Tucker surveyed the gathered throng. I cringed at his smile of satisfaction when he saw me trudging up the hill, veered away from him and tried to maintain an air of indifference as he called out, "See? When something's inevitable, you got no choice but to enjoy it."

He gazed at the slopes below us, and checked his pocket watch with typical impatience. The audience murmured among themselves. Finally a distant gunshot echoed from far below, silencing everyone. Answering shots rang out, each one nearer and nearer. It was the signal from Tucker's messengers that the announcement of the impending flood had been successfully transferred downstream.

"That's it," he said. And with uncharacteristic lack of flair, eyes fixed on the dam, he dropped one hand on the detonator's plunger and pressed it down. It emitted its distinctive mournful whir as the generator spun.

I now learned what Tucker and the foreman had actually been arguing about. It was the amount of blasting powder Tucker had insisted upon placing in the boreholes. Predictably, it was far more than necessary to destroy the dam.

I certainly cannot deny that the result was spectacular. The face of the dam shuddered and lifted as though suddenly transformed from solid rock into a gelatinous liquid. Plumes of rich, orange flame shot out from the rising landmass.

The sound did not reach us for several seconds, then arrived with an astonishing bass thump overlaid with a thunder-like rumble that echoed and re-echoed through the mountains. A concussive wind blasted dust in our faces, tore leaves from the trees, and sent a thousand birds squawking into the skies.

Rising in front of us was an inverted mountain of shattered rock. Its shadow fell across us. And suddenly a distressing truth became apparent.

We were much, much too close.

Luckily, the most massive fragments landed short of our viewpoint, striking the earth like meteors, crushing trees and blasting craters tens of feet across.

But the horde of lesser missiles reached us — a bedlam of deadly stone hail. Onlookers screamed and ran, taking cover under trees, wagons, even burros. As I dropped to the ground and helplessly covered my head, I glimpsed Jenny roll from her rocking chair and hold it over herself. I dared a glance at Tucker, and saw him standing motionless at his table, seemingly mesmerized by the chaos. A chunk of rock five feet broad flattened the table in front of him, but he merely took one cautionary step back as dust and splinters whorled round him.

The thump-and-clatter seemed to last an eternity. Even after it ended, no one moved, lest some late-comer boulder strike him down for his temerity. (Astonishingly, it turned out no one was seriously injured. While I could not help but rejoice in that miracle, a darker part of me cursed Tucker's uncanny luck. Once again, his self-indulgent rashness had proven harmless, at least to other humans.)

Gratefully noting that my head had not been flattened by a remnant of the dam, I rose to my knees. What I thought at first to be a ringing in my ears I realized was a new sound — the hell-inspired roar of the lake's waters unleashed. I gazed in awe upon the next phase of Tucker's engineering.

He had rent an incision so deep in nature's landscape that where one expected to see a waterfall cascading down a rubbled rock face, one instead was presented with an inky black flow one hundred thirty feet wide and sixty feet deep. Its depth kept its surface eerily smooth as it engulfed the stream bed below and rushed unstoppably westward toward distant Lake Maracaibo. I was momentarily baffled by a muted, yet persistent popping sound which punctuated the steady roar, then realized it resulted from trees, invisible beneath the torrent, being snapped off by the water's irresistible onslaught.

CHAPTER SIXTEEN

Tucker's Monster

While the greatest rush of water was gone in the first hours, it took two full days for the fetid lake to be fully emptied. Rather than depart as I had intended, and to my own self-recrimination, I remained in the camp, having convinced myself that the rapid 'draining of an entire lake presented a unique opportunity for the wholesale discovery of bottom-dwelling fauna. After all, I rationalized, don't we often fantasize about discovering what lurks beneath water's cloak?

Tucker and I struck an unspoken and uneasy truce, dealing with one another only on the most businesslike of terms. He remained awake round the clock, trying to be everywhere at once. Sometimes he rowed out to take soundings, as if to reassure himself that the water level was indeed dropping. Others he trod up and down the shores, searching for tracks of any origin. On one of these circuits, he found his lost double rifle, stuck like a flagpole muzzle-down in the mud. Cleaned and oiled, it functioned perfectly and was put back into service, much to his satisfaction.

At all times, teams of men patrolled the expanding shore line. Lanterns, hundreds of them, were lit each night, spaced every fifty feet or so, lest some thoughtless dinosaur try to escape under cover of darkness.

Toward the end of the first day, near the mouth of the stream that had fed the lake, the shallow area we had previously identified showed itself. It was actually two oval mounds, one about a hundred feet long; with a much smaller one some fifty feet from it, closer to the stream inlet. They would have been small islands had the lake been shallower; and they were curious because the lake bottom was otherwise quite flat and featureless.

Unique geography was of no interest to Tucker, of course. He had but one goal. Sadly, very few creatures were revealed other than the occasional turtle or frog; and the primary product of his enterprise was smell. As more and more lake bottom was exposed, a ghastly odor enveloped the land like a suffocating fog. It was vastly worse than the musky smell of a pond gone dry. Indeed, a number of Tucker's employees abandoned us, claiming that no pay was sufficient to endure this unpleasantness.

The odor emanated from a peculiar gray-brown muck — I apologize for finding no more scientific term — that uniformly blanketed the lake bottom. Even fallen water-logged trees were caked in it. It drew flies in the millions, and not sand flies, but rather the sort normally attracted to carrion or dung. Their incessant buzzing was audible a hundred yards from the lake bed.

Another feature of the muck was that it appeared to deny life to reeds, weeds, or other water plants, for none existed. Small snails, worms and water bugs, and now the flies, flourished in it, but little else. My mind returned to my theory of an underwater geyser. Perhaps it spewed forth this inhospitable sediment, along with hydrogen sulfide, which might account for the smell. As more of the shallow area was uncovered, I awaited with increased curiosity the moment that would reveal the source of the spurts of warm water I had catalogued.

But I and Tucker both were to be disappointed. On the eve of the second day, when the last of the water was finally flowing out, neither "dinosaurs" nor geysers had been laid bare. All that remained was the narrow flow of the stream, carving a new channel in the lake bed as it meandered through the evil-smelling muck and out the former dam.

The next morning found me in hip boots, laboriously

slogging through the muck with Tucker. I carried a shovel, and my slung Holland and Holland flopped annoyingly against my back, raising painful welts as I trudged.

We had agreed we would first explore the two mounds. Tucker's hope was that they were a nest or burrow or some other structure built by the now-deceased creature of the lake. Mine was that they might be the source of my suspected geyser.

But again we met only disappointment. There were no tracks or marks around the mounds. Nor was there any indication of a spring or vent. The mounds proved featureless and lifeless, covered like everything else in the lake's singularly foul mud.

Tucker quickly moved on, marching away from me behind the larger mound, determined to explore every inch of the lake bottom for the slightest sign. "Come! We'll walk a grid, no more than ten feet apart."

I was disheartened and not inclined to continue. The smell was incapacitating, ineffectively muted by a rum-soaked bandanna I had contrived to wear across my face, and made worse by the relentless heat of the country itself. I cursed myself for having eaten anything that morning, since the food fought constantly to find its way back up my throat. Flies buffeted round me like a living tornado.

Rather than follow Tucker, I used my shovel to probe round the smaller of the mounds. He called from behind the larger one, complaining that I was taking too long. I was in the midst of reminding him that our goals had long since parted company when a sudden rush of air shot from the mound in front of me, whistling like a cyclone.

"Hah! There it goes!" I shouted in triumph. "It's a geyser, I'm sure!" Indeed, mud had been blasted off several orifices along both sides of the mound. I immediately added to my theory that the mounds had been built up of precipitants left by mineral-rich water from my geyser.

I heard Tucker, already in a foul mood, growl, "Huzzah for the geyser. We're looking for *sign*, Whitney, not geological curiosities."

I ignored him, squinting at the hissing holes in the mud. The mound vibrated, and I waddled clumsily backward in the sticky lake bottom, fearing the current eruption might include boiling water or steam. But the rush of wind slowly subsided and, unexpectedly, air began to suck back into the holes. The hump shuddered again. Then a large slab of mud suddenly flicked *upward*. It took many seconds for me to comprehend what had thrown the slab up — not a burst of air or water, but rather a sort of flap that had raised like a window shade.

It was an eyelid. And I was looking at an eyeball not less than three feet across.

"Stop your lollygagging!" Tucker ordered, completely unaware. "Strike a path east of me. We must be systematic."

The eye rolled around in a disoriented way, its gigantic pupil (a diagonal diamond!) expanding and contracting, trying to adapt to the bright sun. But it soon settled, looking *directly at me*.

Jumbled thoughts skittered through my head like marbles tossed down a staircase; questions silently screamed; fragments of attempted explanations. All the while, logic desperately tried to deny the very sight itself.

"Whitney! Have you gone deaf now?"

I was lurching backward, a brain-numbing fear shooting its tendrils of icy control to every corner of my body. My boots caught in the sucking muck and I fell painfully on my slung rifle. Even so I managed to squeak: "Harry, I think today you're going to get your wish."

"What? What's that? Don't try my patience!" he bellowed back.

Further explanation on my part became unnecessary, for

234

the smaller mound now ripped itself up from the lake bottom, rising on the end of a mud-draped tentacle-like shape that connected it to the larger mound. As these rose higher, Tucker was revealed to me through a cascade of falling mud, slogging round the larger hump. He stopped dead, gaping, as one might expect, at the astonishing site of the hump headed skyward of its own accord.

Not privy to the details I had seen, Tucker did not yet realize that the hump had eyes, that it was connected to the larger mound by a neck, and that the mounds together comprised a single animal some *two hundred feet long* — an unthinkably monstrous version of the "baby" which had pursued us into Pennysmith's laboratory.

The larger mound now moved, and the sodden lake bottom beneath me shook, rippled and jiggled like gelatin. The animal's eight preposterously gigantic legs unfolded and slowly wrenched the body free. The creature was half buried, to a depth of many feet, and another errant question joined those already ping-ponging through my mind, *How long has this thing been lying here?"*

Then next question instantly took precedence over all others: *Does this gargantuan thing have the same ferocious disposition as its smaller predecessor?* If so, I was much too close! I rolled onto my stomach and scrabbled like a hapless toddler toward the distant shore, or rather former shore. My rifle, obviously as useless as had been the Winchester before it, clubbed me vindictively and repeatedly on the back of my head as I crawled.

Tucker now had realized what he was looking at. I heard him shout, "Ready the nets! Ready the nets!" Despite my blinding fear, I glanced ahead to see if, in fact, his men were following the order. Not surprisingly, the sight of a demon surpassing all mythology easily countermanded any request from their formerly intimidating employer. They were running with gazelle-like abandon that would have been funny had I not been twenty feet from the reason.

As I floundered on, a crushing weight suddenly struck me. My brain shrieked, *I am trampled! Dead!* But then realized the blow was but a great clod of mud falling from the creature's flanks as it got to its feet. I kicked and wriggled free, flopping onto my back.

The animal was now at its full height, its head towering sixty feet above me (its neck being proportionally much longer than that of the smaller animal). It weaved unsteadily after what must have been eons of hibernation.

I remained frozen in place, some instinct clamoring that if I did not move, perhaps the titan would graciously ignore the insignificant life form far below.

Through the veritable forest of eight thick legs, I glimpsed Tucker, immobile like myself, his rifle held limply as he craned his neck to gape up at the thing.

Now the creature shook like an enormous wet dog. Mud flew and splatted and plopped in a foul-smelling storm. Then it stood still, drawing in a long, rasping breath for what seemed like minutes. After another pause, it exhaled with the ear shattering roar of a locomotive's blow down. My scientist's mind, a faint flicker in a void of fear-inspired murk, meekly offered, *It is breathing for the first time since becoming submerged here! Amphibious?* Indeed, in that same moment, I became aware of six or seven long slits on either side of its neck. As the creature drew another breath, they closed and became almost invisible. Gills?

The creature surveyed its surroundings, curving its neck first one way, then the other, its massive head swinging out over me like the bucket of a colossal steam shovel. It began to make the most bizarre clucking sound, thrumming guttural notes which literally shook one's body. The sound did not seem aggressive. It was not the fearful French-horn attack-howl we had heard from the smaller animal, so I felt slight hope for my survival.

But in the same moment it suddenly lowered its head down, down, down toward me. I cringed, *Oh God! If I am swallowed whole, how long will I live in the awful wet suffocating blackness!* But the animal had no interest in me. Its head stopped a few feet to my right and tilted awkwardly to one side. This was to bring one set of nostrils (three on each side of its head!) closer to the lake bottom.

The creature sniffed the mud, then snorted — clearly an annoyed sort of snort — blasting a crater three feet deep. Its warm breath enveloped me in a gagging stench that made the lake smell seem almost pleasant. The mouth opened slightly and, as I had on the smaller animal, I saw the white hair-like material on the roof of the mouth. Surely, I now thought, this is for combing and collecting food particles from water forced through it. But also I glimpsed teeth — barrel-sized molars at the back of the jaws.

The leviathan lifted its long neck back up and sniffed the air. Then, cocking its head as though having made a decision, it lurched forward, struggling to pull its many feet one by one from the sucking mud. But its front four legs buckled and it fell heavily on its "chest," shaking the earth. Its hind quarters tilted shockingly in my direction as it fought to regain its footing. At last it righted itself and struggled onward to the southern shore.

It collided with one of Tucker's big nets, but as the animal was some forty feet taller, the effect was rather like a rhinoceros going through a cobweb. The net's massive support poles were yanked from the ground like toothpicks as the creature lumbered obliviously onward and plowed into the forest.

Unexpectedly, it paused. Then, very slowly, it tipped over onto one side. Trees were snapped and flattened, a tumult of leaves billowing up like smoke. I thought perhaps the beast was weak from long inactivity. But then it thrust its eight legs into the air and began to roll from side to side like some outrageous pet of the Gods. It was merely cleaning its back of the caked mud.

When acceptably spruced up, it rolled gracefully upright and moved on. In an astonishingly short time, the titanic animal was lost from our view.

Tucker slogged over to me, bearing the look of one who had had a religious vision. "Tell me *that* is no dinosaur!"

Overwhelmed as I was by the impossible grandeur of what we had just seen, let alone survived, my true opinion seemed to matter not at all. For the rest of my life I would call it simply "Tucker's Monster," since no other taxonomic description fit, even remotely. But instead of voicing this to the enraptured Tucker, I said in a mocking tone, "Ready the nets?"

At that, Tucker exploded with true and rare laughter; and our briefly sundered friendship was restored. In another moment we saw Jenny running along the shore with her rifle, waving to us. Indifferent to the endless fruitless days of searching, she had remained in camp and only learned of trouble when the men came running past. She had just missed seeing the animal.

We would soon learn we were the only humans left in the area. We eventually found some of Tucker's work force far down stream, hiding in the ruins of the recently flooded village. Ernesto, his suit in muddy tatters, was among them. He told us that the rest, when last seen, were still running full tilt toward Lake Maracaibo with no intention of slowing down.

↔↔↔↔↔↔↔↔↔

With the discovery of what I believe to be the largest land animal Earth has ever seen, several things became evident. For one, it explained the poor fishing in the lake. The animal's filter-feeding had vacuumed up almost all life that came down the stream. It consumed not only fish, but crustaceans, insect larvae, and possibly algae and other organic matter. How else could such an immense animal maintain itself immobile on the bottom of the lake?

Not a reptile, it was warm-blooded. The jets of warm water I had assumed issued from a geyser were in fact powerful pulses being forced through the creature's baleen-filled mouth. The odorous "mud" covering the lake bottom consisted of, and I cringed at the thought of how I'd wallowed in it, years of accumulated excrement. Mildly acidic, this offal accounted for the dearth of plant life on the lake bottom.

Of course, the more profound questions cried out in vain. How long had it lain there before we disturbed it? Decades? Centuries? Why was the smaller one foraging in a more conventional manner while the larger remained semi-dormant? Was the smaller one a baby or was it smaller simply because it was a different sex? Did the bizarre creatures have sexes? Did they reproduce by any "normal" method? And above all, most puzzling of all — what on earth *were* these things?

Naturally, Tucker cared little for my musings. As swiftly as possible, he assembled from the least frightened men left in the area a search party with which to pursue the creature.

Ernesto, now in borrowed boots and work clothes, remained on as interpreter, insisting he was fit for the journey. He seemed to be rather enjoying the adventure, despite its hardships.

Gathering and equipping the men took two full days, but Tucker was unconcerned, "Unlikely that we'll lose it, eh? The trail's as wide as a highway!"

I pressed him on his purpose, "You don't mean to shoot and mount the thing, I trust."

"As God is my witness, Whitney, I just want to see it again. I want Jenny to see it. It is my life's work done."

↔↔↔↔↔↔↔↔↔↔

The creature's trail, heading south, was indeed a highway wide; but even so it was exceedingly difficult to follow. The shattered forest was treacherous to navigate. Sometimes it was easier to hack our way through the untrammeled vegetation on either side. Too, where our quarry blithely strode over deep valleys and hills, we smaller beings were forced to slide and tumble, climb and traverse. As I became ever more scratched and bruised, I envied the always practical Jenny who, despite the heat, had chosen to wear the protective fringed deerskin jacket which had gone on every trip with us. On the second day, in an intervening valley, we came upon a small pond that had been thoroughly ravaged. Trees all round it were flattened, and its banks bore deep furrows where, evidently, the creature had done exploratory digging. (With its snout? Its feet?). Had it been searching for food? Merely getting a drink? Questions were endless. We would find two more ponds "explored" in the same way.

Tucker drove our little band hard. But there was no end to the trail of decimated trees. The creature continued almost straight south, mile upon mile, and we seemed unable to overtake it.

In late afternoon of the third day, we had reached yet another valley floor and were debating whether or not to climb to the next hilltop before setting camp for the night. Tucker, of course, was pressing to press on. He judged it to be half a mile or less to the top.

"What's another thousand steps or so?" he demanded.

Ernesto patiently explained that the worn-out and nervous men in our party might abandon us altogether if Tucker insisted. Before Tucker could rebut, he was interrupted by the sound of distant steam whistle, quite unexpected given our extreme isolation — but so welcome!

240

"A locomotive?" he mused, turning to Ernesto. "Are we that near civilization?"

Ernesto answered, "It is I think the Great La Ceiba Railway." (At that time, the La Ceiba ran from Lake Maracaibo to the town of Trujillo).

As Tucker plotted how we might re-supply our search party by train, thus eliminating the need to send men overland back to La Ceiba, the ghostly shrill of the steam whistle was suddenly supplanted by another sound — the harmonic French-horn call of the creature, fully twice as loud, ringing like melodious thunder off the hills. While it was similar to the bellow of the smaller creature, this call lacked the fierceness. It seemed more questioning, or lonely, for lack of some more accurate term.

Then the gunshot crack of snapping trees told us the creature was much closer than we had supposed, just over the hill before us. Perhaps it had been resting. But now it was definitely on the move. The train's whistle shrilled again. And again the creature trumpeted.

"Onward!" commanded Tucker. He, Jenny, and I raced up hill. I glanced back to see that, except for old Ernesto, our men were not following. The unearthly, air-filling call of the creature, and the sound of it felling stout trees as though they were straw, had had an understandably chilling effect.

The hill was steep, the climb laborious, despite the adrenaline urging us on. During these minutes, the train whistle blew several more times. Each time the animal called out, as well — surely, it seemed, as if answering the whistle.

We struggled finally over the hilltop and saw smoke rising from the valley below. We could not see the source through the dense forest, but it was an unsettling amount of smoke, clearly from a very large fire.

We pushed on, zigging, zagging, climbing over felled trees, hurrying down toward the valley. The "trail" veered

241

east briefly, and we entered a broad semicircle of flattened forest, no doubt where the creature had been resting moments before. Tucker and Jenny, always in the lead, did not slow.

Now, over our labored breathing, a distant rumble floated eerily to us. To my surprise Tucker and Jenny both stopped; and therefore Ernesto and I stopped. Tucker turned to his wife, "Pinch me, Dickens, if that don't sound like a stampede." Jenny, concern on her face, only nodded.

Seconds later, we were faced with a herd of cattle charging up the slope. We scattered into the trees on either side, letting the panicked animals rush past. They were terribly battered and cut from crashing helter-skelter through the tangled branches of the fallen trees in the "trail." But worse, an acrid smell assaulted us, that of singed hair; many of the poor creatures were badly burned.

When the stampede had passed, we stepped warily back out into the open. Tucker squinted uphill after the cattle and said dryly, "I did not expect that."

While it was easy to understand that cattle might run from the creature, it was difficult to imagine where they had come from in this mountainous region. Mystified, we continued our rush downward.

At last the forest gave way and we waded into tall dry grass that covered the valley floor, much of it trampled by the stampeding cattle. Pushing through this we came to the railroad tracks.

"It is the La Ceiba line," announced Ernesto. "West is Lake Maracaibo. East is Trujillo."

The smoke was billowing in the east, and the creature's trampled path led toward it. But just as we struck out that way, we heard exciting shouting behind us. It came from two men in engineer's overalls, who gesticulated wildly as they pointed urgently east. Ernesto translated, "They say do not go that way. There is a monster!"

"Tell'em we know," said Tucker.

Ernesto calmly did so. And with no other comment we hurried off, leaving the astonished train men in our wake.

After perhaps a quarter mile, as we went round a long gentle bend, we found the source of the smoke. The valley grass was ablaze. We huddled single file in the center of the tracks to avoid the flames and pressed on.

A hundred yards further we came upon a locomotive. She was on her side, having careened clear off the tracks, steam still whooshing from her cylinders. Coal flung from the firebox had started the fire. (We deduced later that the creature, simply by walking over the tracks, had inadvertently damaged them enough to derail the engine.)

Behind the wrecked engine, shattered cattle cars were scattered like a child's building blocks. The train was the source of the stampede. The jagged line of cars stretched out of sight round the bend.

Now, in recent days I'd seen many things that were competing for the most amazing thing I had ever seen, but yet another now rose to the challenge. As we skirted the hissing locomotive, we heard a deep-throated, air-shaking *huff.* One knew instinctively that it was an exhalation by our quarry. We looked toward the sound, and the head of Tucker's Monster rose high above the treetops before us. It stretched its long neck up and tilted its head back. And I suddenly realized it had an entire cow in its jaws!

The hapless bovine was head-down in the immense maw, hind legs kicking in vain. The monster gurgled and gulped, even seemed to choke as it convulsed its neck, slowly drawing the cow in. Absurdly, the sight reminded me of the eyelash pitviper devouring the tree frog.

But the event was shocking for reasons beyond its preposterous scale. It was shocking on a zoological level. I

243

had been certain that the creature was a filter-feeder, like certain whales, yet here it was devouring prey whole like a snake.

I tore my gaze away to glance at my companions. Ernesto and Jenny were mesmerized, for they were seeing the beast for the first time. But Tucker beamed with pride. He must have felt my eyes on him, for he shot a look right back at me, "Hah! No dinosaur? Bigger than Tyrannosaurus Rex by a long ways, and you can't deny it, Whitney!" Indeed, I could not.

Having at last successfully swallowed the cow, the creature lowered its head out of sight behind the trees.

"Gotta get closer!" declared Tucker. And he headed down the tracks. Jenny chased after and grabbed him. He disengaged her hands with a smile. "I'll not be denied this, Jenny."

Off he went. The rest of us followed hesitantly. When we'd got beyond the area of burning grass, we quietly slipped off the tracks threaded our way among the overturned cattle cars. All the while we heard splintering wood and the frantic mooing of more cattle.

Tucker's Monster came into view, looming over the last of the wrecked train. We learned the source of the sound of breaking wood. The animal lifted the front portion of its body so that its two forelegs were free. It used these to crack open a cattle car like an egg to get at the succulent contents. Some steers were able to stumble out and dash away, but one more was plucked up and swallowed whole in the same unbelievable way we'd just witnessed.

Odd thoughts flickered through my head. *We are mortals trembling before a terrifying god. We are prairie dogs cowering before a grazing bison.*

I marveled at the creature's markings. It was much more ornate than its smaller predecessor. Overall, it was a deep rust red. It had the same jewel-like plates rimming its three eyes and jaws (but blue and yellow, rather than red and green). In addition, it bore four striking blue and yellow stripes, two on each side (made of more of the plates). They ran from the base of the neck across the flanks to the base of the tail, tapering to points at the ends. Oval pinkish spots dotted its belly and trailed down the inside of the legs, growing ever smaller to disappear at the feet. And the feet! Quite unlike those of the smaller creature, they looked like inverted mushrooms. When pressed down, they spread out to twice a leg's diameter, no doubt to help distribute the creature's incalculable weight. The two front-most legs each had two tusk-like spurs sprouting from either side. These aided in ripping apart the cattle cars. The remaining six feet had no nails or claws that I could see.

As the beast tore open the end-most railroad car, it must have been close to satiation, for it somewhat disinterestedly dismembered the one cow it caught, chewing only half-heartedly on the pieces.

Throughout the spectacle we simply stared in a kind of reverent silence. The grass fire, virtually unnoticed under the circumstances, burned itself out against the dense forest. And in the whole time we made only the most banal of comments — "Will you look at that!" "That's something, isn't it?" "Got three eyes, did you notice?" "Aren't those colors something else?" "*Another* cow?! How much can it eat?"

As the sun settled into the haze of dusk, the monster stood up straight, pointed its neck and tail out straight, and indulged in a luxurious stretch. I noted that the tail seemed disproportionately short and fat, but I supposed a thing with eight legs hardly needs a long tail for balance. Next, with studied balletic precision, it carefully folded the left bank of legs under itself and gently, if earth-shakingly, rolled onto its side. Finally, curling head and tail round together like some cyclopean cat, it promptly went to sleep. Soon it was making a sound like the rhythmic rumble of a hundred bass fiddles, snoring we supposed.

So there we were, our quarry "captured," or at least in view, and nightfall upon us. After a time, Tucker grumbled, "Where'd all those men run to? Sure like to have my bedroll."

I asked, "Do you think we should simply stay here? So close to it? Is that wise?"

Tucker smiled, "You think you're not going to hear it if it wakes up?"

Jenny and Ernesto laughed, and I conceded the point with a shrug. We cut some of the tall grass and attempted to make acceptable mattresses.

It may seem odd that we were able to sleep given the unparalleled nature of our adventure. But we were indescribably exhausted from our mad chase through the Venezuelan forest. The sky was moonless. So, even with our immense prize snoring musically not seventy yards away, we were all asleep in minutes, save for a closing comment which came floating out of the darkness from Tucker, "Ernesto, tomorrow you will continue down the tracks to whatever town you come to. Tell everyone you meet, there's twenty dollars American gold waiting for the man who finds me a photographer and sends him here."

↔↔↔↔↔↔↔↔↔

We awoke to tenuous human footsteps, and discovered about half of our previous party creeping toward us out of the morning fog. Shame, or perhaps avarice, had got the better of them, and they'd crept down to the valley to learn the fate of their employer.

Tucker welcomed them without retribution, and we eagerly devoured the arepa they brought. Dawn dimly

246

dappled a cloudy sky, and the men quietly gaped at our sleeping creature. We struck a fire on which to brew some much-desired coffee. Throughout, Tucker's Monster slumbered, motionless, like some fantastical reclining statue.

Ernesto, seemingly as refreshed as if he'd spent the night in a feather bed, stuffed some arepa in his pockets, snatched up a canteen and set off west down the tracks toward La Ceiba to carry out Tucker's orders of the previous evening.

Midmorning approached and still the creature slept. The novelty of the situation wearing off, Tucker became emboldened, "I think I will take a walk round the thing. Get a very close look. Coming Whitney?"

"I remind you that it is a carnivore, a fact proven by the consumption of several thousand pounds of beef."

Jenny spoke, too. "Kiyuga, if it can eat cows it can eat you faster three times."

Tucker slowed and pondered for a moment. Then he said, "What better for my gravestone? 'Harold B. Tucker, devoured by a dinosaur!' Pfhuh!"

Jenny scowled at him. He grabbed her in a hug that lifted her off her feet. "Dickens, when it rose from the lake bed, the beast gave not a second glance to such miniscule morsels as young Whitney and myself, though we were under its very nose. I think anything less than a cow does not interest it in the least."

Jenny glanced at me. I only shrugged. I could think of plausible reasons why the animal might have ignored us on first awakening in the lake bed (and why it might *not* do so now), but what was the point in arguing with Tucker? And, as she almost always did, Jenny relented. Thus, to the amazement of our remaining hunting party, Tucker and I marched toward the creature.

Lancelot could not have been more awed by his foe. We made a slow, cautious circuit. The animal's snoring shook the very air. The brilliantly colored scales along the jaw line shimmered in the morning sun like the wings of a butterfly. The smooth skin was webbed with black veins that pulsed rhythmically below the red surface.

And there was more than size and color and grandeur. A veritable ecosystem of lesser life forms swarmed over and round it. Flies blanketed its blood-stained jaws and viscous liquid oozing from beneath its closed eyes. Repulsive white worms (parasitic? symbiotic?) could be glimpsed slithering in the crevices between the gigantic plates that formed the broad stripes. Birds hopped over its vast flanks, eagerly gobbling up the worms.

Completing our tour, Tucker and I stood again at the head. "A name, Whitney!" he suddenly blurted. "We'll need a good Latin name!"

"What, something like *Tuckerus maximus*?" I kidded.

"No, no, don't have to be named after me," he answered, quite unaware of my joke. Gotta have a great name worthy of the thing. Like 'fantasticus enormium,' or 'outlandious bogglemindium.' Only real Latin, you know?"

I promised to give it some thought.

↔↔↔↔↔↔↔↔↔↔

We remained camped beside the creature for two days, during which time it never stirred. Even as Tucker feverishly formulated plans for announcing his discovery to the world, he fretted that said find would awake and escape him. He pressed me on theories for keeping the animal in this location. If he purchased cattle by the train load, might we not expect that it would become accustomed to dining here and have no wish to move on? I could say only that the limited evidence at hand indicated that course might work.

So, more members of our party were dispatched east and

west along the tracks to carry the message that the rich American was now in the market for cattle, cattle cars, and another locomotive if one were to be had.

Sometime after noon of the second day, we became aware of a curious, faint squeaking sound. At first we thought it came from our sleeping giant; but as it grew louder we realized it emanated from the west, from the direction of Lake Maracaibo. And up the tracks came a railroad handcar, its lever being vigorously pumped by plucky Ernesto.

As we rushed to greet him, I saw there was concern on his face. But this subtlety was lost on Tucker, who had only one concern, "My photographer man! Have you found him?"

Ernesto, not expecting the question, stuttered, "I have sent word to Maracaibo. I am told there is a young man there with the skills and suitable equipment, if he will accept the offer."

"He must! Every day we risk the beast wandering off!"

"Sir, I have a greater worry," blurted Ernesto. At last Tucker saw that delivering news of the photographer was not Ernesto's primary purpose.

"And your worry is?"

"The engineer and fireman of the train came to La Ceiba a day before I. I think they did run most of the distance. They have told everyone of the animal and of the loss of the train."

"Of course. I'd expect they would. What of it?" Tucker snapped.

"In Alto Viento, to the north, there is a — a what would you say, a group — a company of the Venezuelan army. These men have been called to come here. To come here and stop the destruction. To — to attack. With guns — cannons!"

"What?" Tucker exclaimed.

"Mr. Tucker, sir, we are a poor country," Ernesto rushed to explain. "The train, all the cattle, it is a great loss. A great concern to many people."

Later, I would see the humor in poor Ernesto's defense of his countrymen's action, as though, in the rich land of America, news of a monster smashing a train and eating its contents would be viewed as but a minor annoyance. Too, I might have enjoyed the irony that Tucker himself, in younger days, would merrily have gunned the creature down if he could lay hands on an express rifle big enough. But at this moment I shared his alarm that our magnificent, utterly unique animal might be destroyed less than a week from its discovery.

Tucker was shaken. "Bless it!" he whispered. "We gotta stop them!"

Within minutes we had snatched up bread and water, commandeered Ernesto's handcar, and were on our way to La Ceiba. We must have made an inexplicable and entertaining sight — the burly Tucker, myself, and the diminutive Jenny, flying along the rails, taking turns pumping the handcar as though the fate of the world depended upon it.

We made good time. In a few hours we had reached Lake Maracaibo, where the tracks turned north toward La Ceiba. As we pumped onward, we heard a steam whistle. Tucker enjoyed a moment's elation, "Another locomotive! We'll lease it, buy us some cattle, or sheep, or goats, or pigs — whatever they've got. Haul them back up the line and show these people our dinosaur's as manageable as a puppy as long as she's fed, eh?"

But we rounded a bend and were disappointed. The whistle was only that of a traction engine (the very Case engine I'd seen on our arrival in La Ceiba), plowing a large field to prepare for planting in Indian corn. We had no choice but to press on.

Beyond the field, the rail line ran three or four miles in a narrow valley formed by the mountain foothills on the east and a low ridge separating it from Lake Maracaibo.

It was dusk as we emerged from the valley, and at last saw La Ceiba's lantern lights. In a few moments we rolled up to its little train station and breathlessly disembarked from our tiny handcar. There was local word that the Venezuelan Army unit had indeed left Alto Viento. But it had not yet arrived in La Ceiba and, since we knew not which of several roads the unit might take, Tucker immediately sent men up every northern road with the message that we were to be notified the moment the Army contingent was seen.

After that, and after the great rush to get here, there was nothing to do but wait. Ah, how strange the slow pace of life all those years ago in a backward land must seem to the modern reader!

We engaged quarters in the town's tiny hotel. I would like to say that I, like Tucker, deeply concerned, spent the night pacing my room. In truth, thrilled to find myself in a first class feather bed, I plummeted instantaneously into deep sleep.

↔↔↔↔↔↔↔↔↔

Many hours later I was awakened by Tucker pounding on my door, "Whitney! Up! Up! We have word! The Army is coming by the coast road!"

Climbing blearily into the perpetually damp, rancid clothes I had worn for many days, I raced to catch up to Tucker and Jenny. Horses were hired and we set off at the trot to meet the advancing Army.

We could not have met them at a more inopportune spot, for we came upon the men struggling to cross a wide washout that had carried away a broad section of the road. It was a deep, muddy gash at least fifty yards wide, ripped through the forest. One of their heavy cannons was badly mired. The soldiers had hitched up a double-team and were pushing, pulling, whipping and cursing to free it.

As Tucker, Jenny and I took in the sight, we simultaneously realized what had caused the washout. I saw a rare flash of embarrassment as Tucker muttered, "Hmm. The work of my man-made flood."

On the side nearest us, overseeing the slow progress of the cannon, was an officer on foot. He was a trim, middle-aged man with graying beard and temples. Judging from his copper sun-lined skin and walnut-brown eyes, I felt his ancestors must trace back to the people who trod this land before the Spanish. He directed his men with quiet, precise authority, projecting urgency without anger. His uniform was mud-stained, of course, but also bore the fraying of years of service. Venezuela's army at this time was rather unorganized, ill-trained, and ill-equipped. But there was an ongoing effort to train officers, and this man surely rose through that effort.

He noticed us, and suspected immediately who we were. After a brief moment of apparent internal discussion, he strode in our direction. We swiftly dismounted to greet him. He addressed Tucker.

"You are Harold Tucker," he stated, rather than asked. I thought, *Thank God he speaks English*, for we had no interpreter.

"I am," said Tucker, with an apologetic sort of half bow, completely uncharacteristic of him.

The officer nodded curtly in return, "I am Colonel Apolonio Marquez."

"Honored to meet you, sir." Tucker swiftly extended his hand. The colonel responded with a limp shake barely adequate to maintain diplomatic relations. Tucker hurried on, "This is my wife, Jenny, and my advisor in matters of science, Professor Gerard Whitney." (I had received a promotion!)

The colonel gave the two of us a dismissive glance as he

252

continued, looking at Tucker, and waving a hand over his shoulder at the destruction behind him, "You have done this?" Obviously he was fully apprised of our local history.

Tucker responded, "Draining the lake was necessary for the research I'm doing. Research which has borne fruit, I promise you. If I can just explain the full situation —"

But Marquez cut him off, "And now you come north of La Ceiba, maybe to find something *else* to destroy?" While the colonel's command of English was not encyclopedic, sarcasm was well within his reach. Jenny and I braced for Tucker's reaction to the affront, but, surprisingly, he remained calm.

"Sir, we have made a discovery that will forever put Venezuela on the map of the world."

Again Marquez interrupted, "Discovery? Discovery? So tell me, is true, what is say to me, discovery of yours it did broken the La Ceiba train? It did *eat* the train?"

"Well, not the train, of course, no," said Tucker, flustered. "Only the cattle — and not all of'em. Please listen to me, man, the animal is fully under my control."

I cringed. Jenny winced. *Fully under his control?* It is the only time I can remember Jenny wincing.

Marquez pressed on, "And is how big? Big as the mountains, they say to me."

"Oh, no, not nearly. Why it's only," and here Tucker turned to me, "how big would you say, Whitney?"

Trying my best to sound cavalier, I stammered, "Why, I shouldn't think more than — than, say fifty or so feet high." Tucker pierced me with a glare, so I weakly added, "to the very top of its head, I mean. It has a very long, slender, and — and fairly insubstantial neck."

The colonel shot back, "I have — I am give — an order. The order say, if there is an animal, if it is so big to eat the train, and if it is come to La Ceiba, then I kill."

Tucker went pale behind decades of sun tan. "You —

253

you mustn't. It's a dinosaur! Tell him, Whitney!"

I joined in, "Sir, it is indeed quite possibly the most extraordinary biological find in recorded history. There is likely no similar animal known anywhere. As Mr. Tucker says, Venezuela would be famous throughout the world."

Marquez made a disinterested noise, "Famous, but with no trains, no cattle, and no *people*, I think!"

Tucker boomed, "Colonel, don't be foolish. The creature is magnificent beyond imagining!"

The nearer of Marquez's men had become aware of the escalating argument. They dropped what they were doing and moved toward us as Marquez stepped closer to Tucker and countered.

"What about Venezuelan people, hm? If they die?"

"They won't, I swear it."

"What does protect them? Your money?"

"In a manner of speaking, yes. Please understand, the animal is asleep; completely at peace, on the rail line south of La Ceiba. And I intend to maintain it there — restrain it there. At my expense of course. Colonel, I need only procure animals for food and a means of transport. If you and your men will assist me, the job can be done that much more quickly."

Marquez's face went as red as Tucker's had gone pale, "Assist you! If you stay in my way I will *arrest* you! You will be in prison!"

Again, Jenny and I cringed. To challenge our newly invigorated, and obsessed, Tucker in this way was to invite a maelstrom. Several of Marquez's men put their hands on their weapons. I thought, *Dear God, Tucker, don't strike the man. We'll be shot on the spot!*

But I needn't have worried. For instead, to my utter astonishment, Harold B. Tucker did what I would have said was impossible. He simply, quietly begged.

"Sir, please sir, give me just a little time. Let me try to contain the animal. I will make good on this damaged road, on the loss of the live stock, the train. I'll — I'll build schools, or churches, or anything your people —"

"You do nothing, American!" The colonel snapped, and nodded toward the largest of his cannon, now freed from the mud and being hauled past us. "I put my guns in the pass south of La Ceiba. If the animal comes, it is killed!"

He turned away from us, shouting orders to his men. They were jolted into renewed activity, rushing back across the stream bed to the cannons which had yet to be brought over.

Jenny and I stared at Tucker, completely at a loss as to what we should do. In all previous experience, we had only to wait for Tucker to act, then run to catch up.

He glanced at me. He was a most remarkable vision of penance, even fear. "My God, Whitney, what have I done? If he kills the dinosaur — I'll have robbed science — history — future children — the Earth herself!"

While I was touched and surprised by Tucker's anguish, I could not disagree. We struggled through uncomfortable silence until at last Jenny spoke, quiet and definite, "He has not killed it yet."

From that tiny spark Tucker rekindled a flame of hope. "True. True, he has not." In the next instant he was on his horse. He was just as driven as in the past, but with an entirely new goal. "Back to La Ceiba!"

And Jenny and I were running to catch up.

CHAPTER SEVENTEEN

A Worrisome Spot

We were compelled by two fears. The first, of course, was that the most fantastic animal on Earth would be destroyed. But the second was in a way more frightening to contemplate. If the creature *survived* an encounter with Marquez's aged cannons; if it were only wounded, what then? What if went into a vengeful furor like that of its smaller counterpart when stabbed by ill-fated Ximen? Surely, La Ceiba itself would be leveled, with hundreds killed; and who knew how far the destruction might extend beyond that?

We spurred our lathered mounts into town. No one there had heard anything new of Tucker's Monster. Was it still asleep? Was it marching toward us? Marching in some new direction? We did not know.

Nonetheless, Tucker hurriedly formulated plans. He left Jenny and me to purchase animals for food, and to hire wagons and horses to transport same. He acquired a keg of black powder and set off on a fresh horse down the railroad tracks. His thought was: if the creature ventured toward town, he might use explosions to frighten it off, or turn it into the forest, or at least change its course. Even if the colonel were then inclined to pursue the beast, his slow-moving band with their cumbersome equipment could not hope to catch it.

Over the next few hours, Jenny and I found eight slaughtered hogs and three milk cows. We paid dearly for the animals, especially the cows, so precious were they to the local livelihood.

Transport became the more difficult challenge. With planting underway in the fields, a sturdy wagon was not to be found in town; and our own Triumph was still at Pennysmith's former laboratory, miles up in the mountains.

With every wasted moment my concern grew that Colonel Marquez would reach La Ceiba and arrest us for continued meddling. So we hit upon a novel solution. On our arrival the day before, I had noted an empty boxcar on a siding near the train station. While Jenny engaged townsfolk to load our cargo of meat into it, I raced to the livery where we had hired our riding horses and arranged with the liveryman for a four-horse team to pull the car. I did not mention the horses would in all likelihood end up on the menu as well. In support of Tucker's cause, I had become more like him than I cared admit. By afternoon, Jenny and I were leading our horses, two on each side of the tracks, towing the boxcar south.

Our progress was painfully slow. It was two hours before we passed through the narrow canyon into the valley farming area. There the steam traction engine still churned its plodding way back and forth. We garnered some curious looks from the field hands, lumbering along with our horse-drawn train car.

Every few moments the squeak and clatter of the boxcar made me look round, thinking I heard Marquez's company overtaking us. But the tracks behind us remained deserted. I began to feel that perhaps we would succeed in reaching the creature and coaxing it to stay in one spot.

Then an explosion rippled through the hills. From far away it was a curious sound, its long echoes like a sighing wind in evergreens. But it was unmistakably an explosion; and it came from somewhere ahead of us, where the tracks turned east away from the lake. Jenny and I shared a wordless, nervous look and chucked our teams, urging them to pick up the pace. We needn't have bothered, for the situation was coming to meet us at a pace much faster than ours.

First came men, members of the original party that had

tracked the creature with us through the forest. They were now running pell-mell.

"*El monstruo está viniendo!*" they shouted as they flew past us. Trailing the men, but holding his own in the race, was the seemingly unstoppable Ernesto. He stopped to offer the wholly unnecessary translation: "The monster it is coming!"

"Thank you, Ernesto," I said.

The wind was against us, and our horses quickly divined that a carnivore of unique proportions approached. They whinnied and bucked wildly. In but seconds, they'd broken our makeshift traces and were overtaking the fleeing men.

Jenny raced to the boxcar and threw open the doors, "The meat! Get out the meat!" Together we climbed up and struggled to drag a gutted pig from our storehouse. Ernesto clambered up with us to help. The cattle, penned in the rear of the car, mooed in terror.

As we strained to shove out a second pig, a rider burst from the forest ahead. It was Tucker. Seeing us, he bore down, wheeling as he came abreast to peer inside the boxcar.

"This all you got?"

"I'm afraid so," I admitted.

"Hardly a mouthful!"

"I know, Harry!" I said, exasperated.

Jenny stepped forward, "They have no livestock, Kiyuga. They are fishermen."

"Yeah," he grunted. "How far behind you is Marquez?"

I shrugged, "He had not arrived in La Ceiba by the time we left. How far behind you is the animal?"

"Maybe half a mile. I wouldn't be ahead of her now, except she stopped to wallow around in another pond. Stuck her head clear under, thrashing around till she plumb splashed all the water out." (For some reason the creature had become female in Tucker's mind, and so would "she" ever remain.)

The cows mooed. Tucker glanced in at them, "Well, at least you got some cattle. Maybe they'll tide her over." He reined his horse about, pointing at the railroad ahead of us, "I'm gonna set another charge at the bend back there."

"Did your first explosion frighten it — her?" I asked.

"Not so you could tell," he said sourly, and galloped off.

Jenny, Ernesto, and I turned back to the task of wrestling pig carcasses from the boxcar. In a different situation I would have been appalled at the thousands of roiling flies that had discovered our cargo. They swarmed round my face, wriggled down my shirt collar, up my sleeves. I remember them now. Then I hardly noticed them.

As we pitched another swine overboard, I looked for Tucker, and saw that he had dismounted at the bend in the tracks some three hundred yards away and was working to place his charge.

In the field opposite us, I was surprised to notice that the farm hands were still watching us with amused curiosity. The engineer of the steam tractor had even stopped his machine. Their lack of consternation indicated they had not yet heard what was afoot in the area. They were soon to discover it for themselves.

But they had more entertainment in store first. Four riders now appeared from the north, coming along the tracks from La Ceiba. They were soldiers from Marquez's company, and they bore down on us with singular purpose, shouting, "*Alto! Alto!*"

They reined up at the boxcar, weapons drawn and trained upon us. I was embarrassed at how quickly and naturally my hands rose into the air, though Jenny and Ernesto's did likewise.

Surprisingly, the soldier in charge was the youngest of the group. He was very nervous, his revolver shaking in his hand, his cap riding askew on a shock of unruly black hair. The poor fellow had been chosen for this mission solely because he spoke a smattering of English.

He stammered, "Colonel Marquez! He say you to jail! Arrest!" Obviously, upon reaching La Ceiba, Marquez had learned we were not following his orders and had sent this party ahead to put an end to our meddling.

Ernesto, bless him, spoke up immediately. He and the young soldier indulged in a torrent of heated Spanish. It was clear from the escalating tone that the dialogue was not going in our favor. The soldier shouted Ernesto down and then shouted in English, "No! No! You come! You *all* come now!" He cocked his revolver for emphasis. I despaired for our plans, for our creature, indeed for our lives.

But at this moment, one of his men shouted louder than either he or Ernesto, his voice shrill as he pointed down the tracks to the south, "*Mirada allí!*"

The head of Tucker's Monster had appeared above the trees, gliding silently above the forest canopy; so high, so large, one might have thought it some bizarre hydrogen balloon. The effect was enhanced by the fact that the animal's movement, like an elephant's, was unexpectedly quiet (because it was following the rail line and not snapping off trees).

The four soldiers were agog, the plan of arresting the American interlopers temporarily set aside. Their mounts twisted and turned, barely manageable.

Meanwhile, down at the bend in the tracks, Tucker had got back on his horse and was galloping toward us. Ignoring the soldiers, he dismounted on the fly and landed beside me and Jenny.

"I set it," he said, meaning he'd lit his fuse.

One could just make out a wisp of smoke curling up from where he'd placed his charge on the tracks. Jenny and I joined him in staring at the spot with fearful anticipation. The young

260

soldier, spinning round on his spooked steed, made one last game attempt, "You are arrest!"

Without looking at him, Tucker said quietly, "In a minute, son."

The monster rounded the bend and came into full view. I heard screams and exclamations from the nearby field hands, and did not need to look to know they were departing from the vicinity.

Tucker had timed his fuse well. The charge exploded right in front of the advancing creature, almost at its feet — with a bright orange flash and a boiling cloud of white smoke.

The startled monster staggered back a step. The smoke billowed up and enveloped its head, and it instantly jerked its head back with a snort. The three eyes blinked rapidly, (one at a time). The creature drew a long, whistling breath and its head slowly tipped back, further and further, until its neck was practically folded over its back. Then the head shot forward and down with a startling and very loud sound, part musical note and part thunder clap.

It was a sneeze. And the blast from six nostrils the size of sewer pipes tore grass up by the roots.

Two men of the young soldier's group now took off at the gallop, heading not north, toward Marquez's advancing company, but west, toward the ridge that separated this valley from Lake Maracaibo. It is probable they had chosen this moment as ideal for desertion (for many in the army had been "recruited" through impressments). The third man remained, but holstered his sidearm and half stood in his saddle, looking to his young commander with the clear hope that a retreat would soon be ordered.

Unexpectedly, the steam traction engine also came to life, chugging earnestly. The engineer had not abandoned his machine and was now guiding it away from the railroad tracks, no doubt hoping to get clear of danger.

Meanwhile the creature raised its head, sniffed the air, and began shuffling toward us. After all the show, it was quite undeterred by Tucker's bomb. Tucker muttered something uncharitable under his breath, then marched over to the young soldier, grabbing the reins of the man's jumpy horse to steady it.

"How far is the colonel and those guns?" Tucker demanded.

"Y—you, are arrest!" stammered the poor fellow, as frightened of Tucker as of the advancing monster.

"Later, soldier boy!" Tucker barked. "Answer my question!" But Jenny grabbed Tucker's elbow.

"We should not stay by the bait animals. It is coming. It might eat us, too."

Tucker spun round angrily at her interruption, but then saw that his discovery was indeed very close, and fast approaching. He nodded, "Yeah. Better keep clear of her."

Tucker, Jenny, Ernesto and I strode quickly toward the plowed field. The young soldiers and his mate spurred their jittery mounts and rode beside us, perhaps hoping that, if Marquez arrived on the scene, it would look as if we were their prisoners.

Behind us, the animal lumbered up to the boxcar, cocking its head, listening. Certainly it appeared that she was considering another meal. The hysteric mooing of the trapped cattle was piteous indeed.

Tucker turned to the young soldier, "Now you watch this, young fella. This is how I'm gonna save La Ceiba from getting stomped all over. You watch, and you tell the colonel he's gotta help me get more feed for the dinosaur."

Ernesto could see that Tucker's bombast had overwhelmed the boy's limited English, and he quickly began to translate. All the while I was watching the creature. Paused beside the boxcar, it lowered its head and sniffed loudly at the pig carcasses. Then it sniffed at the car itself, nudging it with its snout, effortlessly knocking the car off the rails.

But it did not eat. Rather it raised its head and sniffed the air again, emitting a whistling hurricane breath that I think anyone would have said was a wistful sigh.

"Harry, she isn't eating," I said.

He turned to look, "She's *gotta* eat. She's gotta stay put!"

But the creature did not cooperate. She swung her great head this way and that, sniffing, and sighing. Then she slowly began trudging along her original course, northward along the tracks toward La Ceiba.

"Bless it! Bless it! Why don't she eat?" Tucker raged. "What's she looking for?"

To our dismay, at the very same moment, Marquez's company appeared in the distance, directly in the creature's path, trundling their cannon toward us. Because the canyon leading into the valley was narrow, they came into view of the animal suddenly and, had their purpose not been so deadly, their reaction would have been comical. Some men bolted and ran immediately, with Marquez shouting epithets after them. Any horse not well controlled threw its rider and made tracks for Ecuador.

But Marquez's more seasoned men worked swiftly to unlimber their guns. In minutes they would surely fire on the creature — and one of our two dreaded outcomes would surely unfold.

Tucker dashed toward the army unit, some three or four hundred yards distant. Jenny dashed right after him.

"Kiyuga, no! They will shoot you!"

"Better me than her!"

The two soldiers, still trying to overcome their role as mere onlookers, galloped after Tucker and Jenny, shouting "*Alto*" to no avail.

I simply froze in place, a clamor of thoughts confounding

263

movement. Of Tucker: *How terrible if my friend is killed along with his fantastic discovery!* Of his monster: *Why does it not eat? What is it searching for?*

I reconsidered all it had done up to now, and suddenly seized upon its wallowing in ponds. *Is it looking for another lake, one large enough in which to hibernate? If it saw water, would it turn toward it?* If so, how ironic that the continent's largest lake was just beyond the ridge to the west — a ridge barely two hundred feet high. *What would it do if it knew the lake was there?*

A final thought came, as they say, out of the blue, borne of the memory of the seeming call-and-response we had heard between the creature and the cattle train locomotive.

I spun round to Ernesto and blurted, "Come with me!"

He followed me as I ran for the traction engine. It had traveled only two hundred yards or so from the tracks, trundling along at barely five miles per hour. We overtook it in short order. I glanced back, relieved to see that Tucker and Jenny weren't even half way to Marquez's cannoneers.

As we came alongside the engine, I was startled to see how big it was up close. Some twenty feet long, its steel drive wheels were eight feet high, studded with shovel-sized spikes for added traction. It was truly a "road locomotive," as these machines were sometimes called.

I shouted to Ernesto over the clanking, hissing machine, "Tell the engineer to blow his whistle!"

With a look that told me he had no idea what I was thinking, Ernesto dutifully shouted to the man, "*Sople silban!*"

The engineer, a burly, tan, grizzled character with eyes permanently squinted from a life spent in smoke and steam, was in no mood to attract any more attention than his charge did already. With a fearful glance back at Tucker's Monster, he shook his head and waved us away.

I then did something that, for me, was quite extraordinary. Without thinking, I leapt onto the narrow platform at the rear of the engine and climbed up to the cab. In these times, every boy knew that a locomotive's steam whistle was operated by a cord dangling from the cab roof. The tractor's design proved to be the same. Before the engineer could react, I yanked the cord, unleashing a loud harmonious toot. It echoed long and gloriously.

The engineer quickly overcame his surprise, grabbed me by the shoulders and pitched me headlong from the cab. I landed hard, wind knocked out. But I forced myself to flop over and look to see if my brainstorm had had any effect.

To my joy, I saw Tucker's Monster stop, swivel her majestic head about, and gaze in our direction. Then she answered with a short, tentative, French horn bleat of her own!

And as she did, Tucker and Jenny halted their suicidal run toward Marquez's company. They grasped in an instant what I had demonstrated, that she was attracted to the sound of the whistle, which was similar to her own multi-toned call. They reversed course and ran toward me. Even at this considerable distance, I could hear Tucker shouting.

"Yes! Yes! Blow it again! Keep blowing it!"

Ernesto raced after the tractor, repeating the command to the engineer, whose irate reply went well beyond a simple "no," and I imagine made reference to our ancestors being other than human.

I struggled to my feet and limped after them, calling, "Ernesto, please! Make him understand!"

While Ernesto argued fruitlessly with the engineer, Tucker's Monster eyed the steam tractor curiously, remaining motionless. Unfortunately, this made her a sitting duck for Marquez's guns. And they were nearly ready, the men feverishly setting elevations, ramming charges.

I caught up with Ernesto and the tractor. Jenny and Tucker caught up with me. He swatted me violently on the shoulder and exulted, "Genius, Whitney! The whistle stopped her! What now?"

As the four of us walked briskly along with the engine, I babbled the out rest of my very unbaked plan, pointing to the western ridge. "I think she's looking for water, Harry. Like the lake she was in. If we can lead her to the top of the ridge, she'll see Lake Maracaibo and maybe, God willing, go that way. Of course, Maracaibo is brackish, not fresh water like Pennysmith's lake. So I worry that she may not —"

But Tucker's chin had already jutted, and he cut me off, "It's a plan, Whitney! A fine plan!"

Jenny glanced back at our monster, "She is still not moving! And the soldiers. I think they will still shoot!"

Simultaneously Tucker realized the engineer was refusing Ernesto's entreaties to blow the tractor's whistle. Tucker shouted to the fellow over the machine's symphony of noises. "What are you about there, man? Keep blowing it!"

"He's reluctant, understandably," I yelled.

"*Reluctant?!*" Tucker roared.

He leapt onto the traction engine and gave the engineer the same treatment I'd gotten. Burly though the man was, he no match for an impatient Tucker; and he landed as heavily as I had, rather to my satisfaction.

Tucker started blowing the whistle. The engineer scrambled to his feet, furious and ready for a re-match. But as he charged after us, he found himself staring at Jenny's Colt Army. I knew she would never fire it, but nothing in her ominous demeanor would have told him that. She strode backward with Ernesto and me as we kept pace with the still-moving engine. All the while, Tucker blasted the steam whistle over and over, steering the tractor straight for the ridge.

His monster listened with interest, but did not move. I looked over at the army company. My heart sank as I saw

266

Marquez's arm go up, then drop. It was the order to fire.

But at that same instant the great animal finally turned and took a few tentative steps toward the engine. The slight movement saved her.

The cannons thundered. Marquez's company disappeared behind instantaneous clouds of white smoke. The shells passed within feet of the creature's rump. But miss they did, shrieking on to explode in the forest south of the field. Dull thumps shook the air as trees splintered.

With cannon fire on one side of her and exploding shells on the other, Tucker's Monster flinched, looked right and left in confusion — and stopped again!

Tucker pulled long on the steam whistle cord, shouting to her, "Don't stop! Don't stop, honey!"

Marquez's men worked to reload and re-aim their weapons. Meanwhile, the smoke from their first efforts drifted over to the beast. She shook her head angrily (I can only assume she now recognized the acrid smell of black powder) and marched forward again toward the traction engine, sending forth her own ear-drum rattling trumpets.

"Atta girl!" bellowed Tucker in reply.

The tractor's engineer still marched along behind us, torn between wanting to regain control of his engine and a growing fear of the approaching beast. Tucker, too, was concerned about what might happen if she overtook us. He beckoned to Ernesto.

"Ernesto! Ask him if this puffer will go any faster. Tell him he better run it for all that's in it! Tell him that animal will smash it if she catches us!"

Ernesto relayed this plausible (if wholly theoretical) scenario to the engineer. After a moment's consternation, the fellow made up his mind to join the privateers and swung back into to the cab. Jenny, Ernesto, and I leapt aboard as well, crowding into the cramped space.

Spinning valves, changing gears, and working the throttle, the engineer soon had the ponderous machine clanking along as fast as a man could jog. Next he threw open the fire box, jabbed me in the ribs, and nodded toward a shovel. I guess, as the least intimidating of our group, I seemed the most likely to follow the implied order. And I did, busily shoveling coal from the bins behind us. Smoke and cinders belched from the stack and whirled round us, stinging eyes and skin.

Had she wanted to, of course, Tucker's Monster could have caught us in a few gargantuan steps, but she seemed content to follow and listen and answer the whistle.

Marquez's cannons roared again. But the cumbersome weapons weren't designed to hit a moving target, and this second fusillade missed even more widely than the first. Furthermore, our path up the ridge was taking us behind some trees. The men were forced to roll their guns forward by hand in an effort to reach favorable positions.

Tucker was pleased, "Pfhuh! They'll have a job hitting her now!"

Huddled in the cramped cab, we all had to take care with arms and elbows. Exposed gears whirred in front of us. The spokes of the rear wheels whooshed past us on either side. The thrashing piston spat steam and oil in our faces. Tucker climbed up and leaned out precariously over the furiously spinning flywheel so he could see both forward and back.

The powerful engine effortlessly climbed the steep grade, cleats on the drive wheels digging deep into the soil. The top of the ridge was dead ahead, barely a quarter mile distant. But our newly-recruited engineer watched his gauges with growing worry. I had been dutifully shoveling coal as though born to the task, but now he prodded me in the back and shook his head as if to say, "No more." Kicking the firebox shut, he spoke worriedly to Ernesto, who translated.

"He says the hill is too steep. If the water inside uncovers the crown — I think that is top of the — the place where the fire burns — the boiler can explode!"

Tucker remained in his position beside the flywheel, black steam-laced smoke curling round him. Without looking down, he said calmly, "Tell him I appreciate his concern and I hope that does not happen." He blew the whistle, and nodded with satisfaction as his monster answered.

At last we topped the ridge. There was Lake Maracaibo, glinting less than half a mile below! But Tucker's Monster trailed us by a hundred yards or so, still following, but cautiously. Perhaps something about the engine was off-putting. Or perhaps the pitch of our whistle was not altogether convincing. All of us, save for the nervous engineer, leaned off the back of the traction engine, beckoning and shouting, "Come on! Come on!" In the valley below, Marquez's troops were nearly done resetting their weapons.

The slope on the lake side of the ridge was much steeper. As we tipped forward and down, the engineer furiously threw levers, trying to change to a lower gear to slow us down. But at the same moment, the engine's front roller dropped into a depression. There was an immediate, shuddering rumble from within the boiler. The safety valve erupted with a deafening shriek, shooting a volcanic plume of steam thirty feet into the sky.

The engineer screamed with infectious panic and bounded from the cab, landing at a dead run, positive the engine was about to explode. (I later learned this was not unreasonable. Water sloshing over an exposed overheated firebox generates a sudden dangerous burst of steam.)

Fortunately, the boiler did not explode. But unfortunately, the engineer had left us with all gears disengaged. We began to roll down the slope, gathering speed at a rate quite unbecoming for a twenty-ton machine.

269

Tucker dropped into the cab and grabbed the steering wheel, but the slack chains that "controlled" the front roller allowed little precision. We roller-coastered toward first one tree, then another as Tucker frantically spun the wheel left and right. But he knew well before the rest of us that disaster was imminent.

"Jump!" he commanded. Jenny did so immediately and without question. She landed in a crouched stance that allowed her to tumble rather gracefully down the slope behind us. Ernesto and I hesitated, then made far more ungainly exits. I managed to badly bruise both knees, one elbow, my buttocks and my head. Ernesto faired somewhat better.

Of course, none of that mattered in the moment. We scrambled to our feet and looked with great fear after the speeding tractor. Tucker remained in the cab, spinning the wheel with one hand while blowing the steam whistle with the other. Caring nothing for himself, his only goal was to coax his monster over the top of the ridge.

The traction engine veered suddenly. The front roller had caught in soft earth and the big machine now keeled sickeningly sideways, the drive wheels throwing up spectacular rooster tails of dirt.

We were horrified. The tractor was inexorably rolling over like a capsizing ship.

"Kiyuga!" Jenny barely whispered.

But Tucker, with the remarkable life-saving reflexes I'd seen so often, launched himself from the high side of the cab. His leap carried him just above the spikes of the left drive wheel, and the tractor rolled beneath him. He landed behind the machine, tumbling violently.

The tractor slammed over onto on its right side, skidding down the slope ahead of tumbling Tucker, sheering off several trees before finally stopping in an immense cloud of dust pierced and whorled by jets of rushing steam. As this cleared, I was surprised to see the glint of water through the trees. Due solely to Tucker's tenacity in steering as long as he could, the tractor lay not a hundred feet from the lake shore.

He was immediately back on his feet, limping painfully toward the tractor on a badly twisted right ankle, but nevertheless hell-bent on getting there. I could not imagine why until he kneeled at the crushed cab and reached in to pull the whistle cord — to call to his monster again. The whistle offered up only three more plaintive, disharmonious bleats before steam pressure dissipated from the ruptured boiler.

As Jenny, Ernesto and I raced, or rather hobbled, down to join Tucker, we heard his monster call out from behind us. She was still invisible on the opposite side of the ridge; and her tentative ululation sounded for all the world like a question, perhaps, "Was that you?" or, "Are you still there?"

We all limped out of the trees to the lake shore, from where we could look back and see the ridge top. We prayed we would see her come over it, knowing that Marquez's gunners were hard at work to get her back in their sights.

Quite surprisingly, in this most tense of moments, a man appeared on horseback. He was leading a burro packed with gear, riding along a little-used lake-shore trail. He was perhaps thirty years old, very nattily dressed in tailored jacket, neck-band shirt with waterfall tie, newsboy cap and trendy knickers — an ensemble more suited to a city than this rugged location.

He studied our bedraggled group and quickly settled on Tucker as the one to address. "Mr. Harold Tucker?" he asked eagerly, with a Spanish accent but in carefully enunciated English.

Tucker seemed not in the least amazed that the man had somehow guessed who he was. Eyes riveted on the ridge top, he said only, "Yeah, yeah."

"I am Juan Gongora," the man went on pleasantly. "I have come —"

"Sir!" snapped Tucker, now looking at him, "I'm in something of a worrisome spot! I'd rather not speak!"

But it was Ernesto who spoke next, addressing the newcomer, "Gongora? The photographer?"

"*Sí.* Yes," said Gonogora.

Ernesto turned excitedly to Tucker, "Señor Tucker, he is the photographer I have sent for from Maracaibo."

Gongora leapt from his horse, stepped to his burro and proudly opened a red leather case that contained his fine new Seneca view camera.

"Photographer, you see?" he smiled.

Tucker glanced at him again, now interested, "Well — fancy that."

How had Gongora miraculously managed to meet us at this spot? At this most absurd time? By perseverance. When he had arrived in La Ceiba, he had attempted to follow our route along the railroad tracks out of town. But soldiers posted by Marquez had stopped him. Townsfolk told him he could reach the tracks by following the lake south and crossing the ridge at a suitable point, so he had set out that way.

Now he eagerly pressed us for information, "The animal is near by? Is it as large as people have said?"

"Oh she's large all right," said Tucker.

But the thump of cannon fire interrupted the moment. Our heads jerked round and we again studied the ridge top. Shells whistled high overhead to explode a half mile out in the lake. Still there was no sign of Tucker's Monster.

Tucker shook his head grimly, "I admire your pluck in reaching us, Juan. I hope you have something other than a carcass for your camera."

Gongora was of course trying to catch up to what was

happening, "The soldiers? They are shooting at the animal?"

Tucker nodded.

Jenny voiced the frustration we all felt, "Why doesn't it come? Isn't it looking for water?"

Tucker muttered, "Yeah, you'd think an animal could sense a whole huge lake of it. Smell it."

"That was only a guess on my part," I reminded them sadly. "We really know nothing about her habits. She may *not* be looking for water. She may not even have a sense of smell. And as I was saying earlier, Maracaibo is brackish. She may be suited only to fresh —"

"Enough science, Whitney," Tucker said softly. "Enough."

The unseen guns echoed again. Again shells screamed above us. Still no sign of the creature.

Tucker straightened. "Well, I'll not let it play out settin' on my rump!"

He began to limp painfully up the slope. Jenny hurried after him and put her arm round him, supporting him on her small frame, silently helping him forward. But they had struggled only a few steps when Ernesto pointed up the slope and shouted, "Look!"

The head of Tucker's Monster had at last risen above the ridge. She did not seem in distress, but rather seemed to be searching (for the source of the whistle?). She paused to look all around.

Gongora's mouth fell open in the most classic way. He literally stumbled backward as though physically smitten by the sight.

"*Mi Dios!*" he whispered, then rushed to his burro, determinedly unloading camera, lenses, photographic plates, tripod. The rest of us remained stock still, gazing up at the magnificent creature.

The cannons boomed once more. One shell burst in a tree right next to her. She flinched, vast expanses of skin rippling.

The sun glinted off her undulating rows of colored plates, casting rainbow patterns in all directions, a most unusual sight.

Tucker's Monster then turned toward the smoldering tree, sniffed it, and snorted angrily. Every second she remained still gave Marquez's gunners time to improve their aim.

"For Heaven's sake, *move!*" bellowed Tucker.

To this day I believe she actually heard him, for her neck swung right round and she looked down at us with her three eyes, head cocked to one side like a Brobdingnagian puppy. She emitted a short, bird-like chirp which sounded like surprise. She had spotted the lake.

She surged forward, perambulating smoothly over the ridge top on her eight legs and charging down the slope.

"Atta girl! Atta girl!" huzzahed Tucker, beckoning with broad sweeps of his arms. "Come on! Come on!" Needing no such encouragement, his monster was coming straight for us, faster and faster, following the swath the traction engine had slashed through the foliage.

Ernesto and I nervously began to sidestep out of her direct path. Jenny tried to tug Tucker aside but he did not budge. Instead he glanced round to find Juan Gongora, who was just fitting his camera onto his tripod.

"Juan!" shouted Tucker with a devilish smile. "Are you man enough to take the photograph of your life?"

With no hesitation, Gongora shouldered his camera and tripod, rushed forward, and selected a spot between Tucker and the lake; the only place where he would be able to capture an image of Tucker and Tucker's Monster's together. With the monster bearing down on them, he knew he would have only seconds to capture any image at all.

The ground shook. Trees fell as before an avalanche. I felt a wind on my face, for the approaching monster was actually pushing a shockwave of air ahead of her. Ernesto and I stepped up our sidestepping to get clear.

Gongora set his camera, peered at his ground glass and chose a frame. He slammed home a fresh plate. Trembling, he grabbed his shutter bulb, fumbled and dropped it, stooped, snatched it up again, finally holding it high.

"Ready!" His voice was high and tight.

Tucker swept off his hat and held it behind him with arm outstretched toward the oncoming monster, grinning like a circus ringmaster introducing the grandest act in the world. Jenny, in her incredible adaptive way, said nothing about the insanity, did not object. She stood by her husband, feet braced, hands on his hips, eyes on the monster, ready to push at the last possible moment; ready to die if necessary.

Gongora squeezed his shutter bulb.

"I have exposed it!"

Tucker's Monster was perhaps twenty feet from Tucker himself. Jenny pushed with all her strength. Tucker leaped as best his sprain would allow. The two of them tumbled sideways, but not far enough! The monster galloped right over them!

How eight thundering legs the size of Roman columns left Tucker and Jenny untouched remains a mystery to me. But I saw them rise, unhurt.

One hundred feet further ahead, Gongora tackled his camera and sprinted madly out of doom's path toward me and Ernesto. The three of us cowered in a storm of wood splinters, dirt and rocks as the creature churned past us.

As Tucker's Monster plunged into Lake Maracaibo, she trumpeted more loudly than ever before — an air-shuddering, brain-crushing, yet still melodious cry of utter exhilaration. Her mountainous splash rivaled that of the biggest side-launched battle ship. Spray flew skyward in voluminous billows as though unhindered by gravity. Monumental waves rolled away from either side of her and crashed along the shore.

On she went, deeper and deeper, trumpeting again and again. In a few seconds only her head was visible. She paused then, breathing heavily. Her nostrils blasted mist from the water on either side of her head, reminding one of a steam engine. She looked slowly back at the shore. The slits on either side of neck I'd seen when she first rose from the lake bottom opened again and flapped. I felt sure she was preparing her gills for submersion.

Gongora hurried to the water's edge and set up his camera. He yanked out the exposed plate and slipped in a fresh one. But as he grabbed his shutter bulb, Tucker's Monster slipped beneath the surface.

She would never be seen again.

EPILOGUE

The reader is no doubt left with many frustrating questions. How could something so big just disappear? Were there really only two creatures? Didn't they procreate in some "normal" way? What became of Gongora's photograph?

Still another question would not occur to me until years later, as we gained deeper understanding of the possible origins of life on our planet: Was Tucker's Monster indeed even native to Earth?

One question I can answer. Tucker and I each kept one print of the photograph. I do not know what happened to Tucker's copy. Worse, the original negative remained with Gongora and is, I assume, lost. I no doubt compound the reader's frustration in admitting that, in that distant time, neither Tucker nor myself recognized the importance of acquiring or safe-guarding it.

Yes, my print exists,[3] but one must accept the photograph's limitations. It does not show the whole creature. Tucker and Jenny (her back to the camera) are seen clearly in the lower left corner. But by the time Gongora released his shutter, the beast was already exceeding the edges of his frame. Her magnificent head, bobbing up and down with her galloping gait, dipped low enough to appear in the upper right corner. Only two of her three eyes are visible, giving her a sort of cock-eyed flounder-ish appearance. Her mouth is partially open and the white baleen-like material makes it look for all the world like she is smiling. Maybe she was.

The legs are badly blurred due to movement. You can't

---

[3] Obviously, Grandpop wrote this before the print was damaged.

277

really see eight, or even six for sure. Her tail is curled to the left, jutting across the sky behind grinning Tucker. Though her body literally fills the rest of the image, its brilliantly colored plates and stripes are of course rendered only in the muted shades of black and white.

If one accepts the photo as genuine, one can only say, "Yes, that is certainly large, and could be an incredible creature. But it might also be some elaborate mechanical Chinese dragon." Or, agreeing with the young fellow who unknowingly set me to this task, one can simply dismiss the picture as a cinematographer's sleight of hand.

While I admit that the other questions have never been answered, I submit that my own frustration has been much greater. I was never able to publish a description of the world's most fantastic animal in any recognized scientific journal, for I had not the slightest scrap of evidence to prove the existence of Tucker's Monster. But let me finish my report, such as it is.

In the days immediately following our adventure, boats were hired and a search was made of the area in which the creature initially submerged. Whole cows were weighted, sunk, and offered as bait. Nothing was found. She did not reappear.

I should point out that these efforts lacked the usual Tucker ardor. He and Jenny had repaired to the city of Maracaibo where, while recuperating from his injuries, he directed the search with amused detachment. Indeed, he had become positively serene. For he had found his dinosaur, reveled in the sight, sound, smell and feel of her, saved her from destruction; even been nearly trampled to death by her. He was not burdened by the lack of proof, nor by the lack of public acclaim. His dream had been to discover the thing for himself. That was done. A mere three weeks later, no new sign of her having been uncovered, Tucker and Jenny

278

returned to Oklahoma.

Over the next year, it was G. Winters Wayne's sad task to oversee the dismantling of Tucker's cattle empire. The financial ruin Wayne had often predicted came not from legal turmoil but, ironically, from Tucker's success in his lifelong goal. Not only had he spent prodigiously in the Venezuelan search, he now determinedly followed through on the monetary promises he had made subsequently. He purchased a new train and replaced the lost cattle. He repaired the lake road. He donated two traction engines to replace the one.

He even rebuilt the creek-side village wiped out by his manmade flood, inviting the original inhabitants to return. The village had a school, its own power plant, and electric lights installed by the ever-inebriated Doctor Pennysmith. (In a macabre side note, the doctor managed to electrocute himself while completing this job). The old woman who had tried to warn us of Pennysmith's true nature received a new clapboard house with screened windows. Her name was Maria, and it turned out that her enmity toward him was justified — the body of one of her relatives had been acquired by Ximen for use in the lab.

So, section by vast section, the DH was sold off, divvied up, or given away. None of this mattered to Tucker or Jenny, of course. The ranch was, and always had been, but a means to an end.

The Science Lab was pulled down, my collections sent home with me. I also inherited the Winchester and the Holland and Holland, Tucker enforcing his view that you never knew when you might need a really big gun. They have remained (mostly) silent, gathering dust above various mantels over the years.

While at peace himself, Tucker was not oblivious to my own suffering over the lack of proof. The following year, before his finances were gone, he indulged me in funding a

279

small expedition back to Venezuela with several trained colleagues of mine.

We took with us a "hard hat" diver who went down several times in the area of Lake Maracaibo where Tucker's Monster had submerged. He saw no sign of her. Talks with local fishermen indicated that their catch was normal. If she was still close by, she was not depleting the water of fish (as she had evidently done in Pennysmith's lake).

Finding no trace there, we then combed the entire route of the two known creatures. Dismayingly, Pennysmith's ruined laboratory was already heavily overgrown. Perpetual rain had obliterated all tracks in the original lake's bottom. Undergrowth was rapidly reclaiming the creature's path through the forest and, in any case, a trail of broken trees was no real proof of anything. In our last week, we sounded and fished several other lakes in the region, but found nothing. I'd hoped that we might luck onto some sign of another creature; or at least the remains of a dead one. But it was not to be.[4]

Many years later, when sonar became available, I personally paid for a small campaign to Lake Maracaibo. Many readings were taken where Tucker's Monster was last seen. Divers, now better equipped and much more mobile, searched the area. I'd held out a faint hope that we might at least discover a large mass of bones, but nothing was found. Since then, I have wondered if, finding herself in the vast lake, she began roaming freely its length and breadth, or even perhaps found her way out the strait into the Gulf of Mexico.

---

[4] In Grandpop's time, DNA was not known. Thus, no thought was given to collecting mud or excrement from the creature's original lake bed, which might have contained its DNA. The lake bed is now covered by century-old forest and is not even recognizable.

Long before that final exploration, Tucker and Jenny had retired to a small farm situated in a lovely valley in a corner of the original ranch. We remained in fairly close contact, and I trekked to their place every few years. To my utter surprise, in the second year I found they'd had a daughter, Hope. How Jenny avoided this up to that time is one of many mysteries about her. Hope grew to be a stunning young woman, the exquisite combination of her parents. An avid student, she studied hard and eventually became a noted botanist (I like to think I had some influence there).

Her mam passed at 87 (approximately). And, despite relentless annual predictions of imminent demise, her pap did not leave us until 93.

THE END

.

www.ingramcontent.com/pod-product-compliance
Lightning Source LLC
Chambersburg PA
CBHW021949170626
46808CB00001B/87